Down and Out in Byron Bay

Alex Telman

Published by Alex Telman, 2024.

This is a work of fiction. Similarities to real people, places, or events are entirely coincidental.

DOWN AND OUT IN BYRON BAY

First edition. November 10, 2024.

Copyright © 2024 Alex Telman.

ISBN: 979-8227488633

Written by Alex Telman.

Table of Contents

Preface 1
Author's Note 3
The Saltwater Ghosts 5
Surfboards and Broken Dreams 8
The Rising Tide 11
Coffee Shop Confessions 14
The Uninvited 17
Bonfire Blues 21
The Market Shift 25
A Roof Overhead 29
The Art of Selling Out 32
Echoes of the Past 36
House of Cards 41
The Rave of Ages 45
Whispers in the Wind 49
The Community Pulse 56
An Unlikely Mentor 61
Nightfall Musings 64
The Weight of Expectations 68
Ritual of Release 73
Unfinished Symphony 79
The New Wave 83
Between Two Worlds 89
In the Shadows 92
Glass Houses 96
Fleeting Moments 99
Chasing Shadows 104
The Unraveling 107
Lessons in Solitude 113
Ella 118
Haunted by Hope 120
Silent Screams 126
The Quiet Before the Storm 132

Tides of Change 137
The Artist's Dilemma 143
Lost in Translation 147
Dancing with Shadows 152
Reflections in the Water 158
The Feast of Excess 164
Moments of Clarity 168
The Last of the Hippies 174
Songs of the Sea 178
The Spiral Down 183
A New Dawn 189
Navigating the Grey 192
Embers of Belonging 199
Ricky and Jess 207
The Burden of Dreams 211
Ella 217
An Inheritance of Silence 224
Homecoming 233
Roots and Wings 237
The Final Wave 241

Preface

When the package arrived, postmarked "Byron Bay — 24 April, 2014", an unsettling sense of anticipation washed over me. Something told me this wasn't just another package. My hands trembled as I tore through the tape, and inside, I found an assortment of crumpled papers—notes, reflections, fragments of thought—undated and raw.

They were Finn Sullivan's words.

Finn. A young man I had watched grow up, now a stranger whose life had unfolded beyond my reach for over a decade. But these pages, these pieces of him, felt like a bridge between past and present—a life I had once been close to, now scattered in ink and paper.

It was as if the universe had conspired to give me a chance to understand him again. As I sifted through his writings, a profound urgency took hold of me. What had happened to Finn in all these years? The answer wasn't easy to find; it was a journey in itself—one that I wasn't sure I was ready to take. Finn's story was still unfolding, like an open book, its pages still being written.

His words raw— unfiltered, filled with longing, ambition, and the ache of someone trying to make sense of who they were becoming. It was as if I had stumbled upon pieces of his soul, laid bare in ink.

The more I read, the deeper I sank into his world. These weren't just stories. They were echoes—haunting, beautiful, and heartbreaking. They were a journey I had to share, to honour the boy I once knew and the man he was becoming. Finn's voice was here, in every line, waiting to be heard.

The following letter was enclosed:

Dear Alex,

I've often found myself reflecting on the life that unfolded in Byron Bay—the town that shaped me and became a part of me in ways I can hardly explain. As I sit here, in a small café with the salty air of the ocean in my lungs and the fading light of the day around me, I realize that the stories I've kept buried for so long are not just mine. They belong to Byron, to the people who came here with dreams, to the ones who grew alongside the changing tides of this place.

In a way, sending you these stories was inevitable. I had to share them. The conversation I had with a traveller not long ago made me realize something I hadn't fully understood before: by telling these stories, I'm not simply reminiscing or holding onto nostalgia. I'm preserving something vital—something that needs to be shared, passed down, and remembered. The beauty of this town, the struggles it has faced, the characters that have walked its streets, and the dreams that have lived and died here—these things deserve to be told. And I feel it's my responsibility to do that.

But it's not just about the past. These stories are also about transformation—the kind that's always in motion, just like the ocean that crashes against the shore here. Byron Bay has changed, just as I have. As I've grown, I've watched this town evolve, from a quiet haven for artists and surfers to a booming tourist hub where the past often feels like a distant memory. And in that change, I've found my own growth—my own struggles and triumphs, my own discoveries of who I am and who I want to be.

These stories are more than personal reflections; they are my way of weaving together the narratives of this town—the tales of its bohemian spirit, the highs and lows of its evolution, and the way it has shaped all of us who've called it home. I want you to see that, as I walk this path, I am intertwined with Byron's history, its heartbeat, and its resilience.

I know this isn't just about me. It's about all of us. About the struggles we face, the dreams we chase, and the connections we form along the way. So, as you read these stories, I invite you to join me—not just in reflecting on my life, but in discovering the threads that bind us all together. Our past, our present, and the hope that we carry with us into the future.

Thank you, Alex, for being a part of this. Your friendship has meant more to me than words can express. And as I send you these stories, I hope you can see not just who I've been, but who I'm becoming.

With gratitude, *Finn*

Author's Note

In 1974, at the age of 18, I set out on a driving holiday from Melbourne to Brisbane, following the winding roads along Australia's stunning east coast. It was a journey fueled by youthful exuberance—a chance to explore the natural beauty and vibrant culture that the coast offered. My travels led me to Byron Bay, a quiet seaside town still emerging from its hippie, surfing roots. Back then, Byron was a far cry from the bustling tourist destination it has since become, yet its charm captivated me from the moment I arrived.

During my stay, I found myself at the Emporium Café, one of the town's few retail spots at the time. The café hummed with a warm, eclectic mix of locals and travellers, all drawn together by the aroma of freshly brewed coffee and the welcoming atmosphere. It was there that I met Craig and Carman, Finn's parents. They were young, free-spirited, and full of life, embodying the very essence of Byron. I remember the instant connection we shared—laughter spilling over as we swapped stories about our lives. Little did I know, this chance meeting would grow into a deep and lasting friendship.

At the time, Finn was just a baby, cradled in Carman's arms as we spoke. I was struck by the warmth of their family, and the sense of community that radiated from them. Over the next few days, we explored the beaches, shared meals, and forged a bond that felt as natural and enduring as the waves that lapped at the shore. Those days, filled with sunshine and the salty air of Byron, remain etched in my memory like the taste of fresh fruit—sweet, fleeting, and irreplaceable.

As the years passed, I made it a point to visit Craig, Carman, and Finn whenever I could. Each visit was an opportunity to reconnect, to witness Finn growing up, and to see the life they had built in that idyllic corner of the world. It was a privilege to watch them raise Finn—nurturing him with love and care and instilling in him a sense of wonder about the world. Our friendship deepened over time, anchored by shared experiences and the simple joy of being together in a place that still felt like home.

Sadly, Craig passed away far too soon, and Carman eventually moved back to her hometown of Sydney. Yet, despite the distance, I remained connected to Finn, still visiting when I could, and still bearing witness to the subtle shifts in his life.

As you read this book, I invite you to explore Finn's world through his words. In his writings, you'll encounter the struggles and triumphs of a young man seeking identity, connection, and meaning. Each piece offers a glimpse into his heart—a heart that has wrestled with dreams, disappointments, and the search for solace in creation.

This collection is not just Finn's—it speaks to all of us. It reflects the universal experience of longing for connection, the desire to be understood, and the challenge of remaining true to ourselves amid life's chaos. As you read, I hope you will find echoes of your own journey in Finn's words—a reminder that we are never truly alone in our struggles.

Thank you for joining me on this exploration of Finn Sullivan's life and the ongoing story he continues to write. Together, let us honour the moments that shape us, the friendships that sustain us, and the art that allows us to express our deepest selves. Though the journey may be complex, it is also filled with beauty, hope, and the promise of new beginnings.

Kindest regards,

- Alex

The Saltwater Ghosts

I strolled along the familiar stretch of sand, where the ocean met the shore in a perpetual dance, its salty breath mingling with the fading light of dusk. The waves whispered secrets I had once shared with friends, those sun-drenched days that felt eternal, when laughter echoed against the backdrop of crashing surf. Byron Bay was a different place now, yet the essence of its past lingered like a ghost in the air, evoking bittersweet memories.

I dug my toes into the wet sand, feeling the coolness seep through my calloused skin, a reminder of all the seasons I had spent here—barefoot and wild. In those early days, I had been surrounded by a tight-knit crew of dreamers and wanderers, each of us drawn to the coast by an unquenchable thirst for freedom. We gathered around bonfires, sharing stories and dreams under a sky brimming with stars, our laughter mingling with the sound of the waves.

But the tides had shifted. One by one, my friends had drifted away—some chasing love, others succumbing to the allure of city lights, and a few even vanishing into the shadows of addiction. I could almost see their faces in the water's shimmering surface, like reflections caught between worlds. "You were here once," I murmured to the ocean, "and now you're just a memory."

As the sun dipped below the horizon, the sky transformed into a canvas of deep oranges and purples, hues that stirred something inside me. I remembered Ella, my first real girlfriend, her wild hair whipping in the wind, her laughter ringing like chimes in the breeze. As teenagers, we had shared everything—hopes, fears, and a passion that ignited like the summer sun. But love was fickle, and when she left, I was left with only echoes of her presence.

"Why did you go, Ella?" I whispered to the sea, the words barely escaping my lips, as if speaking them aloud might bring her back. "Why did you leave me?" The waves crashed harder, as though mocking my question, the roar of the ocean swallowing my grief. I turned my gaze to the horizon, where the sky met the water in a blurry embrace, the line between them as indistinct as the space she'd left in my life.

I continued my walk, my heart heavy with the weight of memories. I passed a cluster of beach huts, their faded colors reflecting the passing years. Each one held stories of laughter and love, of heartache and dreams, but now they sat silent, like abandoned ships in a forgotten harbor. I reached for the splintered wood of one, tracing its lines with my fingers. It felt like touching the scars of time, a reminder of both beauty and decay.

The wind picked up, whipping through my hair as I moved further along the beach. I remembered the time we had all come here to surf, a ragtag group of misfits united by a love for the ocean. We had spent the day riding waves, adrenaline coursing through our veins, our laughter mingling with the crash of water. I closed my eyes, the sound of the waves transporting me back to that moment, where everything felt right and nothing mattered but the thrill of being alive.

But the thrill had faded, replaced by a sense of loss. One friend had succumbed to addiction, another had been swallowed by the demands of adulthood. I felt like a sailor lost at sea, searching for a lighthouse that had long since extinguished its light. "What happened to us?" I wondered aloud, my voice barely rising above the wind. "Did we forget how to dream?"

As the stars began to punctuate the night sky, I felt a sense of isolation creeping in, thick like the humidity of the air. I longed for connection, for the warmth of shared laughter, but all I found were shadows dancing in the moonlight. I glanced at the nearby waves, which glimmered under the silver glow, each swell a reminder of the friends I once held dear.

My thoughts drifted to Marcus, a kindred spirit who had always believed in chasing the horizon. We had shared countless nights beneath the stars, discussing everything from philosophy to the perfect wave. Marcus had left, too, leaving behind a note that simply read, "I'm chasing the sun." I had understood, but it had stung, the way all goodbyes did. "Wherever you are," I murmured, "I hope the sun is shining on you."

DOWN AND OUT IN BYRON BAY

I also reminisced about Karen and Joel, my closest companions during those formative teenage years. Karen, with her wild curls and infectious laugh, embodied an adventurous spirit that drew us into the surf and into mischief. She danced barefoot on the sand, her carefree attitude a bright contrast to the weight I often carried. We would spend countless hours on the beach, sharing secrets beneath the stars and crafting dreams that felt impossibly large.

Joel, the thinker of our group, had a way with words that could transform the mundane into something magical. His deep voice resonated with a wisdom that belied his age, painting our lives in broad strokes of hope and possibility. Together, we explored the depths of our identities against the backdrop of a rapidly changing Byron Bay.

When Karen and Joel left for Sydney, it felt as if a part of me had vanished with them. Their absence created a hollow space in my heart, a constant reminder of our shared laughter, dreams, and the unbreakable bond we once shared. I missed those late-night talks, the feeling of belonging that came so easily in our youth. Now, as I navigated my life, I often found myself longing for their presence, wishing we could relive those carefree days and share our journeys once more.

I turned back toward the water, the rhythm of the waves now echoing the cadence of my heartbeat. With each crash, I felt the weight of my loneliness lift, if only slightly. The ocean was a canvas of stories, a collection of souls washed ashore, and in its depths lay the remnants of all I had loved and lost.

"Maybe we're all just saltwater ghosts," I mused, a faint smile creeping across my lips. "Drifting in and out of each other's lives, leaving traces behind like footprints in the sand." I stood there for a moment, feeling the breeze against my skin, as if the universe was wrapping me in an embrace, reminding me that I was never truly alone.

With a deep breath, I turned to leave, the salty air filling my lungs. I took one last look at the ocean, the waves shimmering under the night sky, and whispered a quiet promise to the past. "I'll remember you," I said softly, the words carried away by the wind. And as I walked away, I felt the ghosts of my friends linger just behind me, their laughter echoing in the distance, reminding me that while they may be lost to time, their spirits remained entwined with my own.

Surfboards and Broken Dreams

The air hung heavy with the scent of salt and cedar, a heady mix that clung to my skin as I stepped into the old surfboard repair shop. The dim light cast long shadows, dancing across the faded posters of long-forgotten surf competitions. Here, amid the worn tools and the aroma of resin, time seemed to stand still, encapsulating the spirit of a bygone era—the golden days of Byron Bay, when the waves rolled in like promises waiting to be fulfilled.

I ran my fingers over the surface of a battered board, its once-vibrant colors now muted by years of sun and surf. I remembered the thrill of riding waves with reckless abandon, the rush of adrenaline surging through me as I carved through the water. Those moments felt eternal, yet here I stood, surrounded by remnants of dreams left to collect dust. "What happened to us?" I whispered to the air, my voice swallowed by the solitude.

The old man behind the counter looked up, his weathered face creased like the parchment of a sailor's map, each line a testament to a life spent in the sun. "Lost a few, did ya?" he asked, his voice gravelly yet warm, as if it carried the weight of countless stories. I met his gaze, the piercing blue eyes reflecting a depth of understanding, a shared sense of loss. "Just the ones I thought would always be there," I replied, a bitter laugh escaping my lips.

I watched as the old man worked, deftly applying resin to a cracked board, the glistening liquid pooling like forgotten hopes. "It's funny," I said, leaning against the counter. "We all thought we'd be legends, riding waves that would carry us into the sunset. But instead, we ended up here, patching up broken dreams."

He paused, his hands steady, and looked at me with an intensity that pierced through the layers of nostalgia. "You can't ride the same wave forever, kid. Sometimes you gotta learn to repair what's been shattered." His words hung in the air, a lifeline thrown into the turbulent sea of my thoughts.

A sting of regret washed over me, a tide of memories threatening to drown me. I thought of my friends—Ella with her fiery spirit, Marcus with his reckless ambition, all the souls who had once filled this space with laughter and life. They had believed in the beauty of their dreams, but the currents of time had pulled them apart, scattering their aspirations like leaves in a storm. "I didn't want to end up like this," I confessed, the weight of vulnerability heavy on my chest.

The old man nodded, a knowing look in his eyes. "Life's a fickle wave, lad. You ride it, you wipe out, and then you learn to get back up. But the key is to keep paddling, even when it feels like you're drowning." I took a deep breath, the salty air filling my lungs, mingling with the bitterness of lost dreams.

I glanced around the shop, where surfboards leaned against the walls like weary soldiers, each one carrying its own story of triumph and defeat. The walls were plastered with photographs of surfers long gone, their faces frozen in time, forever young, forever chasing the horizon. "Do you think they ever found what they were looking for?" I asked, searching for some semblance of hope.

"Maybe they did, maybe they didn't," the old man replied, returning to his work. "But you can't let their stories define yours. You've got to carve your own path." His words resonated like the sound of crashing waves, filling me with a mixture of melancholy and determination.

My gaze fell on a surfboard propped against the wall, its surface gleaming like the promise of a new beginning. "Do you ever think about repairing your own dreams?" I asked, feeling the stirrings of a long-buried ambition. The old man paused, his hands still, as if contemplating the weight of my question. "Every damn day," he admitted, a flicker of vulnerability breaking through his grizzled exterior.

With a sudden surge of courage, I stepped forward, running my hand along the smooth edge of the board. "What if I take this one?" I said, my heart pounding in my chest. "What if I try to ride again?" The old man looked at me, a glimmer of approval in his eyes, as if he could see the flicker of hope igniting within me.

"Then you better get to work," he replied, a grin breaking through the lines of age. "You can't ride a wave without a board." My heart swelled with a sense of purpose, the heaviness of regret lifting like the morning mist. In that moment, I felt the stirrings of something beautiful, something worth fighting for.

As I left the shop, the board cradled under my arm, I looked back one last time. The old man was busy at work, a craftsman of dreams, mending the past while preparing for a future yet to be written. I stepped onto the beach, the sun setting behind me, painting the sky in hues of gold and crimson. With the board in hand and the ocean stretching out before me, I felt the tides of change swell within me.

Perhaps tonight, I would ride again.

As I stood there, the board heavy in my arms, I could feel the weight of it pulling me toward the sea. The waves were rolling in with that familiar rhythm—quiet, patient, inviting. The wind picked up, sending a salty spray into the air, and the smell of the ocean tugged at something deep inside me, something I thought I had forgotten. There was a time, not too long ago, when this would have been all I needed. A surfboard, a sunset, the pull of the water. That was all.

But now, with the board in my hands, the thought of paddling out felt like a distant memory. I stood there, frozen between the man I was and the man I wanted to be. The man who used to ride the waves, feel the rush of saltwater on his skin, the freedom of the sea beneath him. The man who used to feel alive. But now... I could only watch.

I stared at the water, feeling the swell of longing rise in my chest. I wanted to be out there, carving through the waves, feeling the rush, the salt, the wind. But the ocean felt like a vast, unknowable force now, something too big for me, too far removed from who I had become.

I shifted the board under my arm, adjusting my grip, my fingers tight on the rails. Maybe tomorrow, I told myself. Maybe tomorrow I'll paddle out, maybe tomorrow I'll feel it again. But even as the words left my mind, I knew better. Tomorrow wasn't certain. And tonight, with the sun sinking low, casting long shadows across the sand, I knew I wouldn't be out there.

The waves kept calling, but they weren't mine anymore. Not tonight.

The Rising Tide

I stood at the edge of the world, where the land met the endless ocean, watching the waves crash with a ferocity that mirrored the turmoil within me. The salt air whipped through my hair, mixing with the scent of freshly cut grass and the faint, acrid smell of construction dust. A bulldozer loomed in the distance, a metallic beast clawing at the earth, tearing apart the very fabric of Byron Bay as it had once been. This was my sanctuary, a place that once thrummed with life and laughter, now choking on the weight of progress.

The sun hung low in the sky, a golden orb casting long shadows over the land, illuminating the scars being etched into the coastline. My heart felt heavy in my chest, like a stone anchored to the seabed, as I recalled the days when this beach was a refuge for misfits and dreamers, a haven where the surf was as wild and free as the spirits of those who rode it. I remembered the sound of laughter mingling with the crashing waves, the warmth of bodies huddled around bonfires, sharing stories that floated into the night like smoke.

"Hey, mate! What do you reckon?" A voice broke through my reverie. It was Max, a local surfer, his tan skin glistening under the sun, a surfboard tucked under his arm. "Can't believe they're building that monstrosity right here, can ya?"

I turned to face him, trying to mask the bitterness that churned within. "It's progress, isn't it? The town's gotta grow." The words felt hollow, echoing the inevitability of change that gnawed at my insides. Max shrugged, his easy smile faltering. "Yeah, but at what cost? They're paving over paradise."

My gaze drifted back to the construction site, where concrete and steel swallowed the last remnants of wild grass and scraggly trees. Each day felt like another piece of my home was swallowed whole, leaving behind only memories, like ghostly echoes that whispered through the air. "This place was ours," I muttered, more to myself than to Max. "Now it's just a cash cow for the rich."

The ocean roared in agreement, waves curling and crashing, a symphony of nature's fury. "You can still surf, you know," Max said, trying to lighten the mood. "The waves haven't changed." But I could only think of how the tides themselves were shifting, how the very essence of Byron was being diluted under the weight of greed and ambition.

That night, as the sun dipped below the horizon, the sky bled crimson and gold, I wandered down to the beach alone. The moon hung low, casting a silvery glow on the water, creating a path of light that beckoned me forward. I slipped off my shoes and felt the cool sand between my toes, grounding me, even as my heart felt adrift.

I sat on the shore, knees pulled to my chest, staring out at the restless sea. The rhythmic crashing of the waves felt like a heartbeat, a reminder that life persisted, even amid the chaos. I closed my eyes, letting the sounds wash over me, a temporary balm for the ache of dislocation.

But as I sat there, enveloped in the darkness, I could not escape the memories that flooded my mind—of laughter that echoed like the waves, of friends who had become shadows, and of a community that felt more like a mirage than a reality. I felt like a relic of a bygone era, a ghost haunting the edges of a town that was moving on without me.

"Finn!" A voice broke through the night. I turned to see Ella, her wild hair illuminated by the moonlight, running toward me. "What are you doing here all alone?"

"Just thinking," I replied, forcing a smile. Ella plopped down beside me, her presence a flicker of warmth against the chill of the night air. "About what? The bulldozers?"

"Yeah," I admitted, gazing back at the waves. "I just... I can't shake this feeling that everything is changing, and not for the better."

Ella sighed, brushing sand from her knees. "I get it. It feels like we're losing ourselves in all this." Her voice trembled slightly, revealing the vulnerability hidden beneath her carefree exterior. "But maybe we can still find a way to hold on to what matters."

I turned to her, her face half-shadowed in the moonlight. "What if we can't?" I asked, despair creeping into my voice. "What if this place becomes unrecognizable?"

"We're not just a place," Ella said, her eyes fierce with determination. "We're the memories, the moments. No one can take that away from us." I felt the truth of her words seep into my bones, a glimmer of hope amidst the darkness.

As we sat together in silence, the waves crashing in an endless rhythm, I realized that perhaps we could not stop the tide of change, but we could embrace the memories that had shaped us. Together, we could fight to keep the spirit of Byron alive, even as the world transformed around us.

The moonlight shimmered on the water, and for the first time in a long while, I felt a flicker of resolve. The tide was rising, yes, but so too was the possibility of reclaiming our story, of carving our path in a world that seemed intent on swallowing us whole.

I took a deep breath, filled with the salty air and the promise of the ocean. "Let's ride this wave, Ella," I said, the spark of determination igniting within me. "Together."

And in that moment, beneath the vastness of the night sky, I felt a connection to something greater than myself, a unity with the land, the sea, and the people who dared to dream. The rising tide would come, but so would the strength to face it.

Coffee Shop Confessions

I stepped into the café, the air thick with the aroma of roasted beans, sugar, and a hint of desperation. As I pushed through the glass door, the chime overhead rang like a bell tolling for the lost souls within. The place buzzed with chatter, laughter spilling over tables, and the clatter of porcelain against wood creating a symphony of the mundane.

I settled into a corner seat, the faded vinyl cushion creaking under my weight, a familiar sound that spoke of countless patrons who had sunk into its embrace. Outside, the sun glinted off the surf, a tantalizing reminder of freedom. Yet inside, the atmosphere felt heavy, a weight I couldn't shake.

Glancing around the room, I spotted a pair of sharply dressed businesswomen animatedly discussing investments in one corner, their voices a mix of enthusiasm and entitlement. "The market is booming, darling," one said, her laughter bright and false, like a facade painted over the cracks of her reality. I turned away, catching sight of an older man in a Hawaiian shirt, his tanned skin sunken against the bone. He was recounting tales of yesteryear, his voice rising above the din. "Back in my day, we surfed for the love of it, not for Instagram likes." That struck a chord, the bitter taste of nostalgia flooding my senses.

As I sipped my black coffee, its bitterness mirrored my thoughts. I felt like an outsider in this temple of commerce and ambition. The conversations around me were laced with dreams wrapped in dollar signs, while I clung to remnants of a life that seemed more poetic than profitable. I was a relic of a forgotten age, a ghost drifting through the modernity that consumed my beloved Byron Bay.

The door swung open, and a gust of salty air swept in, carrying with it a young couple, all smiles and sun-kissed skin. They flopped into seats next to me, their exuberance radiating like sunlight pouring through the windows.

"Did you see that new hotel they're building on the cliffs?" the woman gushed, her eyes sparkling. "It's going to be absolutely stunning! Can you imagine the views?"

My chest tightened as I eavesdropped, the walls of the café closing in around me. "Stunning," I muttered under my breath, bitterness curling like smoke in my throat. I had seen too much beauty lost to development, too many memories sacrificed at the altar of progress. The world had begun to prioritize opulence over authenticity, and the town I loved was becoming unrecognizable.

The man at their table, fresh tan and an arrogant laugh, chimed in. "Yeah, and they say it's going to bring in a ton of tourists. I can't wait to sell my surf shop. I'll be rolling in it!"

The woman laughed, her voice high-pitched and bright, but I could hear the emptiness beneath it. The hustle, the grind—it was all they knew. The rich tapestry of community and connection unraveled, replaced by transactional relationships and hollow aspirations.

"People used to care about the waves, the culture," I found myself saying, unable to contain the words any longer. The couple turned to me, surprise etched on their faces. "Now it's just about how much money you can make off it."

"Who are you?" the man asked, eyes narrowing. "A local? You sound like one of those old hippies."

"Finn," I replied, trying to mask the bitterness that threatened to spill over. "And yeah, I guess I am one of those old hippies." I could feel their laughter cutting through me like a knife, the scorn wrapping around me, suffocating.

"Man, you should get with the times," the woman said, dismissively flipping her hair over her shoulder. "This is how the world works now."

I watched them, their ambition intoxicating yet fundamentally hollow. "Is it?" I asked, more to myself than to them. "Or is it just how you've been told it works?"

Leaning back, I let the weight of their laughter fade into the background, drowned out by the rhythmic clinking of cups and the gentle hum of the espresso machine. Here, surrounded by people chasing dreams I couldn't comprehend, I felt the ache of disconnection gnaw at my insides.

ALEX TELMAN

Outside, the waves crashed against the shore, relentless and free, while I sat tethered to this moment, rooted in a past that felt like a fading echo. The noise of ambition filled the room, drowning out the whispers of the sea, but I could still hear them if I listened closely enough. They called to me, urging me to remember the life that thrived beneath the surface of consumerism.

"Hey, you okay?" Ella's voice broke through my thoughts, her presence a welcome relief. She slid into the seat across from me, a knowing smile on her lips.

"Just... taking it all in," I said, forcing a smile.

"Don't let them get to you. You know what matters."

I nodded, grateful for her grounding presence. "Sometimes it feels like I'm losing grip on it all," I admitted, vulnerability creeping into my voice.

"Then hold on tighter," she said, her eyes fierce with conviction. "You're the one who knows the truth of this place, Finn. Don't let their dreams overshadow yours."

I felt a flicker of hope ignite within me, the warmth of connection pushing against the cold weight of disillusionment. Maybe I didn't need to fight against the rising tide of change; perhaps I could carve out a space for myself, a sanctuary where the essence of Byron could survive.

As the laughter swirled around us, I took a deep breath, allowing the energy of the café to fill me with possibility. The rising tide might threaten to wash away everything I held dear, but I could still stand firm, a lighthouse amid the storm.

"Thanks, Ella," I said, feeling a smile break free. "I needed that."

And as we sat together, the weight of the world felt just a little lighter, the waves of the past mingling with the promise of tomorrow, a reminder that no matter how much the landscape shifted, some things—like friendship and resilience—would remain unyielding.

The Uninvited

I stood at the edge of my garden, the salt-kissed air swirling around me, carrying the familiar scent of jasmine and nostalgia. The sun dipped low on the horizon, casting a golden glow over the wildflowers that danced in the evening breeze. Yet today, the vibrant colors felt muted, overshadowed by an unsettling anticipation.

I had received the call two days ago. "It's been ages, Finn!" my cousin Luke had exclaimed, the excitement in his voice thinly veiling a sense of obligation. "I'll be in Byron for the weekend. We should catch up!"

The weight of those words pressed down on me, the unseen strings of family and expectation tugging at my gut. Luke, with his tailored suits and polished charm, embodied everything I had distanced myself from—a life of surfboards and sunsets traded for boardrooms and bank statements. As the call ended, I felt a knot tighten inside me, a mixture of dread and resignation.

Now, as I wiped my hands on my faded jeans, I heard the low hum of an engine approaching. My heart raced, a primal instinct urging me to retreat, to hide among the hibiscus and bougainvillea. But it was too late; the sound of tires crunching on gravel signaled that the moment had arrived.

The car—a sleek, black sedan—pulled into the driveway like an unwelcome specter. I forced myself to breathe, the air thick with the scent of impending confrontation. I stepped forward, bracing for the onslaught of unfamiliarity.

"Finn!" Luke's voice rang out, warm yet laced with an undertone of condescension, as he exited the car. With a smile that could melt glass, he was a walking embodiment of a life I had forsaken. Luke strode onto my veranda with an air of effortless confidence, his crisp linen shirt sharply contrasting the weathered charm of my cottage. The fabric glimmered in the sunlight, tailored to perfection, hinting at a lifestyle that felt foreign to me.

His designer running shoes, pristine and expensive, squeaked lightly against the worn wooden floor, a stark reminder of the polished streets from which he hailed. Luke's hair was neatly styled, each strand in place, and his easy smile carried the weight of privilege, yet beneath the surface lay a subtle tension. Despite the contrast in our worlds, I felt a flicker of nostalgia for our shared childhood, even as I grappled with the differences that had emerged over time.

"Hey, Luke," I replied, trying to match his enthusiasm but feeling more like a ghost haunting a party. Our hug was brief, an awkward collision of worlds, and I could feel the difference between us as palpable as the summer air.

"Your place is still... rustic," Luke remarked, looking around with feigned admiration. "I didn't expect it to be so... earthy."

My home was a rustic cottage on a small lot, its weathered wooden walls adorned with peeling paint that told stories of sun and rain. The roof, patched with corrugated iron, gave it a charming haphazardness, while a small veranda out front offered a view of the swaying palms and distant waves. Inside, mismatched furniture created a cozy, lived-in feel, with stacks of books spilling off shelves and art supplies scattered about. A vintage record player hummed softly in the corner, filling the air with a nostalgic warmth. Sunlight filtered through the dusty windows, casting a golden glow on the memories etched into every corner.

"Yeah, well, I like it that way," I said, bitterness creeping into my tone. "Nature's got a charm that... you know, money can't buy."

"Right," Luke chuckled, brushing it off as if I had just made a joke. "Anyway, I'm here for some fun! Let's grab a drink, hit the beach. You know, the good life."

The contrast between us was stark, a chasm created by choices and chance. I felt a swell of resentment bubble up—a cocktail of envy and sorrow. I watched Luke stride toward the beach as if he owned the sunset, his back straight, confidence radiating like the dying sun.

I followed, my feet dragging through the sand, each grain a reminder of the weight of my own decisions. As we reached the shoreline, the waves rolled in, foaming and crashing like the unrelenting tide of expectations that Luke represented.

DOWN AND OUT IN BYRON BAY

"So, how's work?" Luke asked, a casual inquiry that hung heavy in the air. "Still writing?"

I balanced my days between part-time manual work and my true passion for painting and writing. Most mornings, I often found myself hauling timber at a local building site, the physical labor grounding me amidst the swirling thoughts crowding my mind. The sun beat down on my back, the scent of sawdust mingling with the salty air, each nail I drove reminding me of the structure I was trying to build in my own life.

By afternoon, I retreated to the dim light of my cottage, where the clutter of unfinished manuscripts and scattered notes lay in disarray. Here, I poured my heart into words, transforming the chaos of my experiences into poetry and prose. Each sentence was a step toward my dream, a whisper of hope against the backdrop of uncertainty. Despite the challenges, the struggle between earning a living and nurturing my artistic spirit fueled my determination to craft stories that reflected the beauty and complexity of life in Byron Bay.

"Still writing," I replied, the words tasting bitter on my tongue. "Keeping things afloat."

Luke laughed, a bright, hollow sound. "I mean, that's great and all, but when are you going to get serious? There's a whole world out there. You could be making real money!"

I felt the urge to recoil. "Money isn't everything," I said, a quiet defiance in my voice. "I'm happy, you know? This place... it's home."

"Home," Luke scoffed, his tone dripping with condescension. "You're still holding onto that hippie dream, aren't you? The surf, the sun, it's all... well, it's child's play."

I turned to face the ocean, letting the salty spray sting my face. "And what's your dream, Luke? To climb the corporate ladder until you're too exhausted to enjoy the view?"

For a moment, the air thickened between us, a silence punctuated only by the crashing waves. I could see the irritation flicker across Luke's face, like a candle threatening to extinguish. "You're being dramatic," he finally replied, his voice strained. "I'm just trying to look out for you."

"Look out for me?" I snapped, the words bursting forth like the tide. "Or look out for your own guilt? You left this place, Luke. You chose your path. Don't pretend it's for my benefit."

Luke stepped back, his facade cracking, revealing a glimpse of vulnerability. "I didn't leave because I wanted to," he admitted, his bravado slipping. "I left because that's what was expected of me. You think it's easy to—"

"To what? To wear a mask?" I interrupted, the rawness of my emotions spilling over. "To pretend that all of this"—I gestured broadly to the beauty around us—"isn't enough?"

The moment hung between us, suspended like the sunset casting its fiery glow across the horizon. For an instant, I saw Luke not as a cousin lost to the currents of ambition but as a kindred spirit, grappling with his own fears and insecurities.

"You don't get it," Luke said, his voice low. "I'm trying to succeed, to make something of myself. You think I don't miss this place? I do. But you can't just cling to dreams when reality is—"

"Reality is what we make it," I interjected, my heart racing. "And right now, you're making it into something soulless."

Luke looked at me, and for a moment, we were just two lost souls on a beach, the weight of our choices crashing over us like the waves.

"Maybe we're both lost," Luke whispered, the admission heavy with truth.

I took a breath, the cool air filling my lungs, mingling with the warmth of the setting sun. "Then let's figure it out together," I said softly, a fragile thread of connection weaving between us.

And as the sun dipped below the horizon, painting the sky with shades of orange and purple, we stood side by side, the chasm between us narrowing ever so slightly.

In that moment, I realized that family could be both an anchor and a sail, pulling you under while lifting you up. It was a balance I'd need to navigate, but for now, standing on the edge of the world, I felt a flicker of hope ignite amidst the uncertainty—a reminder that the ties that bind can sometimes lead you home.

Bonfire Blues

I stood on the edge of the bonfire's warmth, the flames dancing like ghosts in the dark, illuminating faces that shifted like shadows. Laughter erupted, a mix of carefree joy and the heavy weight of nostalgia, swirling in the air like smoke. At the edge of the beach, the salty breeze ruffling my hair as I watched the waves crash against the shore. My mind was a tangled mess, weighed down by thoughts of what I hadn't done, what I should be doing, and the vast expanse of ocean before me, offering both freedom and fear in equal measure.

The night unfurled like a tattered flag, the sky painted with a thousand stars, each flicker a memory lost to the salty breeze. The beach, once a sanctuary of sun-kissed days and starlit nights, felt both familiar and foreign. I glanced around, the flickering light casting a warm glow on the gathering—a motley crew of old friends and new acquaintances, each harboring their own stories, their own burdens.

A familiar voice called out, pulling him from his reverie.

"Hey, Finn!"

I turned and there she was, Jess, strolling down the path.

Jess had been my neighbor for as long as I could remember. Growing up, she was more than just the girl next door—she was a constant in my life, a friend who had witnessed my most awkward teenage years, and someone who had always known me in ways no one else did. Her laugh was familiar, like the sound of the ocean crashing on the shore—warm, comforting, and ever-present.

She married Ricky, and together they became fixtures in my life. But Jess—she had a way of grounding me, of reminding me that things could still be simple, even when everything else seemed to be unraveling. Even with Ricky by her side, Jess had never stopped being my closest friend, even when the years and the distance between us threatened to pull us apart. She was the one who always knew how to make sense of the chaos, a steady presence in a town that was constantly shifting.

Her hair was a wild mess, her skin sun-kissed from hours spent in the surf. Her grin was wide, carefree as if the world was a place meant for adventure, not introspection.

"You surfing?" she asked, surprised. "I thought you traded your board for a writing desk?"

Finn forced a smile, but inside, he felt the usual tightness in his chest. He hadn't surfed in weeks. Months? Maybe longer. "Yeah, I still surf," he said, the words feeling distant, like a part of him that was just out of reach. "Just haven't had the time."

Jess raised an eyebrow, clearly unconvinced. "Time? Or maybe it's just the motivation that's been a little... lacking?" She asked with a grin that could outshine the moon. She stopped a few feet away from me, hands on her hips, a challenge in her eyes. "You know, the waves aren't going to wait forever."

I chuckled, the sound caught somewhere between honesty and sarcasm. "Nah, I'm still riding the waves. Just... waiting for the right one to come along."

Jess leaned against the makeshift seating—a cluster of driftwood and beach blankets. "Waiting, huh? You know life's too short for waiting, right?" Her eyes sparkled, but behind them was a flicker of something deeper, a challenge laced with vulnerability.

"Yeah, I get it," I replied, my heart heavy with the weight of unsaid words. "But sometimes it feels like the waves are all breaking in the wrong direction."

Around us, the fire crackled, sending sparks spiraling into the night sky, as if trying to escape the gravity of the moment. I watched as others shared their tales, the air thick with camaraderie and unspoken fears. Each story laid bare was a piece of the tapestry we once wove together, now fraying at the edges.

I turned my gaze toward the flames, losing myself in the flicker and dance. "Remember when we used to come here every Friday? Just us and the stars?" I mused, nostalgia washing over me like the tide.

"Yeah, and we thought nothing could ever change," Jess said, her voice softer now, tinged with melancholy. "But look at us. Jobs, responsibilities... it's all so... mundane."

"Life isn't mundane; it's just... complicated," I replied, my tone sharper than intended. "We grew up, but did we really have to leave all of this behind?"

The fire crackled in response, the sound echoing the uncertainty hanging in the air. Just then, a newcomer joined our circle—a tall figure with sun-bleached hair and an infectious laugh. "What's this? The philosophers of the beach?" he teased, plopping down on the sand.

"Just contemplating our lost youth," I replied dryly, but the newcomer's energy was contagious, pulling us back into laughter.

"Ah, youth! The one thing we never really lose; we just bury it under our responsibilities," he said, his grin disarming. I found myself chuckling, but there was a sting beneath the humor, a truth we all knew too well.

As the night wore on, stories of carefree days melded with confessions of regrets. I listened, a silent observer to the unfolding tapestry of lives intertwining. Each tale was a thread, weaving together our shared history, yet also highlighting the distances that had grown between us.

Jess spoke again, her voice breaking the quiet. "I sometimes wonder if we've become the very thing we swore we'd never be. Look at us—talking about life over a bonfire like we're in some movie. Where's the spontaneity?"

I pondered her words, the truth resonating like the distant crash of waves. "Maybe we're just... adapting. This place is changing, and so are we. But is that really a bad thing?"

"Is it? Or are we just making excuses for ourselves?" Jess shot back, her passion igniting a fire of its own. "We can't let the world swallow us whole, Finn. We owe it to ourselves to fight for what we love."

The words hung in the air, heavy with the weight of shared understanding. I felt a stirring within me, a flicker of defiance against the encroaching shadows of conformity. "Then let's not just sit here and talk about it. Let's do something—start a project, clean up the beach, revive that old surf club. We can create our own community, one that feels right for us."

The group fell silent, the crackle of the fire a gentle reminder of our collective heartbeat. One by one, eyes met in the glow of the flames, a tentative spark of hope igniting.

"Yeah, let's do it," Jess said finally, her voice firm. "No more waiting for the perfect wave. We'll create our own."

As the fire crackled and the night deepened, I felt a sense of purpose begin to unfurl within me, like dawn chasing away the shadows. The tide of change might be relentless, but in this moment, surrounded by old friends and the promise of new beginnings, I felt a flicker of connection—a reminder that amidst the chaos of life, community could be a refuge against the storm.

And as laughter mingled with the sound of crashing waves, I realized that the essence of Byron Bay—the wildness, the warmth, the beautiful chaos—still thrived in our hearts. It was not lost but transformed, waiting for us to embrace it, to shape it into something new.

But that felt like so long ago. Nothing really happened after that night. Everyone became too busy with their small lives, caught in the grind of jobs and responsibilities that pulled them further from the dreams we once shared. Days turned into weeks, and weeks into months, as I watched the vibrant energy of that night dissolve into the mundane. The surf club remained abandoned, its peeling paint and rusting metal a testament to forgotten aspirations. The beach, once a sacred space for laughter and connection, slowly decayed with the remnants of a community too tired to care.

Sitting in my rustic cottage, surrounded by crumpled pages and half-finished drafts, I longed for that fire-lit night, for the sense of belonging that slipped through my fingers like sand. It gnawed at me, that yearning to reclaim the connection we had. Each word I wrote was infused with the hope that somewhere, somehow, we might rediscover that spark and breathe life into our dreams once more.

The Market Shift

The sun hung low over Byron Bay, casting a golden haze across the bustling local market. I stood at the fringes, hands buried deep in the pockets of my faded jeans, my heart heavy with the weight of change. The air was thick with the scent of freshly cut fruit and the sharp tang of spices, mingling with laughter and the low hum of conversations. Once, this had been my sanctuary—a vibrant tapestry of community woven from shared stories and dreams. Now, it felt like a foreign land.

Stalls that once showcased hand-carved trinkets and organic produce from local artisans were now adorned with polished, imported goods—soulless baubles glimmering under the midday sun. The joyous chaos of the past had been replaced by a sterile order, a sanitized version of what Byron Bay used to be. I watched as well-dressed families ambled by, their designer shoes crunching over the cracked pavement, each step echoing a privilege I couldn't relate to.

A woman in a pastel sundress, her hair cascading like a waterfall of gold, examined a ceramic bowl with exaggerated delight. She turned to her companion, a man with a neatly trimmed beard, and exclaimed, "Oh darling, this would look perfect in our sunroom!" I felt a tension tighten in my chest. What sunroom? The beach was our sunroom, the saltwater air our ambiance, not these overpriced commodities.

"Hey, Finn!" A voice broke through my reverie. It was Liam, a fellow surfer from the old days, his sun-kissed skin a testament to countless hours in the water. "You still haunting these markets, man?"

"Yeah, just soaking in the vibe," I replied, forcing a smile. "Seems like the vibe's changed, though."

"Tell me about it," Liam scoffed, gesturing toward a stall selling artisanal granola. "When did we start paying twenty bucks for a bag of nuts? It's like they're selling us our own memories back at a premium."

I nodded, feeling bitterness seep into my veins. "And look at those people," I said, nodding toward a group huddled around a food truck, each holding a paper cup of overpriced coffee. "They're living in a bubble, oblivious to what's happening around them."

Liam frowned, a flicker of concern crossing his face. "We can't fight it, man. Change is part of life. Maybe we're just getting old and grumpy."

"Or maybe we're watching the soul of this place get ripped apart," I countered, my voice rising slightly, drawing curious glances from nearby shoppers. I took a deep breath, trying to regain my composure. "This used to be about connection, about community."

"Maybe we need to find our own connection then," Liam said, his tone shifting to one of encouragement. "We can still make our own memories."

I watched as Liam melted into the crowd, leaving me once again in the midst of the shifting landscape. I wandered deeper into the market, the sounds of laughter and chatter becoming a distant murmur. As I passed a stall overflowing with exotic fruits, I couldn't help but feel like an outsider in my own home.

A young couple strolled past, arms linked, laughter spilling from their lips like champagne. They stopped at a vendor selling handcrafted jewelry, their eyes sparkling with excitement as they admired the shiny trinkets. I felt a pang of envy—not for their possessions but for the carefree joy they exuded, something I struggled to grasp in the shadow of my discontent.

I turned my back on the crowd, seeking refuge at the edge of the market, where the grass met the sand—a place that still held the essence of Byron Bay. I sank to the ground, the cool earth grounding me, and took a moment to breathe. The waves crashed rhythmically in the distance, a soothing balm for my troubled spirit.

As I sat there, I recalled the days when the market was a gathering of dreamers—artists, surfers, travelers—sharing their hopes, their crafts, their lives. I remembered the warmth of community, the shared meals under the stars, the music echoing late into the night. That warmth felt like a distant memory, replaced now by the sterile glow of neon lights and plastic smiles.

DOWN AND OUT IN BYRON BAY

A couple of kids raced by, barefoot, their laughter ringing out like bells, momentarily breaking through my haze of despair. I watched them, their joy infectious, a reminder that innocence still thrived amidst the encroaching shadows. Perhaps there was hope yet, a flicker of life that could not be extinguished by the weight of materialism.

Suddenly, a familiar tune drifted through the air, the gentle strumming of a guitar blending seamlessly with the sound of the waves. I looked up to see an old friend, Sam, sitting cross-legged on the grass, his fingers dancing over the strings. A smile tugged at my lips; the music wove through me like a warm embrace.

"Come on, Finn! Join me!" Sam called, his voice an anchor in the tide of change. "Let's remind these people what it's all about."

As I approached, I felt a spark of rebellion ignite within me. Perhaps the essence of Byron Bay hadn't vanished entirely; maybe it was just waiting for those who still believed to breathe life back into it. Sam began to play an old protest song from the 1960s, the sound of the guitar resonating in the air, drawing a few curious onlookers. I joined in, singing with a rawness that echoed the unfiltered spirit of our youth.

The notes soared, intertwining with the salty breeze, each lyric a reminder of the power of community and resistance. People began to gather, drawn in by the familiar melody, their faces reflecting nostalgia and curiosity. My voice cracked, but I pressed on, channeling the pain of lost dreams and forgotten connections into every word. As we sang, laughter erupted and memories flowed, weaving a tapestry of hope amid the encroaching shadows. In that moment, I felt the pulse of Byron Bay, alive again, as if the town itself was awakening alongside us.

Laughter returned, blending with the music, transforming the sterile market atmosphere into something alive and beautiful. I sang with abandon, pouring my heart into the chorus, reclaiming a piece of the town's spirit that still lingered in the cracks of its facade.

In that moment, surrounded by friends and the rhythm of the past, I understood that the heart of Byron Bay was not entirely lost; it simply needed to be nurtured, cherished, and fought for. The commercialization might encroach upon the shore, but the soul of the community could be revived by those who refused to surrender.

ALEX TELMAN

As the sun dipped below the horizon, painting the sky with hues of orange and purple, I felt a renewed sense of purpose. Change was inevitable, but so was the resilience of those who dared to stand against the tide.

A Roof Overhead

I stood at the entrance of the new café, the scent of freshly ground coffee wafting through the air like a siren's call. This place, with its polished wood counters and eclectic art lining the walls, felt foreign yet oddly familiar. Just a year ago, I had wandered these streets with sun-kissed hair and an unyielding spirit, savoring the freedom that came with a life unbound by convention. Now, I was about to step into a world that demanded a price for that very stability.

As I pushed the door open, the chime of the bell echoed—a signal of my arrival that felt more like a warning. Inside, the café hummed with the chatter of customers, laughter bubbling up like the froth on the barista's cappuccino. I took a moment to absorb the scene, watching a couple in the corner share whispers over their lattes, their fingers entwined like vines. I envied their ease, the way they navigated life with such nonchalance.

I had arrived early for my shift, a mix of anticipation and dread churning in my stomach. This job as a barista was my first step toward a more stable existence. But with it came the shackles of routine, the dulling of my once-vibrant spirit. I thought of the sun-soaked days spent surfing, the nights filled with impromptu gatherings by the beach, where dreams flowed as freely as the waves.

"Hey, Finn!" called out Tara, the café manager, her voice bright and cheery, pulling me from my reverie. Her enthusiasm felt like a double-edged sword, slicing through my memories. "Ready to get started?"

"Yeah, sure," I replied, forcing a smile. The warmth of her presence was inviting, yet it reminded me of the compromises I was making.

As I moved behind the counter, the rhythm of the café swept me up. I learned to grind the coffee beans, steam the milk, and craft lattes with hearts etched in foam. Each cup felt like a small achievement, yet with every order filled, I sensed a piece of my freedom slipping away. I watched as the customers came and went, their faces fleeting like clouds across the sky, and wondered if they even noticed me.

Amidst the steam and chatter, I spotted a familiar face—Liam, my friend from the old days. My heart swelled with a mix of joy and guilt. Liam strolled in, a tattered surfboard under his arm, sunburned and carefree. He approached the counter, eyes sparkling with mischief.

"Hey, look at you! All buttoned up and serving coffee now. What happened to the Finn I used to know?" Liam teased, leaning against the counter.

"I'm just trying to survive," I replied, my tone more defensive than I intended. "Gotta pay the bills, right?"

"Pay the bills, sure," Liam chuckled, "but at what cost? You used to laugh in the face of responsibility."

I felt a pang in my chest at the truth of Liam's words. "It's just a job, man. A way to get by until I figure things out."

"Figure things out?" Liam raised an eyebrow, concern creeping into his voice. "You're not going to lose yourself in this place, are you? This isn't who you are."

The moment hung between us like a fragile thread, and I felt the weight of expectation bearing down on me. The café buzzed around me, each sound becoming a reminder of the life I had traded for security.

"I don't know, Liam. Maybe it's time to grow up," I said, my voice wavering. "Maybe chasing the sunset isn't as fulfilling as I thought."

"Don't let them take your light, Finn," Liam urged, a fire igniting in his eyes. "This town is changing, but you don't have to change with it. You can find a way to keep both—a roof over your head and the freedom to live."

I glanced around the café, at the people lost in their routines, faces glued to screens instead of engaging with the world around them. The irony struck me like a cold wave crashing against the shore: I had secured a job, but in doing so, I had locked away a part of myself, buried beneath the espresso machine and the responsibilities that came with it.

As the shift wore on, I poured cup after cup, a mechanical rhythm setting in. Each drink served felt like a reminder of my constraints, my heart pulling me back to the beach where I belonged, where the sun dipped below the horizon, painting the sky in hues of orange and pink. But here, the walls felt suffocating, the chatter too loud, drowning out the whispers of the ocean.

At closing time, the café emptied, and the lingering smell of coffee began to fade. I wiped down the counters, the monotony of the task reflecting my inner turmoil. Tara came up beside me, her demeanor relaxed now that the rush had passed.

"You did great today, Finn," she said, her tone genuine. "We're lucky to have you."

"Thanks," I replied, though the compliment felt like a hollow echo. "I just... it's different, you know?"

"I get it," she said, leaning against the counter. "But you'll find your groove. It takes time to adjust."

I nodded, but uncertainty lingered like the last rays of sun slipping beneath the waves. I stepped outside into the cool evening air, the sky a deepening indigo. I glanced up at the stars beginning to emerge, their distant twinkles a reminder of the vastness beyond the walls I had erected.

I wandered to the beach, my feet sinking into the soft sand. The sound of the waves rolling in was a balm for my weary spirit. I took a deep breath, the salty air filling my lungs, and closed my eyes, letting the sound of the ocean wash over me. Here, I felt the remnants of my freedom, the pulse of life that once flowed through me so effortlessly.

In that moment, I realized that perhaps the struggle for balance wasn't about losing one for the other but finding a way to weave them together. A roof over my head didn't have to mean the end of my journey; it could be a new beginning. The tides of life ebbed and flowed, and as long as I could still feel the sand beneath my toes, I knew I could navigate the changes ahead.

As the waves whispered secrets to the shore, I smiled softly to myself, understanding that every choice led me somewhere new, and that I still had the power to choose my path.

The Art of Selling Out

I stood at the edge of the bustling Byron Bay markets, a kaleidoscope of colors and sounds swirling around me like the painted canvases hung from weathered wooden stalls. The sun draped its golden light over everything, turning the scene into a mirage of joy, but underneath it lay a dissonance that made my heart ache. The laughter of children mixed with the strumming of a guitar; scents of spices and fried food mingled with the salty tang of the ocean breeze. It should have felt vibrant, alive, but instead, it felt like a performance—a façade hiding the growing rift in my beloved town.

I watched as a local artist, once known for her raw, expressive pieces that captured the wild essence of the coast, now painted smiling koalas and surfboards, each stroke a compromise, each brush dipped in a color of conformity. I felt the weight of disillusionment settle in my chest like a stone. Art was meant to be a reflection of the soul, not a tourist's trinket.

"Hey, Finn!"

Her voice snapped me out of my thoughts, and I turned just in time to see Marla approach me from her market stall, her wild curls bouncing with each step. A small woven basket swung casually at her side, likely full of whatever she'd found on the beach today, some sort of inspiration she was turning into art.

"You've got to check out my latest pieces! I think you'll love them!" she called, grinning widely as she drew closer.

I managed a smile, though it felt tight on my face. "Sure, Marla," I replied, trying to keep my tone light and absently glancing at her stall. "What are you working on these days?"

"Oh, you know, just some more 'beachy' stuff. The tourists eat it up." She rolled her eyes, but there was that familiar gleam in her expression, that little spark of pride, even in her cynicism. "It's all about the market, right? If I want to make a living, I have to adapt."

I nodded, more out of reflex than actual agreement. Marla was a good artist, I knew that much. But there was something about her work—how commercial it had become—that rubbed me the wrong way. I could see the conflict behind her eyes, though. She wasn't stupid. She was just doing what she had to do to survive.

"But isn't that selling out?" I asked before I could stop myself, the words slipping out like an old habit. There was a slight edge to my voice, an undercurrent of skepticism I couldn't quite hide.

Her expression shifted, just for a second, and I caught the vulnerability in her eyes before it vanished behind a wall of defiance. "Maybe," she replied, chewing on her lip for a moment. "But what's the alternative? Starving in a studio, hoping someone will appreciate the 'real me'? I have bills to pay."

I winced, feeling a flicker of empathy. She was right, in a way. She was making it work, even if it wasn't in the way she'd originally imagined. And maybe that was the price of living in a place like this—where the surfboards and sunset paintings sold better than anything more abstract or complex.

She paused, her eyes narrowing slightly as she shifted the conversation. "What about you? You been working on anything new lately?"

I hesitated, the question suddenly feeling loaded. I wasn't ready to talk about my work—about the unfinished canvases, the half-formed ideas that seemed to have no clear direction. Everything I'd been trying to paint felt off, like I couldn't get the brushstrokes to match what was in my head. I didn't want to explain that to her.

"Uh, yeah, you know... just some stuff," I muttered, scratching the back of my neck. "Nothing really worth showing yet." I offered her a half-hearted grin. "I've got a lot of... unfinished pieces piling up, actually."

Marla raised an eyebrow, her expression turning knowing, but she didn't press it. Instead, she leaned in a little closer, her eyes glinting. "Are you selling anything? Or is it just piling up in your studio?"

I shrugged, avoiding her gaze, my mind spinning for a reason, an excuse, something to deflect. "Not really," I said vaguely. "Haven't gotten around to it. You know how it is—life gets busy. Maybe someday."

ALEX TELMAN

It wasn't a lie, but it wasn't the whole truth either. The truth was, I hadn't been 'trying' to sell my work. Not recently, anyway.

She let out a soft laugh, like she knew better, but didn't want to call me on it. "Well, when you're ready to part with something, I'll be your first buyer. I love your stuff, Finn. Don't sell yourself short."

Her words hung there between us, a little too generous, a little too kind, and I almost believed her for a second. Almost. But the knot in my stomach didn't loosen. I wasn't ready to part with anything, especially not with someone who could see the vulnerability I tried to hide behind my art.

"Thanks, Marla," I said, my voice softer now, and I gave her a nod of acknowledgment. "Maybe one day."

But deep down, I wasn't sure when—or if—that day would ever come.

I watched as she walked back to her stall, filled with paintings that no longer resonated with the raw spirit she once created. I knew this struggle too well—the line between passion and practicality growing thinner by the day. The beach that had once cradled our dreams now felt like a distant memory, eroded by the tide of commercialization.

As I meandered through the stalls, I couldn't shake the sense of loss that enveloped me. An old man sat hunched over, carving wooden figures of dolphins and surfboards, his gnarled hands moving with the grace of a dancer. I admired the craftsmanship but felt a twinge of sadness. The man's art was genuine, yet it, too, catered to the tourists—the very people who took from the town without understanding its soul.

"Good work you've got there, mate," I said, my voice rough like the sandpaper the man used on his carvings.

The old man looked up, eyes crinkling into a smile. "Thanks, son. It's what pays the bills. But I do it for the love of the craft, too."

I pondered his words, searching for wisdom hidden within them. "Is it still art if it's for profit?" I asked, the question heavy on my tongue.

The old man paused, his hands still, as if the weight of the world rested on his shoulders. "Art's like the ocean, young man. It ebbs and flows. It can be both a wave of expression and a current of commerce. The trick is to ride it without losing your balance."

I felt a flicker of hope amidst the darkness that seemed to surround me. Perhaps it was possible to navigate this new reality without losing myself entirely. Maybe I could carve out a space that honored both art and survival, authenticity and practicality.

As the day wore on, I found myself in front of a stall adorned with vibrant fabrics—batik prints and tie-dye, the colors a riot against the dullness of my thoughts. A woman with sun-kissed skin and a smile that could light up the night stood behind the table, weaving stories with her words as easily as she wove the fabric.

"Welcome! Looking for something special?" she asked, her voice like honey.

I picked up a scarf, its colors swirling together in a dance of vibrancy. "What's the story behind this?" I asked, holding it up to the light.

"It's about freedom," she said, her eyes sparkling. "Each piece reflects a moment, a feeling. I want people to feel the spirit of Byron when they wear it."

I nodded, feeling the fabric slip through my fingers like sand. "But don't you think it's a bit commercialized?"

She laughed, a sound that bubbled up like laughter at the beach. "Everything changes, love. But if you pour your heart into what you create, then it's yours, regardless of who buys it."

Her confidence struck a chord within me, and I realized I was witnessing the essence of true artistry—not merely in the product, but in the intent behind it.

As the sun began to set, casting a golden hue over the market, my heart began to soften. I could see a glimmer of possibility amid the challenges. The changes in Byron Bay might threaten the authenticity of its artistic soul, but perhaps it could be preserved through the spirit of those who refused to compromise their passion.

I turned to leave the market. My shift at the café was starting soon, and my steps felt lighter, the weight on my shoulders dissipating like the evening mist. I was ready to embrace the duality of my existence, to find a balance between the tides of commerce and the wildness of my heart.

With the last rays of sunlight dancing across the horizon, I felt a spark ignite within me—a determination to remain true to myself in this evolving landscape. The art of selling out didn't have to be the end; it could be a new beginning, a canvas waiting for my unique brushstrokes.

Echoes of the Past

I leaned against the weathered railing of the Byron Bay boardwalk, the wooden slats creaking under the weight of both time and memory. The ocean spread before me, an endless expanse of blue, shimmering under the sun like a promise long forgotten. I closed my eyes, allowing the salty breeze to sweep over me, carrying whispers of the past—the laughter of friends, the scent of bonfire smoke, the warmth of a world untainted by ambition.

The boardwalk was a relic of the old Byron, where surfboards were made of dreams, and the only currency was camaraderie. But as I opened my eyes, I saw the encroachment of luxury—yachts bobbing in the distance, developers circling like vultures. The landscape had shifted, and so had the people.

"Finn?" A voice cut through my reverie, familiar yet strange. I turned to see a figure emerging from the shadows of a clump of ragged palm trees, the sun catching the glint of hair that had once danced in the wind during carefree days. It was Mark, my old friend, a ghost from a life that felt both near and impossibly distant.

"Mark! It's been ages!" I said, feigning enthusiasm, my heart drumming with a mix of joy and apprehension. We embraced, but it felt more like a formal handshake—both of us grappling with the weight of years spent apart.

"Yeah, too long," Mark replied, stepping back to take me in, the lines on his face deeper than I remembered. "How's life treating you?"

"Same old, you know. Just trying to keep my head above water," I said, a forced smile plastered on my face. "You?"

"Just got back from Sydney. The hustle there—it's a different world," Mark said, his voice tinged with a hint of envy. "People chasing dreams, but it's all plastic, you know?"

I nodded, recalling our youthful idealism when we believed we could change the world with our art and passion. "What about your painting?" I asked, hopeful to steer the conversation back to the spark we once shared.

Mark shrugged, a flicker of sadness passing over his face. "I'm in advertising now. Art is about what's selling now. I create what sells. You have to, to make a living. No one wants the raw stuff anymore. They want something pretty to hang on their wall or what sells the next tube of toothpaste."

His words hung between us, heavy with regret. I felt a pang in my chest, longing for the time when we believed our work could mean something, when we poured our hearts into every stroke. "You remember that mural we painted down at the old youth center?" I asked, nostalgia flooding my voice. "The one that made the front page of the local paper?"

Mark chuckled, but it was bittersweet. "Yeah. We thought we were changing the world. Now it feels like we were just kids playing with paint."

"Maybe we were," I replied, my voice quiet. "But we had something back then—a sense of purpose, of community. Now it's like... everything is for sale."

I watched the waves crash against the pier, the white foam bubbling and dissipating. It mirrored my thoughts—ideas that once surged with vigor now fizzled out like fireflies in the night. The vibrant community I loved was being swallowed by a tide of consumerism.

"Do you ever miss it?" Mark asked, his gaze fixed on the horizon. "The way things used to be?"

"Every damn day," I admitted, my heart aching with the weight of truth. "But I feel lost. I don't know where I fit anymore. This town isn't the same."

Mark turned to me, his eyes a mixture of understanding and pain. "You know, I think we all feel that way. But you can't let it eat you alive. You have to find a way to create, even if it means adapting."

My thoughts spiraled. Could I adapt? I looked at Mark, who seemed both a reflection of my past and a reminder of what had been lost. "What if adapting means losing yourself?" I asked, the question a raw nerve.

Mark opened his mouth to respond but paused, lost in thought. "Maybe it doesn't have to," he said finally. "Maybe it's about blending the old with the new. Find a way to keep the spirit alive, even in this changing world."

I must have looked doubtful.

"You know? Like you write poetry, but why not write poetry for people who to sell toothpaste?"

The conversation hung between us, a fragile thread woven from shared memories and unspoken fears. I felt the weight of the past pressing down on me, but amidst the nostalgia, there was a glimmer of hope—a flicker of what could still be. "Maybe…"

As we spoke, the sun dipped lower in the sky, casting long shadows across the boardwalk. The world around us began to soften, the harshness of reality blending into the warmth of camaraderie. We reminisced about our dreams, our laughter ringing out like music carried on the wind.

But the laughter faded into silence, the specter of reality creeping back in. My heart sank as I realized that those days might be gone, but the longing for connection remained. The boardwalk, with its peeling paint and weathered wood, stood as a reminder of the resilience that still lingered within me.

The words Mark had said lingered in the air long after he'd gone, like the salt breeze that never quite left the skin. "Let's keep in touch," he'd said. "We could do something that honors what was while still reaching for what could be." It sounded perfect, didn't it? So full of potential, a path forward that blended past and future. But the longer I stood there, alone on the boardwalk, watching the waves shift and pull against the shoreline, the more I felt the weight of doubt creeping in, inch by inch.

I had promised myself that I wouldn't let this moment slip away. That I wouldn't let it become one more empty promise, another "what if" tucked into a drawer that never saw the light of day. But even as the thought crossed my mind, I could feel the familiar pull of excuses wrapping around me.

I've always got good intentions, I told myself. But good intentions don't pay the bills. Maybe I could still try to work with Mark on some kind of advertising project that was 'real'+— maybe. But then what? The city, the community, the expectations of everyone around me, including myself… it felt like everything was already too much. The noise of life, of unfinished business, was overwhelming. I'd promised to get back to my writing… to start writing again, to 'finish something'—anything— 'but'…

DOWN AND OUT IN BYRON BAY

I exhaled sharply, pushing the thought aside. Maybe I was just making excuses. Again. It felt like I had been putting things off for so long that now even the idea of moving forward seemed like a monumental task. Mark had been right: we 'had' talked about creating something meaningful, something that mattered. It had been easy to believe in the idea when we were younger, sitting around drinking beer late into the night, talking about dreams that felt like they were within arm's reach. But now? Now, the weight of everything—the bills, the obligations, the pressure to be "someone"—felt suffocating.

I'm not the same person I was back then, I thought. Back then, we had endless time, endless possibility. Now, everything feels like it's slipping through my fingers.

The echoes of the past that had once felt like a source of strength now felt like chains. And with the weight of those memories hanging over me, how was I supposed to make space for anything new? How could I carve out time for a creative partnership or the passion to write when there was always something else pulling me in a thousand directions?

The worst part? I could feel myself slipping into the same pattern. I was already rationalizing, already finding reasons not to follow through.

Maybe Mark won't follow up anyway, I thought. Or maybe we'll just talk about it forever, never actually doing anything. People always say they'll keep in touch, but they don't. I'll just let this one fade out like all the others.

I tried to push the thought away, but it stuck to me like sand to skin, gritty and impossible to shake. The truth was, I wasn't sure if I could follow through anymore. I had my writing, sure, but it felt like it belonged to someone else. Someone more 'alive' in it, someone who wasn't tangled in knots of self-doubt and fear of failure. I was a prisoner between writing and the idea of writing.

As I stood there, the fading light of the sunset casting long shadows on the water, I realized that the idea of creating something with Mark wasn't the problem. The problem was me.

I'm not ready, I thought. I'm not ready to take that leap again. I'm not ready to put myself out there—again—and risk falling flat on my face.

I'd been burned before. Not by Mark or by anyone else, but by myself. The countless times I'd said, "I'll do it tomorrow," and then tomorrow turned into next week, then next month, and eventually, 'never'. I had a lifetime of unfinished projects stacked up, abandoned with every excuse I could think of.

And yet, there was something about Mark's enthusiasm, his belief that we could still do something together, that stirred something inside me. Maybe this was my last shot to reclaim some of that lost spirit. Maybe, just maybe, I could step up and try again. Maybe I could just show up and see what happens.

But the longer I stood there, the more I felt the familiar weight of my own hesitations wrapping around me like a thick fog. The truth? I wasn't ready to get my hopes up. I wasn't ready to risk disappointment again. The flame of possibility that Mark had sparked seemed so bright, but it also felt 'dangerous'.

I took one last deep breath, forcing myself to let go of the spiraling thoughts. I'll think about it, I told myself. I'll call him. I'll reach out.

But even as I promised myself that, I could feel it. I could feel that familiar, gnawing certainty in the pit of my stomach. Nothing would come of it. It would slip through my fingers, just like all the other opportunities. Just like everything else.

I turned away from the water, heading back down the boardwalk, my footsteps echoing hollowly beneath me.

Maybe someday, I'd get around to it. Maybe someday, I'd believe in something again. But today wasn't that day.

And I couldn't shake the feeling that nothing ever really would come of it.

House of Cards

I stood at the edge of the driveway, the concrete stark and cold beneath my feet. The house loomed before me—a sprawling, sun-soaked monstrosity with white walls gleaming in the fading light, an architectural echo of the wealth and ambition that had transformed Byron Bay. I felt like an intruder, an artifact from a bygone era, clutching a six-pack of beer like a talisman of my simpler past.

Laughter drifted through the open doors, a symphony of joy tinged with hollowness. As I approached, the sound wrapped around me, seductive yet dissonant, like a siren's call promising pleasure but hiding the peril beneath its surface.

Inside, the party erupted into a kaleidoscope of color and movement. Friends from my youth mingled with the new bourgeois elite, their laughter mingling with clinking glasses, the air thick with the scent of expensive perfumes and roasted meats. I scanned the room, my heart tightening as I recognized familiar faces transformed by tailored suits and designer dresses. I felt like a ghost haunting a place I once knew intimately.

"Finn! You made it!" Claire, an old friend, rushed over, her cheeks flushed with a mix of wine and exuberance. She embraced me, and for a fleeting moment, warmth seeped back into my bones.

"Of course! Wouldn't miss it for the world," I replied, my voice laced with forced enthusiasm. "Nice place you've got here."

"Oh, it's just a little something," she said, waving her hand dismissively, but her eyes sparkled with pride. "You know how it is—hard work pays off!"

I smiled, though it felt more like a grimace. Hard work? I had seen too many friends trade their authenticity for comfort, too many ideals suffocated under the weight of success. I glanced around the room, taking in the glittering chandeliers, the expensive art lining the walls, and the laughter that felt rehearsed, scripted in a play I had never agreed to join.

As the night wore on, I found myself cornered by a group of Claire's new friends—stockbrokers, real estate agents, and other purveyors of wealth, each one a polished façade hiding the cracks beneath. They regaled tales of their latest acquisitions, their voices booming with bravado, drowning out the deeper currents of longing that swirled beneath the surface.

"Finn, you should invest!" one of them said, clapping me on the back. "You can't live off memories, man. You have to capitalize on the future!"

A flash of anger surged through me, mixed with profound sadness. "What if the future isn't what it seems?" I replied, my voice barely above a whisper, the words lost amidst the laughter.

Another friend chimed in, "Come on, man! We're living the dream! Look at us!" He gestured grandly, encompassing the lavish surroundings as if they were proof of fulfillment. But to me, they felt like a house of cards—beautiful, intricate, but so easily toppled.

The conversation shifted to vacations, lavish getaways that felt like a retreat from the very existence they had crafted. Tales poured forth, a stream of excess and indulgence, each story punctuated with laughter that rang hollow in my ears. I felt myself slipping, a shadow retreating from the light, caught between two worlds—one I had loved and lost, and another that felt foreign, unreal.

"Do you ever think about what we used to do?" I asked Claire, pulling her aside as the party swirled around us like a tide. "The beach bonfires, the art shows we created... everything felt so real back then."

She hesitated, her eyes darting as if searching for the right words amid the chaos. "Of course, but you have to move on. This is the life we wanted, right?"

A pang shot through my chest. Did we really want this? Or had we simply traded our dreams for a safe harbor, forsaking the wildness that once defined us? "I don't know," I said, vulnerability creeping into my voice. "It all feels... empty."

Her smile faltered, and for a moment, I saw the truth lurking behind her facade. But it was quickly masked by the laughter of others, pulling her back into the swirl of bourgeois revelry. She excused herself, leaving me standing alone, feeling more disconnected than ever.

I wandered through the house, searching for something—perhaps a glimpse of the past or a sign that authenticity still existed. I found myself in a room adorned with paintings, each piece a stark representation of the struggle between reality and illusion. One caught my eye, a wild landscape, colors bleeding into one another, raw and unrefined.

"This one's beautiful," I murmured, stepping closer.

"It's the artist's rendition of the old Byron," a voice said from behind me. It was Noah, Claire's husband, a man with a polished exterior that felt like glass. "But you know, it's not really marketable. People want what looks good above all else."

My heart sank. "What about the truth?" I asked, my voice barely steady. "What about the struggle?"

"Struggle doesn't sell," he replied with a shrug, turning to mingle with other guests, leaving me to grapple with the reality that the world had shifted beneath my feet.

I stepped out onto the balcony, needing air, the cool breeze hitting my face like a slap of reality. Below, the waves crashed against the shore, a reminder of a world that thrived on authenticity rather than pretense. I leaned against the railing, the wood rough against my palms, grounding me in the chaos of the night.

As I stood there, watching the ocean churn, the weight of my loneliness settled in. I had tried to reconnect, to find some sense of belonging among these people who had lost their way. But the truth was clear: I couldn't join them in their masquerade.

The laughter echoed behind me, a reminder that the party continued without me. Yet here, at the edge of the world, I felt a flicker of clarity—a spark of hope amidst the rubble of my nostalgia.

Maybe I didn't need to fit into their world. Maybe I could carve my own path, honor the past while shaping a future that resonated with my spirit.

I turned back toward the party, the lights twinkling like stars in the night sky, and realized that while I might not belong to this new Byron Bay, I could still forge connections grounded in authenticity. With that thought, I

ALEX TELMAN

stepped back inside, ready to face the crowd, but this time, with a renewed sense of purpose.

The Rave of Ages

I stood outside the old community hall, a relic of better days, its paint peeling like the memories that clung to its walls. The flickering lights inside spilled out onto the pavement, casting shadows that danced like ghosts from the past. The air hummed with the distant thud of music—a beat pulsing through the cool night, echoing the vibrant life that once thrived in Byron Bay.

As I entered, the familiar scent of cheap beer and sweat washed over me, reminding me of long-forgotten nights where laughter flowed as freely as the ocean waves. It felt both inviting and suffocating, nostalgia wrapping around me like a warm but constricting blanket. The hall was packed, a sea of familiar faces illuminated by colorful lights, each lost in their own moment of joy or regret.

I moved through the crowd, feeling like an observer in a world that had once felt like home. The music surged, a blend of classic rock and punk, a soundtrack to the memories echoing in my mind. I spotted Claire, her hair wild and eyes bright, lost in conversation with a group of friends who seemed to float between laughter and nostalgia.

"Finn! Over here!" She waved me over, her smile radiant but tinged with a hint of something I couldn't quite place—was it desperation or delight? My heart pounded as I walked toward her, the rhythm of the music melding with the rhythm of my insecurities.

"Good to see you!" she said, her voice barely audible over the chaos. "It's been ages since we've had a night like this!"

"Yeah, feels like a reunion," I replied, trying to mask the tightness in my throat. "Everyone looks... happy."

"Happy?" She laughed, the sound a little too sharp, a little too forced. "Maybe just trying to forget."

I caught a glimmer of something deeper in her eyes, a hint of shared disillusionment beneath her laughter. The night was a throwback, a revival of everything that had once defined us—music, friendship, rebellion. Yet, I felt like an intruder in this celebration of a past I both cherished and mourned.

I grabbed a drink from a nearby table, the cheap lager bubbling over the rim of the plastic cup. As I sipped, the taste was bitter, a reminder of the choices I had made—the sacrifices for stability that had slowly eroded my sense of freedom. I glanced around, watching as old friends embraced, sharing stories and laughter that felt as fleeting as the bubbles in my drink.

"Come on, let's hit the dance floor!" Claire tugged at my arm, pulling me toward the center of the hall where bodies swayed and bounced, each movement a celebration of life in its rawest form. I followed, though my feet felt heavy, like they were mired in the mud of my own discontent.

As we danced, I observed the way the lights flickered, illuminating the faces of people lost in joy and oblivion. There was something beautiful in their abandon, a fleeting glimpse of the freedom I craved but couldn't quite grasp. I caught snippets of conversations—plans for the future, dreams that still burned bright despite the weight of their realities.

"Can you believe how far we've come?" Claire shouted over the music, her smile wide, infectious. "Look at us! We're still here!"

"Yeah," I replied, though my heart felt heavy with the truth of it all. "But at what cost?"

"What do you mean?" She leaned in, concern creasing her brow.

"Everything feels... different now. We're different. It's like we're holding on to ghosts." My voice was raw, but the truth lingered in the air between us, palpable and unsettling.

Claire's gaze faltered, and in that moment, I saw the flicker of doubt cross her features. The music swelled around us, and I could feel the weight of our unspoken fears pressing against my chest. I had longed for connection, but here it felt frayed, the threads of our past unraveling in the face of our present.

We danced in silence, the pulsating beat thumping against my ribcage. I tried to lose myself in the rhythm, but the more I moved, the more acutely aware I became of my own displacement. I watched as couples swayed together, bodies entwined like vines, their laughter drowning out the reality of the night.

"Remember when we used to dream about changing the world?" I asked, the words slipping from my lips before I could stop them. "Now it feels like we're just... existing."

Claire's expression shifted, and for a moment, we were both lost in the weight of our shared history. "Sometimes I think we've lost our way. Maybe we traded our dreams for something... safer."

Her words hung in the air, heavy with resignation. I felt the truth resonate within me, a painful acknowledgment of the compromises we had made. The night was a celebration, yes, but it was also a reminder of everything we had sacrificed—the fire in our souls dimmed by the mundane rhythms of adulthood.

The music shifted, an anthem of rebellion blasting through the speakers, and I felt a surge of energy. I pulled Claire closer, the two of us spinning into the fray, letting the chaos consume us. For a fleeting moment, I felt alive—alive with the pulse of the night, the warmth of friendship, and the memories that were at once beautiful and heart-wrenching.

"Where's Noah tonight?" Claire's eyes flickered with surprise, then darted away, as if seeking an escape from the weight of the question. "He's back in Sydney... meetings," she replied, her voice barely above a whisper. There was an edge of vulnerability in her tone, a hint that their marriage was not as happy as it seemed. I watched her closely, noting the way her fingers played nervously with the hem of her dress, and I wondered if she felt as trapped as I did. The night wrapped around us, thick with unspoken possibilities. "Did it ever feel like you were just... going through the motions?" I asked, my heart racing.

But as the song faded and the next began, I caught a glimpse of the room through the chaos—laughter mingling with tears, joy hiding behind smiles. It was a tapestry of humanity, flawed yet beautiful, and I realized I was still searching for my place within it.

Before the next song began, I stepped outside for a breath of air, the coolness washing over me like a wave. The stars sparkled overhead, bright and indifferent to the struggles below. I closed my eyes, listening to the muffled sounds of the party behind me—a mix of laughter, music, and the occasional shout of joy.

In that moment, I felt the weight of my own dreams pressing against me, a mixture of hope and despair. I could still see the flickering lights through the door and hear the echoes of the past calling me back inside. But this time, I carried the weight of my choices with me, embracing both the beauty and the pain of my existence.

The pulsating beats of the rave faded behind me, replaced by the cool night air that wrapped around me like a whisper. I leaned against the rough wooden railing, the stars twinkling above, mocking my turmoil. Claire's laughter echoed in my mind, a siren song pulling me back inside. But guilt wrapped around me like a heavy shroud. She was married, and yet the connection we shared felt electric, intoxicating. Should I risk it all for a fleeting moment of passion? The tension between desire and morality coiled tightly in my chest, leaving me breathless and uncertain.

As I turned back toward the hall, I took a deep breath, ready to face the night. It was a celebration of the past, yes, but also a reminder that there was still time to forge a new path. With that thought anchoring me, I stepped inside, ready to embrace the chaos, ready to reclaim my place among the living. The thrum of music enveloped me like a warm embrace, the laughter and chatter swirling around me, each sound pulling me deeper into the vibrant tapestry of life. I felt the flicker of possibility ignite within, urging me to dance, to connect, to feel again.

Whispers in the Wind

I trudged along the narrow, winding path that hugged the coastline of Byron Bay, each step muffled by the golden sand, damp from the ocean's embrace. The sun hung low, a burnt orange orb melting into the horizon, casting long shadows that stretched like fingers across the shore. The air was thick with salt and nostalgia, each breath igniting memories long buried beneath the weight of responsibility and expectation.

I paused, allowing the ocean's roar to wash over me—a tempestuous symphony that echoed the tumult within my soul. The waves crashed against the rocks with a ferocity that mirrored my own restless heart. It was a reminder of the wildness I once craved, the free-spirited youth who roamed these shores, lost in dreams of art and rebellion, unshackled by the mundane.

"Come on, Finn," I muttered to myself, the words tumbling out like the waves. "Remember who you are."

The wind whipped around me, a fierce companion that tugged at my clothes, urging me forward. It seemed to carry whispers—fragments of conversations I had once had with friends who shared my hunger for life, for meaning. Those late-night talks beneath the stars, where hopes and fears intertwined like the strands of a fraying rope.

I thought of Claire, her laughter ringing like chimes in the wind, her dreams igniting my own. But as the years rolled on, our ideals had faded into the background, dulled by the grind of everyday life. Now, the only laughter I heard was the hollow echo of social gatherings, where conversations revolved around property values and the latest trend. The world had changed, and somewhere in that shift, Claire and I had drifted apart.

I remembered the way she looked at me that night at the rave, as if the world had paused just for us. The way her eyes sparkled with something that felt like an unspoken promise. Our one night together was everything I had ever imagined—full of the energy and passion of what could have been. We had connected in a way I hadn't felt in years, like two kindred spirits rediscovering each other after too long apart.

But she was married and as unhappy as she was, the reality of her life and commitments rushed in like cold water, washing away the warmth of what we'd shared. It wasn't just the truth of her relationship—it was the guilt that gnawed at me, the knowledge that for all the beauty of that night, it was fleeting. A stolen moment.

I'd tried to push the memory of her out of my mind, telling myself that the connection had been one-sided, that she was just as lost as I was in the chaos of life. But deep down, I knew the truth. She had felt it too. That night, her touch had lingered in my thoughts long after she left, and no matter how many years passed, it would always be there, tucked away like an unfinished poem, never fully resolved.

But she was married. She had a life—a husband, a house, responsibilities that I couldn't even begin to understand. We had once spoken about leaving it all behind, about chasing our dreams with no fear of what others thought. But life didn't work that way. Not for most people. And certainly not for Claire.

I exhaled slowly, pushing the thought of her back into the recesses of my mind, where it could quietly haunt me without consuming me. It was hard, though. Hard to let go of something so perfect, so tempting, and so utterly impossible.

But life was a series of impossible choices, wasn't it?

Maybe that was the thing. Claire's laughter, her presence in my past, was a reminder of what I could have had, what I could have been. A reminder of who I used to be before I let fear dictate my choices. I wanted to be that person again—the one who could take risks, the one who wasn't afraid to fight for what mattered.

"You're thinking about her again, aren't you?" I looked around and there was Ella staring at me. Her voice was gentle but direct.

I didn't answer right away. There was nothing to say. It wasn't just Claire—it was the life I had once imagined for myself, the one that had slipped through my fingers without my even realizing it.

"Yeah," I finally muttered. "I think I am."

"Well, you're not going to find it by standing here, you know," she said, her tone light but firm. "If you keep waiting for things to happen, you'll miss them. You've got to make a choice, Finn. You can't keep looking back. It's time to move forward."

"Maybe I'm just not ready," I whispered, though even I wasn't sure who I was trying to convince.

Ella didn't respond right away. She just stood there, watching me. And in her silence, I felt the truth settle in like a weight I had been carrying for far too long.

It wasn't the past or the dreams I once had that were holding me back. It was me. I was the one keeping myself stuck.

I took a breath, then another, feeling something stir in me—a faint flicker of resolve, a small but insistent reminder that I had a choice. I could either stay here, wallowing in what had been, or I could start again. I didn't have to wait for life to come to me. I could go out and find it, just like I had once done.

"I'm not ready to let go of everything," I said quietly, "but maybe it's time to start something new."

Ella nodded, her smile softening as she saw the shift in me. "That's the spirit."

And just like that, I knew it was true. Nothing was going to happen unless I made it happen. Nothing was going to change unless I decided to take the first step. It wasn't about Claire or the life I had once imagined. It was about me—my own choices, my own future.

I turned back to the ocean. Whatever I created next, whatever came from this moment, would be mine. And for the first time in a long time, I was ready to see where it would take me.

The salty breeze kissed my face, a reminder of a promise I made to myself long ago—to never lose sight of who I was. But the world had a way of reshaping dreams into obligations, expectations into chains.

I continued down the path, each step stirring the sand like the unresolved feelings in my heart. I reached a rocky outcrop where the waves battered against the stone, white foam spiraling into the air like the chaos of my thoughts. I watched as the tide surged and receded, a reminder of life's relentless ebb and flow.

"Why do we allow ourselves to be swept away?" I whispered into the wind, as if seeking an answer from the universe itself. The ocean responded with a crashing wave, a frothy explosion that doused my legs, startling me out of my reverie.

I laughed, a sound that felt foreign yet liberating, the saltwater mingling with the sweat on my skin. The ocean had always been my sanctuary, a place where I could shed the layers of conformity that clung to me like barnacles. Here, I was reminded of the fierce independence that once defined me.

I recalled the nights spent under the stars, the fire crackling beside me, friends gathered close, sharing dreams and fears like offerings to the universe. It was during those moments I felt truly alive, each laugh a rebellion against the mundane.

"Hey, you!" a voice broke through my thoughts, pulling me again back to the present. I turned to see Ella walking behind me. "What are you still doing out here?"

"Just... thinking," I replied, the weight of my words hanging between us.

"Thinking or wondering?" Ella's grin was wide, but I caught the underlying concern in her eyes.

"Both, I guess. Trying to remember who I used to be."

Ella nodded, her expression shifting. "I get that. Sometimes it feels like we've sold out. This place is changing, man. It's not what it used to be."

I glanced out at the ocean, the horizon a blur of blues and gold. "Yeah, it's like we're all caught up in some dream that's turned into a nightmare."

"Or a party we weren't invited to," Ella added, a hint of bitterness lacing his tone. "Remember when we used to create art that mattered? Now we just shuffle through life, pretending it's enough."

The honesty of Ella's words struck a chord deep within me. We stood together, two souls adrift, both yearning for something more—a connection to our past, a spark of inspiration that felt all but extinguished.

"Let's do something," I said suddenly, the idea bursting forth like a wave crashing against the rocks. "Let's revive the art scene here. Bring back the music, the poetry... the heart of Byron."

Ella's eyes brightened for a moment, but then the doubt returned. "And what? Watch it get swallowed by the same tide that's swallowing everything else? We're not kids anymore, Finn. This is real life."

"Real life?" I echoed, the bitterness rising in my throat. "What's real about a life spent chasing money and status? We used to believe in something greater than that."

As we stood there, the wind howled around us, a furious reminder of the storms we had weathered. I felt a surge of rebellion rising within me, a fierce longing to reclaim the wildness that had been lost.

"Maybe we can't change the world," I said, the fire in my voice igniting a flicker of hope. "But we can start right here, right now. We can create a space for the dreamers, for the artists, for those who refuse to settle."

Ella hesitated, uncertainty flickering across her face. "What if it fails?"

"Then at least we'll know we tried," I replied, feeling the tide of possibility rising within me. "We owe it to ourselves. To the dreamers we once were."

The ocean roared in agreement, waves crashing against the shore as if cheering us on. I looked out at the expanse of water, the whispers of the wind now urging me forward.

"Let's do it," Ella said finally, the resolve returning to her voice. "Let's bring back the spirit of this place."

Together, we stood on the edge of the world, the sea stretching out before us like an uncharted territory, brimming with potential. I felt the warmth of possibility wrap around me, a promise that perhaps, amidst the changing tides of life, there was still room for rebellion, for creativity, for the wild heart of Byron Bay.

But as I looked at Ella, I realized she wasn't there. Her presence, so full of life just moments before, had evaporated. She had gone, disappeared into the fading light, with nothing more than the breeze to mark her departure.

I glanced around, searching for her, but the beach was empty now, the last traces of the sunset slipping into the horizon, leaving only the lingering hum of the ocean. The feeling in my chest shifted, turning from warmth to something colder, something that felt like a quiet ache. Where had she gone? Had I imagined it all?

The conversation we'd shared—about dreams, about art, about creating something new together—was supposed to be the spark. I thought we had connected, that we were standing on the same ground. But now, standing there alone, I couldn't shake the feeling that I had misread it. That maybe, just maybe, Ella had seen something in me that wasn't really there.

I had always been good at imagining possibilities. It was easy to dream when you didn't have to face reality head-on. But the reality was, I was standing on the edge of something that felt like a precipice, and the weight of it, the weight of all the things I hadn't done, was starting to sink in.

Ella had her fire, her spark. She could dance with the tides, with the changing rhythms of life, and not be afraid. She didn't carry the same doubts I did, the same weight of all the things left undone. Her enthusiasm was contagious, but now, with her gone, I couldn't help but feel that maybe it wasn't meant for me.

I stood there, still as a statue, watching the last of the twilight fade. The waves rolled in, gentle and steady, but I wasn't sure if they held the promise I thought they did. I didn't have Ella's fire. I didn't have her drive. I had a notebook full of unfinished words, a gallery full of half-painted canvases, and a heart full of 'what ifs'.

Why can't I just follow through?

I thought about the things she'd said. About rebellion. About being real. About making something of myself in a place that was so full of life, so full of possibility. But then, in the quiet after she left, I realized something: maybe it wasn't about rebellion at all.

Maybe it was about facing the hard truth that I didn't have what it took to keep going.

I took a deep breath, watching the last of the light disappear from the sky. Maybe I wasn't cut out for this anymore.

The thought didn't sit right with me, but it felt true. And that was the part that stung the most—the quiet, bitter truth that, despite everything, I wasn't sure if I still had the fight in me.

Maybe Byron Bay, with all its wildness and freedom, was a place I had outgrown. Maybe I had outgrown the person I used to be—the person who believed in endless possibilities, who took risks, who 'created'.

I turned away from the beach, my feet dragging in the sand. As I walked back toward the cottage, I glanced at the empty street, the stillness of it suddenly overwhelming. The world felt big, but I felt small, like I had been waiting for something to happen for too long and had missed it.

DOWN AND OUT IN BYRON BAY

Was I just waiting for a sign?

I could almost hear Ella's voice again, her laugh, her energy. But it felt distant now, like a song I couldn't quite recall. Maybe she was right. Maybe I needed to find that spark again. Maybe the wild heart of Byron Bay was still here, still waiting for me. But for now, it felt like I was just another one of its faded memories, clinging to the past instead of reaching for the future.

I pushed open the door to my cottage, stepping inside. The familiar walls, the smell of salt air, the quiet of it all—they felt like both comfort and prison. I sat down at my desk, my gaze falling on the stack of unfinished paintings, the empty canvas that stared back at me like a challenge.

'Maybe tomorrow.' I told myself, but even as I said it, I knew.

Tomorrow wasn't enough anymore. I needed to take the first step, and I needed to do it now.

But for some reason, I couldn't make myself move.

The Community Pulse

The sun hung low over Byron Bay, casting a golden haze across the soft contours of the landscape. The air was thick with salt and sweat, mingling with the scent of eucalyptus and the distant sound of crashing waves—a constant reminder of the wild heart of this place. I stood at the edge of the community hall, watching as the crowd began to gather, their voices rising and falling like the tide.

It was a Saturday afternoon, the kind of day that should have felt lazy, filled with the blissful echoes of surfboards slicing through water and laughter spilling from the beach. Instead, it buzzed with tension. A development company had announced plans to pave over the very heart of our town, replacing the beloved local market with a sterile shopping center—a steel and glass monstrosity that threatened to choke the spirit of Byron.

I felt the weight of the world pressing against my chest, a familiar ache stirring long-buried memories of rallies, banners, and the fierce passion that once ignited my youth. I had wandered away from those days, lulled into complacency by the slow drift of life. But now, the pulse of community was beckoning me back, like an old lover whispering secrets of rebellion in my ear.

"Oi, Finn!" A voice jolted me from my thoughts. It was Jess, her hair a wild halo of curls, her face flushed with enthusiasm. She had a way of igniting something inside me, a spark that reminded me what it meant to truly feel alive.

"Are you coming?" she asked, gesturing toward the throng of people milling about, some clutching makeshift signs, others shouting slogans that resonated with raw fervor.

DOWN AND OUT IN BYRON BAY

I nodded, swallowing hard, the lump in my throat a mix of excitement and fear. "Yeah, I'm in."

As we stepped into the crowd, I could feel the energy swirling around us—voices rising, hands gesturing passionately. It was a mix of old friends and new faces, a tapestry of humanity woven together by a shared love for our home. Yet beneath the surface lay a current of anxiety, the fear that our voices might not be enough to halt the encroachment of development.

"Look at them," Jess said, her eyes scanning the crowd. "It's beautiful, isn't it? We're all here for something greater than ourselves."

A swell of emotion rose within me—an overwhelming longing for connection. I had spent too long in isolation, trapped in my own doubts and the monotony of my life. Here, amidst the shouts and cheers, I felt a flicker of hope ignite within me, a reminder of the power of community.

The rally began to unfold, words cascading like waves, washing over me. I found myself clutching a sign that read "Save Our Bay," the cardboard cutting into my palm as I held it aloft. Each chant felt like a heartbeat, the pulse of the town resonating with my own longing for purpose.

"This is what we need, Finn!" Jess shouted, her voice rising above the noise. "This is your chance to stand up for what you believe in!"

But amidst the fervor, doubt gnawed at me. What if we failed? What if all this passion amounted to nothing more than a fleeting moment of noise in a world that thrived on silence? The thought made my stomach churn, but I pushed it away, allowing the collective energy to sweep me along.

Hours passed, filled with speeches and impassioned pleas. The sun dipped lower, painting the sky in hues of orange and pink, as if the heavens themselves were igniting in support of our cause. I watched as the crowd swelled, strangers embracing, tears of determination streaming down faces etched with both hope and despair.

"Finn!" Jess's voice cut through my reverie. "You've got to say something!"

"What? Me?" I recoiled at the idea. "I'm not a speaker. I can't—"

"Just speak from your heart," she urged, her eyes glistening with conviction. "People need to hear your voice."

With every heartbeat, I felt the walls I had built around myself begin to crumble. Memories of my younger self surged back—fierce, unyielding, a warrior for the voiceless. I took a deep breath, the salty air filling my lungs, and stepped forward, the crowd parting as I moved to the front.

"Uh, hi," I stammered, gripping the edges of the sign like a lifeline. "I'm Finn, and I guess...I just wanted to say that this place—this community—is everything to us. It's our home, our history, our identity. And if we let them tear it down, what are we left with?"

My voice trembled, but the words flowed, raw and unfiltered. "I've spent too long sitting back, thinking it wouldn't make a difference. But look around! This is us fighting for what matters! We can't let them take our spirit away. We're not just fighting for a place; we're fighting for who we are!"

The crowd erupted into cheers, a wave of energy washing over me, fueling my courage. In that moment, I felt alive—like the weight of the world had shifted, the burdens I had carried for so long lifting just enough to allow a glimpse of possibility.

As the night wore on, the rally concluded with a sense of unity that hung in the air like the scent of rain on dry earth. Jess and I joined arms with the others, a circle of faces illuminated by the flickering glow of lanterns, laughter mingling with the sounds of the ocean.

"This is just the beginning," Jess whispered, her breath warm against my ear. "We'll keep fighting. Together."

I nodded, feeling a profound connection to the people around me, to the very essence of what it meant to belong. The weight of my past still lingered, but it felt lighter now, infused with purpose and the promise of change.

As we began to disperse, I caught a glimpse of the stars peeking through the twilight sky, their brilliance cutting through the haze of uncertainty. For the first time in a long while, I felt the pulse of community within me—a heartbeat that resonated with the wild, untamed spirit of Byron Bay.

And the words I'd spoken that night still echo in my mind today. The buzz of voices, the clinking of bottles, the rustling of banners—it all feels like a distant hum now, as if I were moving through a dream. The applause, the cheers, it had all felt so real in the moment, like a spark igniting something deep inside me. But as I stepped away from the gathering, the weight of reality started to settle back in.

DOWN AND OUT IN BYRON BAY

Jess was beside me, her energy still alive, still pushing forward with the rallying cry of change. Her smile, full of hope, was contagious, but I couldn't ignore the creeping sense of unease building in my chest.

She shook my arm, her voice full of that fire I'd come to admire. "That was amazing, Finn. You really stirred something in them. You've got the heart of a true leader."

I offered her a smile, trying to match her enthusiasm, but inside, I felt disconnected, like I was playing a part rather than living it. "Yeah, but... I don't know, Jess. I don't think I'm cut out for this. All these people, all this energy... I'm not sure I can keep up."

She shot me a look, her eyebrows lifting in playful challenge. "Are you serious? You've got everything it takes. You just need to believe it."

The truth? I wanted to believe her. I did believe her, in that moment. But as soon as the applause had died down, the mask I'd been wearing started to slip. I could feel the weight of the excuse already creeping back in. "I've got too much going on. I'm not a full-time activist. I can't drop everything and keep this momentum going. I've got bills, unfinished projects, my own messes to sort out."

Jess just chuckled, completely unaware of the knot tightening in my stomach. "You don't have to be full-time, Finn. We can make this work together. I'll help. We just need people like you to push forward."

Her optimism made my heart ache with guilt. She didn't understand that this wasn't my fight, not in the way she needed it to be. I was a man of words, of fleeting dreams, not of lasting commitment. I could speak my truth, but when it came time to follow through? That was another story.

As we walked down the path, my thoughts drifted back to the words I'd said on stage. The community. The spirit. I did believe in it, I did feel the weight of the land beneath my feet and the pull of the ocean beside me. But how long could I keep pretending I was part of this fight? How long could I say yes to the world and keep hiding from my own doubts?

I watched Jess chat with the others around us, her words easy, her laughter flowing. She was so sure, so certain in the cause, in herself. And I hated myself for not being able to say the same.

I had said what was needed to be said. The crowd had responded. But deep down, I knew. The next time they asked for more from me—more time, more energy, more of myself—I would have an excuse ready. I would convince myself that it wasn't my fight anymore. That I was too old for this. Too tired. Too detached.

And the guilt would creep in, but I would bury it, like I always did. The same way I buried my writing, my art, my passions—waiting for a perfect moment to revive them, when deep down I knew that moment never came.

"Yeah, let's talk more tomorrow," I said to Jess, my words hollow even to my own ears. "I'm sure we can brainstorm something, get more people involved."

But as we walked away from the hall, my steps dragging, the truth gnawed at me. This wouldn't be a new chapter. It wouldn't be a resurgence of my purpose. The rally was just another moment in a long string of fleeting ideals I'd tossed aside over the years.

I wasn't ready to commit to anything—not to the rally, not to my art, not to my writing, not to anything that required more of me than I was willing to give. I'd stood up in front of those people, I'd spoken the words that resonated with the crowd, and they'd cheered for me. But for all the passion I'd felt in the moment, I knew I'd fade into the background once the dust settled.

Nothing would come of this. I'd let them down. And I'd let myself down. Again.

As we made our way through the night, the promise of the community pulse, of something greater than myself, felt like a ghost fading in the mist. Byron Bay would keep changing, as would I. But we weren't destined to change together.

I just couldn't commit—not to this, not to anything that asked me to leave behind my doubts and dive into something bigger. And that was the bitter truth I'd have to live with, as I walked away into the night, the sound of the ocean a distant reminder of all I wasn't willing to fight for.

An Unlikely Mentor

The sun hung heavy in the late afternoon sky, the orange hues stretching across the horizon like a painter's brushstrokes on an unfinished canvas. I stood by the rocky outcrop overlooking the ocean, the salty breeze tousling my hair and tugging at the edges of my worn shirt. It felt like a moment suspended in time, yet inside me churned the weight of unresolved thoughts—loss, discontent, and the nagging feeling that I was adrift in a world relentlessly moving on without me.

As I stared into the abyss of the waves crashing against the shore, I caught sight of a figure hunched over near the base of the rocks. An old man, his back curved like the trunk of a gnarled tree, sat on a piece of driftwood, fingers digging through the sand as if searching for lost treasures. His clothes were tattered, and his beard—a white cascade—danced in the wind. Something about him compelled me to approach, even though I had always preferred the solitude of my own thoughts.

"Hey there," I called out, unsure if I'd be met with a gruff reply or a dismissive wave.

The old man looked up, his eyes a cloudy blue that seemed to hold the weight of ages. "Did you lose something, son?"

I hesitated, taken aback by the question. I glanced down at the worn-out sandals on my feet, the weight of my struggles hanging like a heavy fog in the air. "Not really. Just... wandering, I guess."

"Aren't we all?" he chuckled, a sound bubbling up from somewhere deep within him, rich with experience and sorrow. "You got a name?"

"Finn."

"Finn," he repeated, savoring the syllables like a rare vintage. "I'm Arthur. Nice to meet you."

ALEX TELMAN

I took a seat on the driftwood beside Arthur, the roughness of the wood contrasting against the softness of the sand. We fell into a comfortable silence, the ocean's rhythm lulling us both. The air was thick with the scent of brine and the occasional whiff of cigarette smoke, remnants of a life lived on the edge.

"Thought about the weight of progress?" Arthur's voice cut through the tranquility, sharp and probing.

"What do you mean?" I turned to him, curiosity piqued.

"Look at this place," he gestured vaguely toward the shore. "Once, it was untouched—wild and free. Now it's just a postcard for tourists. All shiny and new, but hollow at the core." He paused, letting his words hang heavy in the air. "You can't progress without losing something. That's the cost."

I nodded slowly, grappling with the realization. I had watched Byron Bay transform over the years—the rise of boutique shops and cafes, the influx of people drawn by the allure of paradise. But what had we sacrificed? The essence, the soul of the community began to fray like an old tapestry.

"Have you ever thought about what you're losing in your own life, Finn?" Arthur pressed, his gaze piercing through my facade.

His question struck a nerve, and I felt exposed, the layers of my life peeling back like the bark of a tree. "Yeah, I guess I have." I let out a soft laugh, tinged with bitterness. "I used to think I'd be someone—an artist or a writer, you know? Now I'm just... lost."

"Lost isn't a bad place to be," he said, his voice a gravelly whisper. "It means you're searching. And searching means you still care."

I looked out at the horizon, where the sun was beginning to dip below the water, casting a golden path across the waves. "But what if I don't find anything?"

"Then you keep searching," Arthur replied, a twinkle in his eye. "It's the journey that shapes you, not the destination. You learn resilience along the way. Each wave that crashes against you builds your character, even when you feel like you're drowning."

His words hung in the air like the last notes of a haunting melody. I felt a flicker of something—hope, perhaps, or the faintest hint of determination. The burden of regret lifted just slightly, revealing the soft underbelly of possibility.

"Tell me, Finn," Arthur continued, his voice gentle yet firm, "what is it that you truly want?"

I sighed, the weight of the question heavy on my heart. "I want to create something that matters. I want to feel alive again."

"Then do it," he said, leaning forward, his eyes alight with fervor. "Stop waiting for the perfect moment. It's never going to come. You have to carve out your own path, even if it means getting your hands dirty. The world needs your voice, your vision."

In that moment, I felt a surge of conviction. The vibrant colors of the sunset reflected in my mind, illuminating the shadows of doubt that had plagued me for so long. The thought of creating, of expressing myself authentically, ignited something within me—like a long-forgotten ember coaxed back to life.

"Thanks, Arthur," I murmured, feeling warmth spread through me. "I needed to hear that."

"Just don't forget, Finn," the old man said, a twinkle still in his eye. "Progress isn't a straight line. It's a winding road with plenty of bumps. But if you keep your heart open and your feet planted in the sand, you might just find your way."

As the sun finally slipped beneath the horizon, painting the sky with deep purples and blues, I felt a renewed sense of purpose. I stood up, the sand cool beneath my feet, and turned to face Arthur. "I'll remember that."

"Good," he replied, a satisfied smile breaking through his weathered features. "Now go, before the stars steal your courage."

I laughed, the sound ringing out against the darkening sky. I walked away, leaving the old man behind but carrying his words like a talisman. Each step felt lighter, the weight of the past lifting as I embraced the unknown ahead.

As I looked up at the emerging stars, I whispered a silent promise to myself. I would create, I would search, and I would never forget the lessons of resilience taught by an unlikely mentor beneath the vast, eternal sky of Byron Bay.

Nightfall Musings

The sun dipped below the horizon, staining the sky with shades of blood orange and deep indigo. I sat on the weathered veranda of my small cottage in Byron Bay, the wood creaking beneath my weight, each sound a reminder of the passage of time. The air was thick with the scent of salt and something sweet—perhaps the remnants of the day's blooms fading into night. I traced the grain of the wood with my fingers, feeling the roughness of life's choices, each knot and splinter a testament to moments I could never take back.

As twilight enveloped the world, the cacophony of the day began to fade, replaced by the distant whispers of the ocean. The waves rolled in like soft sighs, crashing against the shore in a rhythm that echoed the beat of my heart—a heartbeat that often felt out of sync with the world around me. I took a drag from a cigarette, the smoke curling upward like fleeting thoughts, dissipating into the evening air.

It was during these hours of solitude that the weight of my loneliness pressed down hardest, like an anchor tethering me to the ground. I looked out at the beach, now a canvas painted with shadows, the flickering lights of distant houses reflecting the quiet bustle of lives lived just beyond my reach. The familiar pang of yearning washed over me—a desire to be part of something greater, to break the invisible chains that kept me at bay.

"Hey, mate," a voice called from the path leading to the beach. It was Ricky, my neighbor and Jess's husband, stumbling toward me with a half-empty bottle of beer clutched in his hand like a lifeline. "You out here all alone again?"

"Looks like it," I replied, forcing a smile that didn't quite reach my eyes. The weight of the day lingered, heavy and unyielding.

DOWN AND OUT IN BYRON BAY

"C'mon, let's hit the pub. I'll buy you a drink." Ricky's enthusiasm was infectious, a spark of life in the encroaching darkness. I knew I should join him, but the thought of the bar—the laughter, the music, the clinking of glasses—felt overwhelming, like trying to swim against a riptide.

"Maybe later," I murmured, my voice barely above a whisper.

Ricky shrugged, sensing the distance I had built around myself. "Suit yourself, but you're missing out. The world's out there waiting for you, mate."

As Ricky walked away, the weight of his absence settled deeper into my bones. I admired his carefree spirit, the ease with which he moved through life. In contrast, I felt like a ghost haunting the remnants of my past. Each choice I made seemed to echo in the hollow chambers of my heart—a symphony of regret and longing.

My mind wandered back to the choices that had led me here, to this moment of stillness, and I felt the familiar ache of nostalgia wrap around me like a cold blanket. Memories danced at the edges of my consciousness—laughter shared with friends, stolen kisses beneath the stars, dreams that once felt so tangible now reduced to whispers in the night.

The irony wasn't lost on me. Happiness had once felt like a warm embrace, a promise of brighter days. But now, it felt elusive, slipping through my fingers like sand, leaving only the stark reality of my solitude. I took a deep breath, the salty air filling my lungs, and closed my eyes, surrendering to the pull of memory.

A soft rustle interrupted my thoughts. I opened my eyes to find a young woman standing at the foot of the porch steps, a silhouette against the deepening dusk. Her hair flowed like liquid gold, and her eyes sparkled with the mischief of youth. She looked like Ella, but it wasn't.

"Is this seat taken?" she asked, her voice melodic, cutting through the stillness.

I shook my head, surprised by her sudden appearance. "No, it's all yours."

She climbed up, perching herself on the edge, her bare feet dangling just above the floorboards. Her smile brightened the shadows around us. "I saw you sitting here and thought you looked lonely."

"Lonely is one way to describe it," I admitted, studying her with curiosity. She seemed to radiate an energy I had almost forgotten existed.

"I get that," she replied, her gaze drifting out to the ocean. "But sometimes loneliness can lead to the best conversations."

"Is that so?" I leaned in, intrigued. "What's the best conversation you've ever had?"

She paused, a contemplative look washing over her face. "It was with a stranger at a party. We talked about our dreams, our fears... everything. It felt like we were the only two people in the world."

I felt a pang of longing—an echo of those late-night conversations filled with the promise of the future. "And what did you learn from it?"

"That people are complex, but we're all searching for the same thing—connection. Sometimes it's just buried beneath layers of fear and expectations."

I nodded, absorbing her words. They resonated deep within me, illuminating the corners of my heart that had grown dim over time.

"Why do you think we let fear take over?" I asked, vulnerability creeping into my voice.

"Because it's easier," she said softly. "It's safer to hide away, to stick to what we know. But that doesn't lead to happiness, does it?"

I looked out at the horizon, where the last rays of the sun faded into darkness. "No, it doesn't. Happiness feels like a fleeting memory."

"Then maybe it's time to chase it," she suggested, her voice gentle but firm. "Life's too short to let it pass you by."

I considered her words, a flicker of hope igniting within me. The night had settled around us, but her presence felt like a beacon in the dark—a reminder that connection was still possible, that I could still reach for something beyond the confines of my solitude.

As the stars began to twinkle overhead, I felt the burden of my choices shift, just slightly, as if a path had opened before me. "You're right," I said, a newfound determination swelling in my chest. "I've been waiting for something to change, but maybe I need to be the one to change."

She smiled, a bright light against the encroaching night. "That's the spirit."

Together, we sat in silence, the weight of loneliness lifting as we shared the space—our hopes, our fears woven into the fabric of the night. And in that moment, I felt a connection blooming amidst the shadows, a small but undeniable flicker of light guiding me back to myself.

As the stars blinked down, I understood that even in the depths of solitude, there existed a pulse—a rhythm of life that beckoned me to dance once more.

The Weight of Expectations

I stood on the veranda of my weathered cottage, the salt-laden breeze tousling my hair like a mother's gentle reprimand. The sun hung low in the sky, casting long shadows across the wooden planks, each creak beneath my feet echoing a sense of impending confrontation. The air was thick with the scent of damp earth and fading flowers—remnants of a once vibrant garden I had neglected, much like my own ambitions.

Today, my mother was coming to visit, a rare occasion that always seemed to stir up a mix of anticipation and unease. It had been three years since she'd been here, since she left for Sydney, and with each visit, it felt like more time had passed between us, like the distance between the two cities had somehow stretched into something bigger.

I could already feel the weight of her expectations pressing down on me, heavy and unyielding, like dark clouds rolling in off the ocean, threatening storms. I took a deep breath, the salty air filling my lungs, a momentary escape from the tension building inside me. It had been years since I'd seen her; years since I'd felt the sting of her disappointment.

The day dragged on, the sun inching closer to the horizon, as if reluctant to bear witness to our meeting. I poured myself a drink, the amber liquid swirling in the glass, mirroring the turmoil in my heart. As I stared into it, memories washed over me—the childhood dreams that had blossomed under the warmth of her affection, now wilted under the harsh glare of reality.

When she arrived, her figure appeared at the end of the street, a silhouette against the fading light. My heart raced as she approached, each step punctuated by the soft thud of her sandals against the pavement. Her expression was a mixture of love and expectation, her arms laden with gifts—homemade cookies wrapped in crinkled paper, a tattered photo album filled with memories I had long since tried to forget.

"Finn!" she called, her voice slicing through the evening air. "Look at this place! You're still living in this old shack?"

The cottage belonged to my grandmother, who'd moved back to Sydney years ago, leaving it to gather dust and memories. When my father passed away, and my mother returned to Sydney, I was a teenager, still trying to find my footing in a world that felt like it had shifted beneath me. My grandmother had offered me the cottage to live in. She always called it "quaint," but to me, it was more than that—it was a refuge, a place that wrapped me in its comfort when everything else felt uncertain. It wasn't much—barely more than a modified shed—but it was my space; my only reguge. And for a long time, I hadn't seen any reason to change it.

I stiffened, and forced a smile that didn't quite reach my eyes. "It's cozy," I replied, the words hollow even to me. The walls, the faded paint, the dust that clung to everything— it all felt like a reflection of where I was in life. Stagnant. Stuck.

She stepped inside, her eyes sweeping over the clutter of my world: scattered notes, half-filled notebooks, and crumpled pieces of paper strewn across the table. Pens and pencils were scattered in chaotic disarray, some uncapped, some broken, like forgotten thoughts waiting to be reassembled. Pages of unfinished ideas leaned against the walls, their corners curling as if they, too, were unsure of their place. It was a mess, but it was mine—each fragment a reflection of the things I hadn't yet figured out; mostly a collection of forgotten promises.

"You still writing?" she asked, her voice tinged with disappointment. "I thought you'd be doing something more... stable by now."

I shrugged, trying to downplay the sting in her voice. "Yeah, I'm still writing," I said, my words a little sharper than I intended. "It's not a nine-to-five, but it's what I've got," I muttered, pouring her a glass of lemonade that was too sweet, a sickly reminder of childhood summers spent in her kitchen.

Her gaze lingered on the scattered papers, a flicker of concern crossing her face. "Finn, you can't live like this forever. Your father would've wanted you to have more stability, more direction."

I forced a smile, but it didn't quite reach my eyes. "I'm working on it, Mum. Just... not in the way you expect."

Her silence was the heaviest thing in the room, like she was trying to figure out whether I was lost or just stubborn. I knew she didn't understand. But then again, I wasn't sure I did either.

"Finn," she said, her voice softening, "I just want you to be happy. I worry about you."

"I want to be happy, too, mum." I swallowed hard, the bitterness of her concern mixing with the sweetness of the drink.

"Happy? Is that what you call this?"

I gestured around the room, the chaos of my life laid bare. "I'm a writer, not a businessman. I'm not cut out for your world of nine-to-fives and mortgages."

"Then why do you make it so hard for yourself?" Her eyes searched mine, an ocean of disappointment threatening to drown me. "You have so much potential. I just don't understand why you wouldn't want to use it."

"Use it for what? To conform to a life that wasn't meant for me?" The heat of my anger flared, a fire sparked by years of unmet expectations. "I'm not going to spend my life chasing what everyone else wants me to be."

Silence fell between us, thick and suffocating, a chasm filled with unspoken words and regrets. I watched her as she fiddled with the photo album, flipping through pages filled with laughter and joy from a time that felt so distant it could have belonged to someone else. There we were—young, carefree, the world at our feet—but that world had shifted, leaving me stranded in a reality that felt foreign and heavy.

"I just don't want you to be alone, Finn," she finally said, her voice breaking like a wave crashing against the shore. "You have so much love to give. Why don't you want to share it?"

I looked away, unable to meet her gaze, the weight of her question hanging in the air. Love felt like a commodity I had long since given up on—too complicated, too messy, like the paint splatters that dotted my floor. "It's not that simple," I replied, my voice barely above a whisper. "Life isn't a straight line, Mom. It's a series of choices that can lead to nowhere."

"Or somewhere," she countered gently, her eyes pleading for understanding. "What about your friends? What about... what about family? You can't keep pushing everyone away."

I clenched my fists, the rawness of her words piercing through my defenses. I thought of Ella. I thought of Claire. I thought of my neighbors Ricky and Jess, the fleeting connections that felt like fireflies—beautiful but ephemeral. The world outside continued its rhythm, the sun now a mere sliver on the horizon, signaling the onset of night.

"I don't know how to let people in," I admitted, the vulnerability of the truth wrapping around me like a shroud. "Every time I try, I end up feeling... empty. Like I'm trying to fit into a mold that doesn't suit me."

"Maybe it's time to break the mold," she suggested, her voice imbued with a warmth that seemed to melt the ice encasing my heart. "You have the power to choose, Finn. You can decide how to live your life. You can be an writer without losing yourself in the process."

"Maybe you're right," I said softly, the words carrying a weight I hadn't expected. "Maybe I can find a way to make it all fit."

Her expression softened again and she sighed, her voice dropping to a quieter, more concerned tone. "Finn, there's something you need to know." She paused, as if the words themselves weighed more than she could carry. "Grandma's not doing well. She's very ill. I think you should contact her."

I froze, the words settling in like stones in my chest. My grandmother had always been a distant, silent presence in my life, but the thought of her being sick, of her fading, hit me harder than I expected.

"Is it... serious?" I asked, though I already knew the answer.

She nodded, looking down at her hands. "The doctors aren't optimistic. I just thought you should be prepared, that's all."

I swallowed, feeling a knot tighten in my throat. "I'll call her." The words felt hollow, like a promise I wasn't sure I could keep.

I met her gaze, and for the first time, I saw not just a mother, but a woman who had weathered her own storms. Her eyes reflected my fears, my dreams, and the possibility of connection that lay just beneath the surface. In that moment, I felt a flicker of hope, a recognition that perhaps I wasn't as alone as I believed.

As night descended, the room filled with a gentle glow from a single lamp, casting shadows that danced along the walls. We talked late into the evening, the walls that had kept us apart slowly crumbling with each shared story, each laugh, each moment of vulnerability.

In the quiet of the night, I realized that the weight of expectations might never fully lift, but perhaps it could transform—into something lighter, something that allowed me to breathe. As we shared cookies and memories, the burdens of the past began to feel less like chains and more like the fabric of a life woven together with threads of love and understanding.

And for the first time in a long while, I felt the stirrings of a future—a story not yet planned, a novel not yet written, full of possibilities waiting to be explored.

Tomorrow, I will call my grandmother. Tomorrow, I will take the first step back into the light.

Ritual of Release

The sun sank slowly behind the waves of Byron Bay, a molten orb bleeding orange and pink into the indigo sky. I stood on the weathered beach, my bare feet sinking into the cool, damp sand, feeling the pulse of the earth beneath me. The ocean roared like an old friend, its salty breath a reminder of the wildness that once thrummed through my veins. I could taste the brine in the air, a sharpness that brought with it memories of laughter and warmth—connections now frayed like the edges of my tattered journal.

Tonight, I was supposed to find solace in a healing ceremony at the edge of the forest, where the eucalyptus trees whispered ancient secrets. A flicker of hope danced within me, but it was accompanied by the weight of uncertainty. What if the night only served as a reminder of the emptiness that had taken root in my soul? I brushed those thoughts aside and turned my gaze toward the gathering, a huddle of figures illuminated by the flickering light of a bonfire.

The air crackled with anticipation as I approached, the scent of burning sage curling through the atmosphere, mingling with the earthy smell of damp foliage. The participants, a motley crew of seekers and wanderers, were draped in flowing fabrics that caught the breeze like sails, their laughter a mixture of joy and nervousness. I felt like an intruder, a ghost haunting the edges of their shared experience, but I stepped forward anyway, drawn by an unseen force.

As I joined the circle, the facilitator—a woman with wild hair and piercing eyes—spoke softly, her voice weaving a tapestry of intention that enveloped us all. "Tonight, we honor the land and each other. We release the burdens we carry and invite healing into our lives." Her words flowed like water, soothing yet powerful, and I felt the tightness in my chest loosen just a fraction.

I took a seat on the cool ground, the grass damp against my skin. The ceremony began with a rhythmic chant that vibrated through the air, echoing the heartbeat of the earth. I closed my eyes, surrendering to the sound, feeling the energy of the group weave around me like a protective cocoon. The world outside faded, the noise of the ocean replaced by an internal symphony of longing and release.

Images flooded my mind—Anna's laugh, the way her hair danced in the wind, the feel of Joel's hand on my shoulder as we planned our future. I had pushed them both away, chasing a dream that felt increasingly hollow. As the chant deepened, I confronted the weight of those choices, the loneliness that had become a familiar companion. My heart ached with regret, a dull throb that matched the rhythm of the drumming that echoed through the gathering.

When it was my turn to speak, the words stumbled out like uninvited guests. "I... I'm Finn. I feel lost. I've been chasing something, but I don't know what it is anymore." The honesty was raw, naked in the moonlight, and I felt exposed under the gazes of the group. Yet their expressions were not judgmental; they were understanding, reflective of the struggles that bound us all.

The woman with wild hair nodded, her eyes softening. "We're all searching for something, Finn. Let's release those burdens together. You're not alone."

As we began a guided meditation, I focused on the ground beneath me, imagining roots extending from my body into the earth. With each breath, I envisioned the burdens I carried being drawn from me, sinking into the soil where they could be transformed. The image was powerful—a cleansing of sorts.

The chanting resumed, a harmonious echo that danced in the cool night air. The flames of the bonfire flickered, casting playful shadows that seemed to come alive, merging with the spirits of the past, present, and future. I surrendered fully, allowing myself to feel everything—the pain, the love, the longing. Each breath became a release, a promise to reconnect not just with the land, but with myself.

As the ceremony reached its peak, I felt a surge of energy, a warm current that coursed through my veins. The world seemed to blur around me, and for a fleeting moment, I wasn't burdened by the weight of my past. I opened my eyes and saw the faces around me—people who had come here for the same thing I had: a release, a chance to shed something old and worn. Their vulnerability was like an unspoken language, a bond we shared that didn't need words.

The fire in the center crackled, sending spirals of orange and red into the air, and I could feel the energy of the land, the earth beneath me, alive and humming. I had always thought that spirituality was something distant—something abstract that only other people seemed to understand. But tonight, in this circle of souls, it became something very real. It wasn't just about the land or the earth beneath our feet; it was about the connections I had let slip away, the bridges I had burned. It was about choices, choices I could still make, people I could still reach out to, if I allowed myself to.

As the ceremony ended, a heavy silence settled over the group, the kind that comes when something sacred has just been experienced. The flames danced in the firepit, their light flickering across the faces of those around me. Everyone seemed lost in their own thoughts, reflecting on what had just transpired.

Then, I felt her.

It was subtle at first—just a shift in the air—but as I turned my head, my heart skipped a beat. There, standing at the edge of the firelight, was Ella. Her presence was like a ghost made flesh, a blur of memories and regrets that pressed against my chest. She looked exactly as she had the last time I saw her: wild, untamed, and impossibly beautiful.

For a moment, I thought my mind was playing tricks on me. But no, this was real.

I stood slowly, my legs a little unsteady, unsure whether I should approach or not. She met my gaze, her eyes soft and knowing, as if she could read every hesitation in my heart. I swallowed, but the lump in my throat wouldn't go away.

"Ella..." My voice cracked, barely a whisper, as I took a hesitant step forward.

She smiled, but it wasn't the carefree smile I remembered. This one was tinged with something deeper, a kind of quiet understanding.

"You look different," I said, unsure of what else to say, my words fumbling. I wanted to reach out, but I didn't trust my hands not to tremble.

"I feel different," she replied, her voice light but edged with something weighty. "You're still holding on to so much, Finn. You know that, right?"

Her words hit me like a wave, and for a moment, I was back in that old place—trapped in the cycle of my own doubt and self-doubt, spinning around a life that didn't feel like mine. But now, standing before me, she felt so close, so real, that it was impossible to ignore the truth in her words.

"I don't know how to let go," I confessed, my voice low, laced with a bitterness I couldn't shake. "Every time I think I have it figured out, I find myself stuck again."

Ella's gaze softened, and she stepped a little closer, her presence somehow grounding, even though I knew she wasn't really here in the physical sense. It was like she had slipped between the cracks of my memories, an echo of a past I wasn't sure I was ready to face.

"You don't have to figure it all out right now," she said gently, her eyes searching mine with that familiar intensity. "You've spent so much time trying to solve everything, but maybe you need to just 'be' with it for a while. Be with the mess, the uncertainty. It doesn't have to be fixed. Not yet."

I wanted to argue, to tell her that I couldn't just let go of the past—of the dreams I'd abandoned, of the guilt that wrapped around me like chains. But as she spoke, something in her tone softened that hardened part of me. Maybe she was right. Maybe I didn't have to have all the answers today. Maybe I just needed to feel the questions without trying to drown them out.

"Do you ever feel like... like you've been living someone else's life?" I asked before I could stop myself. The question tumbled out, raw and unrefined, but it felt like the truth.

Ella looked at me for a long moment, as if she were seeing something I couldn't. "I think you've always been afraid to live your own," she said softly. "It's easier to let the world push you around than to stand up and claim your space, your story."

Her words cut through the haze in my mind, and I was quiet for a long moment. I hadn't realized how much I had been waiting for something to give me permission to be myself—to step into my own life, my own choices. Instead, I had been drowning in my own excuses, caught in a loop that kept me safe, but never alive.

"I've been so afraid," I admitted, my voice barely above a whisper. "Afraid of failing. Afraid of being nothing more than a dreamer with nothing to show for it."

Ella smiled again, her expression filled with something I couldn't quite place—love, maybe, or forgiveness. "You're more than just your fears, Finn. Don't let them define you. You have everything you need to move forward. You just have to trust yourself, even if it means walking into the unknown."

Her words were like a balm, soothing the raw parts of me that I had spent so long neglecting.

"I wish I could see myself the way you do," I murmured, a lump forming in my throat.

Ella reached out, her fingers brushing my arm lightly. "You will, Finn. You just need to stop hiding from what you're capable of. And don't be afraid to reach out to the people who care about you. They're still here. You just have to let them in."

I felt a tear slip down my cheek, but it wasn't sadness—it was something else. Something lighter. Something that felt like release.

"Thank you," I whispered. "For showing me... showing me that it's not too late."

Ella's smile widened, and for the briefest moment, I felt like she was really there, standing in front of me, a piece of my past brought back into the light.

"I'll always be here, Finn. In the memories. In the lessons. You're not alone."

And with that, she stepped back, fading into the shadows of the night. But even as she disappeared, her presence lingered, a quiet promise that maybe, just maybe, it wasn't too late for me to finally start living the life I was meant to live.

As the night deepened, I found myself laughing, the sound a buoyant echo against the vastness of the universe. The laughter felt new, like a spring thawing the winter in my heart. I was still flawed, still searching, but for the first time in a long while, I felt the stirrings of hope—a hope rooted in the very earth beneath me, in the people beside me, and in the possibility of tomorrow.

Unfinished Symphony

The sun dipped below the horizon, casting a fiery glow over Byron Bay, where the whispers of evening promised music and memories. I stood at the entrance of the local music festival, the familiar scent of salt and earth wafting through the air, mingling with the sharp tang of beer and fried onions from the food stalls. Laughter and distant melodies swirled around me, a vibrant tapestry that tugged at my heartstrings.

As I wandered through the throng, each step felt like a step back in time, to a version of myself I barely recognized anymore. I brushed past a group of teenagers, their laughter bubbling like champagne, carefree and unencumbered. They were lost in the moment, and I envied them—a ghost haunting the edges of their vibrant existence. I remembered when I had danced in the rain and strummed my guitar until my fingers bled, when life had felt like an endless symphony.

I paused by a makeshift stage, where a band of scruffy young men played an off-kilter version of a familiar tune. Their voices were raw and unpolished but filled with an energy that sparked something inside me. The music flowed through the air, wrapping around me like a warm embrace, igniting the embers of dreams long buried. I closed my eyes, letting the notes wash over me, each chord a reminder of the melodies I once conjured in the quiet of my bedroom.

"Hey, Finn! You gonna join us or what?" A familiar voice broke through my reverie. It was Ricky with Jess, their laughter ringing out like bells, clear and carefree, echoing through the warm evenings of the festival. It was the kind of laughter that made you feel lighter just by hearing it, a sound full of shared joy and comfort. Ricky and Jess, always so in sync, had this effortless way of being together—whether they were at the beach, making spontaneous plans, or just lounging in their backyard, their happiness was contagious. You couldn't help but smile when you saw them, two people completely at ease in each other's company, like they had unlocked a secret to life that few ever found.

I approached them, a smile creeping onto my face, but it felt heavy, burdened by the weight of unfulfilled promises. "I was just soaking it all in," I replied, trying to match their enthusiasm. "Feels like a throwback to simpler times."

"Yeah, before we all got lost in the grind," Jess said, her eyes sparkling with mischief. "You used to play, remember? Why don't you get up there and show them how it's done?"

I hesitated. The guitar sat in the corner of my mind, dusty and abandoned. I hadn't touched one in years, not since that night... the one where I'd promised myself I'd focus on something real, something practical. Music had always been my escape, but somewhere along the way, it became just another thing I left behind.

"I don't know," I said, looking down at the worn strings of the instrument by the stage. "I haven't picked up a guitar in so long, Jess. Besides, these guys are way more in tune with the vibe than I am."

"Oh, come on," she teased, nudging me with her shoulder. "Don't tell me you've forgotten how to jam. You used to be the heart of this town's music scene. Show them what you've got."

Before I could protest, a hand slapped my shoulder, and I turned to find Ricky grinning at me.

"Finn, mate! You're not backing out, are you? Come on, get up there. We've heard about your 'soulful' sound for years—time to prove it," Ricky said, his voice full of laughter but with an edge of challenge. He always had that way of pushing me when I wasn't sure I wanted to be pushed. His big grin felt warm, but it also carried that persistent energy, the kind that could make you feel like you owed it to the universe to step up.

I shifted on my feet, awkwardly scratching my head. "I don't know, Ricky. Been out of practice for too long. You know how it is."

Ricky's grin didn't waver. "That's the thing, Finn. You've always known how it is. And you've never let a little rust stop you before. Just get up there, even if it's just for the hell of it."

I felt a mix of guilt and longing twist in my stomach. Ricky was right in one sense—music had been my way of letting go, of connecting with the world when nothing else made sense. And yet, in the time since I'd buried it, I'd somehow convinced myself that it wasn't worth the effort. Maybe because, deep down, I knew it was easier to stay on the sidelines, to not try, than to face the disappointment of another abandoned dream.

But standing there, with Jess's infectious energy and Ricky's damn near irresistible challenge, I knew I had to make a choice. I couldn't keep dodging everything, least of all my own potential.

"Alright," I said, my voice steadier than I expected. "I'll give it a shot. But no promises." I didn't know if I was making that promise to Jess, to Ricky, or to myself.

Jess's face lit up with excitement. "That's the spirit!" she cheered, practically bouncing on her feet. "Just remember, this town remembers the magic, Finn. It's still there."

I stepped up to the stage, my hands sweaty and unsure as I picked up a guitar that felt foreign, despite how familiar it should have been. The strings felt stiff under my fingers as I adjusted them, the fretboard too smooth, too quiet.

As the band started up again, I hesitated, feeling the weight of my silence. But when the music swelled, I found my footing—slowly at first, then with more confidence. I strummed, the sound a little ragged but real. The crowd around me began to sway, to feel it. My fingers found the rhythm, and the memories started to come alive again. The ghosts of old songs, of forgotten words, whispered through me.

And then I found the song I used to play, the one that always made me feel like I was truly alive.

It came to me like muscle memory, the notes falling effortlessly from my hands. I looked up, meeting Jess's gaze across the firelight, and saw that same spark, the one that had always been there. Ricky gave me a thumbs-up, his face alight with approval, but I wasn't playing for them anymore.

In that moment, I was not just a man on a stage; I was the music. Each note I played resonated with the echoes of my past—the lost dreams, the friendships, the pain, and the love. The sound soared, filled the air, and wrapped around me like a warm blanket, enveloping me in a sense of belonging I hadn't felt in years.

I was playing for myself.

By the time the song ended, the crowd was clapping, some cheering, and for a moment, it felt like the world had opened up just enough to let me in. Jess was grinning, Ricky was laughing, and I was alive again in a way I hadn't been in so long.

When the song faded, I lowered the guitar, my breath coming fast, my heart still beating to the rhythm of what I had just unleashed. "Alright, that was... that was better than I expected," I admitted, looking at Jess and Ricky.

Jess stepped forward, eyes sparkling with joy. "See? I told you! You've still got it. The magic was always there, Finn."

Ricky clapped me on the back, laughing. "Not bad for a guy who said he was rusty."

I smiled, the weight of the past lifting just a little. Maybe this was the first step back to the person I used to be—or maybe even the person I was always meant to become. And with Jess and Ricky there, encouraging me, pushing me, maybe I wasn't as alone in this journey as I'd thought.

For the first time in a long time, I felt like I was on the right path again, no matter how uncertain or winding it seemed.

The New Wave

I stood on the sun-bleached sand of Byron Bay, where the ocean stretched endlessly, a vast blue canvas interrupted only by the frothy whitecaps dancing like restless spirits. It was a new century, a time when surfboards and bohemian vibes mingled with something else, something that felt both exciting and suffocating. As the waves crashed against the shore, I felt the churn of a different kind of tide—a new wave of tourism washing over the town, reshaping it into something unrecognizable.

The beach was a mosaic of bodies, many unfamiliar, their laughter piercing the salty air like shards of glass. Families clad in matching swimwear and sunburned tourists snapped pictures, their wide-brimmed hats and sunscreen-clad noses glistening under the harsh Australian sun. To me, it felt as if the soul of Byron was being smothered beneath a veneer of superficiality, each wave that lapped at the shore pulling away the essence of what made this place my home.

I wandered past market stalls selling trinkets and overpriced smoothies, each more garish than the last, the aroma of burnt sausages mingling with the scent of coconut oil. A group of backpackers laughed loudly, their carefree spirits infectious, yet I felt like an outsider watching a play unfold from the shadows. "What's it to you, mate?" one of them shouted, noticing my scowl. "It's all good vibes, right?"

I couldn't respond. Instead, I turned away, the weight of unspoken words pressing down on my chest. Regret and nostalgia rose like bile in my throat. Once, this had been a sanctuary for dreamers, artists, and surfers—a refuge for those who sought connection with the land and each other. Now, it felt like a carnival, a stage set for a show I no longer wanted to watch.

Making my way toward the cliffs, the wind whipped through my hair, and the ocean roared below—a powerful reminder of nature's indifference.

Standing at the edge, I stared down at the waves crashing against the rocks, thinking of the stories hidden beneath the surface, the memories that lingered like whispers in the wind.

"Hey, Finn! You alright?" It was Leo, an old friend, his voice tinged with genuine concern. Leo had always been the pulse of Byron, the embodiment of its spirit, and now he stood beside me, his gaze fixed on the horizon.

"Just thinking about how much this place has changed," I replied, my voice heavy with disillusionment.

Leo chuckled, but it rang hollow against the crashing waves. "Change is inevitable, mate. We can't hold onto the past forever. Remember the nights we'd sit on the beach, strumming guitars and dreaming?"

I nodded, but the memory felt distant, like a faded photograph. "Yeah, but it wasn't just about the music, was it? It was about the connection, the authenticity of it all. Now it feels like a stage for tourists, and we're just... spectators in our own lives."

Silence stretched between us, filled with the roar of the ocean and the laughter of strangers. The weight of the world pressed down on me, each breath heavy with the burden of unfulfilled dreams. I had watched my friends drift away, swept up in the currents of ambition, while I clung to the remnants of our shared history like a drowning man grasping at straws.

"Maybe we need to create our own wave," Leo suggested, his voice brightening. "We could throw a festival, bring back the spirit of what Byron used to be."

"A festival?" My brow furrowed. "But wouldn't that just become another spectacle? A way to cash in on the superficiality?"

"Or it could be a way to reclaim it," Leo countered. "We could infuse it with the rawness, the grit, and the soul that made this place special. A chance to gather the old crew, share stories, and make music again."

A flicker of hope ignited within me, but it quickly dimmed under the weight of reality. "And what happens when the tourists show up? Will they drown it out again?"

"Maybe. But what if we create a space where they can feel that spirit? Where they're part of it, not just observers?" Leo's eyes sparkled with passion. "You've got to believe there's still beauty to be found in this mess."

DOWN AND OUT IN BYRON BAY

I stared out at the turbulent sea, the waves crashing against the rocks with a fury that mirrored my own turmoil. It was true—the ocean had always been both beautiful and destructive, a force of nature that didn't care about human intentions. But it also held the potential for rebirth. I thought of laughter, strumming guitars, and the warmth of friendship. Could we really capture that spirit again?

"Alright," I finally said, my voice steadier now. "Let's do it. Let's bring back the spirit of Byron."

Leo grinned, the weight of my words hanging in the air, full of possibility. "That's the spirit! We'll gather the old crew, reach out to the locals, and make it happen."

As we stood together, I felt a renewed sense of purpose wash over me, mingling with the salty breeze. I realized that while the waves of tourism might crash against the shore, I didn't have to let them drown me. I could ride them, reshape them, and forge connections anew.

With the sun setting behind us, painting the sky in hues of orange and purple, I turned to Leo. "We'll need a name for it, something that captures what we want to create."

"Let's call it 'The New Wave,'" Leo suggested, his smile contagious. "A celebration of what's to come, but rooted in the heart of Byron."

I smiled back, feeling a spark of excitement ignite within me. The New Wave wouldn't just be an event; it would be a reminder of what we had lost and what we still had the power to reclaim.

As the conversation with Leo lingered in the air, a spark of excitement flickered within me. The New Wave! The idea seemed so simple yet so monumental. A festival—our festival—to bring back the heart and soul of Byron. It felt like the kind of thing that could ignite something inside the town, something genuine, something that wasn't tainted by the commercialism that had slowly smothered the spirit of the place.

Leo's words echoed in my mind: "We could infuse it with the rawness, the grit, and the soul that made this place special. A chance to gather the old crew, share stories, and make music again." I could almost see it: a gathering under the stars, guitars strumming, faces lit by firelight, laughter flowing as freely as the ocean breeze. It sounded like the kind of revival I had been yearning for—the kind of energy that made me fall in love with this place in the first place.

"Alright," I had said to Leo, my voice carrying a quiet surge of determination. "Let's do it. Let's bring back the spirit of Byron."

Leo's grin had been electric, a mirror of the excitement surging through me. But as the words left my mouth, a shadow fell over my thoughts. My mind flickered with doubts, a steady undercurrent of uncertainty threatening to pull me under. What if we did bring the spirit back only to watch it drown in a sea of shallow commercialism? Would it even be possible to reclaim something so fleeting?

The more I thought about it, the more I could see the cracks, the holes in the dream. The festival could start off with the right intentions, but soon enough, the tourists would flood in, drawn by the same allure that had destroyed so much of what I loved about this place. What would stop the event from becoming just another package for people to consume—a hollowed-out version of what it was supposed to be?

Maybe they would drown it out again, I thought, the excitement I had felt moments ago beginning to dissipate like smoke in the wind. The bigger the festival got, the more it would lose its meaning. People wouldn't care about the rawness, the grit, the realness of Byron. They'd just want the Instagram photo, the easy experience, the next shiny thing to add to their list of "adventures."

I looked at Leo, his eyes still sparkling with enthusiasm, and felt the weight of my own doubts. Could I really get behind this idea? Could I truly commit to something that had the potential to be consumed and spat out, like so many other good intentions? What if I failed to capture that essence, that spark? What if it was all for nothing?

"Leo," I said, my voice quieter now, laced with uncertainty, "what happens when the tourists show up? When they start crowding in, buying their overpriced kale smoothies and yoga mats, will it just become another spectacle?"

Leo's grin faltered for a moment, but he quickly recovered. "Maybe. But what if we create a space where they can feel that spirit too? What if we show them that Byron isn't just a place to visit, but a place to 'experience'—in its raw, imperfect, real form?"

I wanted to believe him. I wanted to believe that somehow we could capture that spark, carve out a space where the essence of Byron was alive and well. But the truth was, my heart felt heavy with doubt. It was easier to stay cynical, to protect myself from the crushing disappointment of expectations unmet. It was easier to let the dream stay just that—a dream, one that I didn't have to risk breaking my heart for.

I turned away, my gaze drifting back to the ocean, its waves crashing against the rocks in relentless pursuit of the shore. The ocean was wild, untamed, and unpredictable. It could be beautiful one moment and terrifying the next. Just like this idea. Could we really take on the tide? Could we ride the wave and make it our own, or would we be swept under, caught in the undertow?

I felt a deep ache in my chest. What's the point of starting something if you can't see it through?

Leo's voice broke through my thoughts, his optimism a lifeline I wasn't sure I could hold onto. "Finn, you've got to believe in this, man. There's still beauty to be found in the mess. We can create something real, something that'll remind people what Byron used to be. What it still could be. If we do it right."

I let out a slow breath, trying to sort through the conflicting emotions inside me. Part of me longed to dive into the project, to be a part of something that could bring life back to this town. But another part of me hesitated, afraid of the vulnerability, of the possibility that it could all fall apart. That the tourists, the commercialization, the inevitable sell-out would swallow it whole.

"You're right," I said, my voice flat, the excitement gone, replaced by the weight of what I knew was coming. "But we're not the only ones trying to reclaim this place, are we? It's always going to be a battle against the tide, Leo. And I don't know if I can keep fighting it."

Leo's smile dimmed slightly, but he didn't push. He didn't have to. I could see the understanding in his eyes, the knowing look that said we'd all been here before—fighting for something we believed in, only to have it slip through our fingers. The dream of Byron was becoming more and more like a ghost, haunting us but never staying long enough to let us truly embrace it.

"We'll talk about it again," Leo said, a bit of his earlier enthusiasm flickering back. "We've got time, Finn. Don't give up on it just yet."

But as I stood there, staring out at the crashing waves, the weight of the world on my shoulders, I knew deep down that the dream of "The New Wave" might never come to fruition. At least, not in the way we imagined. Maybe the reality of Byron, the world we lived in now, was simply too far gone. Too many forces working against us. Too many compromises to be made. I had my doubts. And the longer I held onto them, the harder it would be to let go.

For now, I stood there with Leo, watching the sun dip beneath the horizon, casting the sky in hues of gold and purple. I wasn't sure what the future held, but I could feel the weight of indecision in my bones, heavy like a stone. And I knew one thing for sure: the waves were coming, but I wasn't sure if I had the strength to ride them anymore.

Between Two Worlds

I stood at the edge of the bustling Byron Bay market, where the scent of ripe mangoes mingled with the salty tang of the ocean breeze. The morning sun hung low in the sky, casting a warm golden hue over everything, but it felt more like a spotlight illuminating the divide I couldn't escape. Laughter echoed around me as families strolled past, their smiles bright and carefree, while I felt a weight in my chest that no amount of sun could lift.

The stalls were vibrant, overflowing with artisan goods and handmade crafts—each piece a testament to the burgeoning upper class that had begun to claim this slice of paradise. I watched as tourists, adorned in designer swimsuits and oversized sunglasses, snapped pictures of each other, their superficial joy contrasting sharply with the memories I held tightly like an old photograph tucked away in a dusty drawer. This town had once celebrated grit and heart, a sanctuary for the weary and the wanderers. Now, it was being swept up in a tide of affluence that felt foreign and cold.

"Oi, Finn!" A familiar voice pulled me from my reverie. It was Jake, a friend from my school days, a surf bum turned real estate mogul, now dressed in khakis and a button-up shirt that screamed of privilege. "You still hanging around? Thought you'd be off chasing waves or something."

I forced a smile, the kind that didn't reach my eyes. "Just taking it all in," I replied, my voice strained. "How's the market treating you?"

"Can't complain! Byron's booming! You should get in on it—buy a place, make some real money," Jake said, clapping me on the shoulder as if we were still kids kicking around a beach ball.

"Yeah, right," I muttered, glancing around at the families with their pristine beach towels and laughter that seemed to float above the fray like a bubble about to burst. "Not everyone's interested in joining the rat race."

Jake shrugged, oblivious. "Suit yourself, mate. Just remember, this place won't stay cheap forever. You either get in or get left behind." He sauntered off, leaving me standing alone, the weight of his words heavy in the air.

My gaze drifted toward the shoreline, where the waves rolled in with a relentless rhythm, crashing against the rocks like a heartbeat. I remembered the days when Byron felt like home—an embrace of salt and sand, where my friends and I would gather by the fire, sharing stories that lingered like smoke curling into the night sky. But now, that warmth had been replaced by a chill, a sense of alienation that wrapped around me like a thick fog.

I wandered through the market, picking up pieces of fruit and examining them absently. The vibrant colors reminded me of a time when life felt alive and unfiltered—before I felt caught between two worlds, before I had begun to measure my worth against the glitzy expectations of success. I tossed a bruised peach into my bag, the softness reminding me of the decay lurking beneath the surface of this vibrant facade.

"What's this?" A woman's voice broke through my thoughts. It was Marla, a local artist whose paintings depicted the raw beauty of the coast. Her hair was a wild mane of curls, and her eyes sparkled with the kind of energy I had always admired.

"Just trying to navigate the madness," I replied, my voice tinged with fatigue.

She laughed lightly, but there was an edge to it. "You and me both. It's like a carnival now, isn't it? Everyone's trying to cash in on the dream."

"Yeah, but what about the people who made the dream?" I felt a fire ignite within me. "This place isn't just about surfing and sunshine. It's about community, about grit. I feel like we're losing that."

Marla nodded, her expression shifting to something more serious. "You're right. We have to remind people of what Byron used to be. Otherwise, we're just ghosts in our own town."

Our conversation felt like a lifeline, a reminder that not everyone had surrendered to the tide. We began to speak of ideas—of gatherings, of art festivals, of reconnecting with the roots that had nurtured us. I felt a flicker of hope amidst the despair, as if a spark had been reignited within me.

But as we spoke, I couldn't shake the feeling of being caught between two worlds—the old and the new. I wanted to be part of the future, to help shape it, but the path forward felt fraught with challenges. The pull of ambition and the love for my home tugged at me, each vying for dominance in a battle I didn't know how to win.

Later that evening, I sat alone on the beach, the waves lapping at my feet, their rhythm a soothing balm against the tumult of my thoughts. The sky had turned a deep orange, and I could see silhouettes of surfers riding the last waves of the day, their movements fluid and free. I remembered when I was one of them, riding the waves not for fame or fortune, but for the sheer joy of it.

A small group gathered nearby, the sound of laughter mingling with the surf. They were locals, people I had grown up with—the ones who still held onto the spirit of Byron like a life raft in the rising tide. They welcomed me with open arms, their energy infectious as they shared stories and laughter that filled the air like music.

I felt myself relax, the tension slowly dissipating. As the sun dipped below the horizon, I realized that perhaps I didn't have to choose between worlds. Maybe I could forge my own path—one that embraced the roots I cherished while navigating the new realities around me.

As darkness settled in, the stars began to twinkle above like distant dreams waiting to be realized. I looked around at the faces illuminated by the flickering firelight, the warmth of our connection wrapping around me. I didn't have all the answers, but I felt a sense of belonging—something that had eluded me for too long.

In that moment, I understood that I could honor the past while stepping boldly into the future. Byron was changing, but I was still part of it, a thread woven into the fabric of its identity. And as I gazed out at the endless ocean, for one moment I felt the weight of uncertainty lift, replaced by the quiet certainty that I would find my place in the world—between two worlds, and yet entirely my own.

In the Shadows

I stood at the edge of the beach, the golden sands stretching before me like a forgotten promise, the sun dipping low and casting its last warm rays over the scene. It was the kind of day Byron Bay was known for—postcard perfect, the sky an unbroken expanse of blue, the waves gentle and inviting. But somehow, I felt like an outsider in the very place I called home. I watched as surfers danced across the waves, their laughter carried on the breeze, a sound that felt as old as the land itself. Yet, I felt far removed from it all—more like a ghost lingering on the outskirts of a celebration that wasn't meant for me.

I turned away from the sun-soaked scene and wandered toward the rocks on the far side of the beach, where the manicured edges of the coastline gave way to the untamed wild of the ocean. The crowds thinned here, the noise of the tourists fading into whispers lost in the wind. It was a space where I could breathe a little easier, even if the air still felt thick with something I couldn't quite name—something that gnawed at me from the inside.

My fingers brushed against the rough, weathered surface of the rocks as I walked, the texture grounding me in a way that nothing else seemed to. It reminded me of the life I used to know—of days spent on these same shores, surfing, laughing, feeling free. But now, standing amidst the jagged stone and the creeping tide, I felt a hollow ache in my chest. The waves kept crashing against the rocks with a furious rhythm, as if trying to make me listen to something I'd long ignored. I was a product of Byron's transformation—just another face in the crowd, but one who had forgotten the pulse of the place that once gave me life.

That's when I saw them—three figures huddled together by the rocks, their skin bronzed from the sun, their laughter loud and unfiltered, spilling over like water from a broken dam. They were surfers, but not the polished kind you saw in the cafes or the glossy boutiques. These were the ones who lived in the fringes, in the places Byron had forgotten, where life still felt raw and real.

"Oi! You're not from around here, are you?" A voice called out, breaking through my reverie. It was a wiry man with dark, tangled hair and a beard that looked like it had never met a razor. His eyes twinkled with a spark of mischief, a stark contrast to the grayness that had settled over me.

I hesitated, then stepped closer. "Just... trying to escape the noise," I found myself admitting, surprised by how true the words felt.

The man chuckled, as if that was the answer he'd been waiting for. "Join the club. Name's Paul. This here's Benny and Lisa." He gestured to the other two, who both flashed wide, unguarded smiles. There was something about them—something untainted by the world outside this little patch of earth—that made me feel just a little lighter.

"Finn," I said, the tension in my shoulders easing, if only for a moment.

Lisa gave me a warm look, her voice like the sun itself. "Welcome to our little corner of paradise. What brings you out here? Chasing waves or running from something?"

"Bit of both, I guess," I replied, and before I knew it, the words were flowing out, the truth coming easier than it had in months.

We spent the next hour or so talking—about everything and nothing, our words spilling out as naturally as the tide rolling in. They spoke with a freedom I hadn't heard in years—no pretensions, no small talk, just stories about life lived on their terms. Late nights under the stars, the simple joy of the sea, and the fleeting beauty of moments when you're not trying to be anything other than yourself. It was a sharp contrast to the conversations I'd grown used to—the ones that danced around the truth, hiding behind smiles and polite chatter. With them, there was no artifice. There was only rawness and laughter, like music that made the air hum with life.

"Most people think we're crazy, living like this," Paul said, tossing a stone into the surf. "But we're just chasing something real. You know?"

I nodded, feeling a sudden kinship with them—a deep sense of connection to people who didn't need to be anything but themselves. For too long, I'd been lost in a world of curated images, fake smiles, and hollow achievements. These surfers, these outsiders, they were living without the weight of expectations. They were living in a way that felt... free.

As the sun dipped lower in the sky, the ocean turning from gold to deep blue, I felt a sense of peace I hadn't experienced in ages. The weight of my discontent, of all the choices that had brought me here, seemed to lift, even if just for a moment. There, by the rocks, in the company of people who knew what it meant to truly live, I felt something stir inside me again—a flicker of connection, a reminder of what it was like to feel 'alive'.

But as the evening settled into night, I could feel the darkness creeping in, bringing with it a reminder I couldn't ignore. The surfers began to roll out sleeping bags and gather their things to camp by the rocks. They had no plans beyond the horizon. No schedules. No commitments. Just the waves, the stars, and the simple joy of being. The thought of joining them stirred something deep within me—longing, yes, but also fear. Fear of abandoning everything I had left behind, fear of losing myself completely.

"Are you going to sleep here?" I asked, my voice hesitant, betraying my inner conflict.

"Why not?" Lisa grinned, her eyes sparkling with that wild, untamed energy. "It's better than any hotel. You wake up to the sound of the waves and the smell of salt. No rules, just freedom. Join us?"

My heart raced at the thought of just letting go, of slipping into this unstructured existence where nothing was expected of me. But the pull of my own life—the responsibilities, the choices, the weight of everything I had to build—was too strong. It was like an anchor that refused to let me float free. I glanced back toward the distant lights of Byron, where life went on, disconnected from the moment I was living in now.

"Maybe tomorrow," I finally said, and I could see the change in their expressions—understanding, but also a hint of pity. It was in their eyes, the recognition of a man caught in the web of his own choices, unable to break free.

As I stood to leave, Paul called out, his voice light and easy. "Hey, Finn! You don't have to have it all figured out. Sometimes just being here is enough."

DOWN AND OUT IN BYRON BAY

I turned back, the warmth of their camaraderie wrapping around me like a soft blanket. "Thanks," I replied, my voice thick with gratitude. "I needed this."

I walked away slowly, the sound of their laughter trailing behind me like a haunting melody. The stars were just starting to emerge, twinkling above as the night deepened. The weight of my own choices was still there, heavy in my chest, but for a moment, it didn't feel quite so suffocating. For that brief span of time, in the company of people who hadn't lost their way, I felt something stirring—a glimmer of hope, a whisper of possibility.

I didn't know what tomorrow would bring, or if I could ever fully embrace the freedom they had. But for the first time in a long while, I felt alive. And in the heart of Byron Bay, between the chaos and the calm, I knew I wasn't completely lost. Not yet.

Glass Houses

I stepped onto the gravel driveway, the crunching stones beneath my feet like a chorus of whispers, warning me of the facade that lay ahead. The house loomed before me, a sprawling structure of glass and steel that caught the late afternoon sun, fracturing it into a kaleidoscope of blinding reflections. It stood as a monument to success, a gleaming testament to the world I felt increasingly alienated from. Yet here I was, drawn into its orbit by the gravitational pull of old friendship.

As I approached, an uneasy feeling crept over me, tightening around my chest. The manicured lawns stretched endlessly, bordered by perfectly trimmed hedges, while fountains gurgled in rhythm to the laughter echoing from within. It was a world so polished it seemed almost unreal, a shiny wrapper hiding the emptiness inside.

I pushed open the glass door, and a chill of air conditioning washed over me like an artificial tide. Inside, the space opened up like a vast ocean, with high ceilings and art that screamed sophistication. It felt like a gallery of excess, where every piece seemed curated for Instagram rather than the soul. My friend Julian, lounging on a designer sofa, looked up and grinned, a flash of white teeth that contrasted sharply with the dim lighting.

"Finn! Man, you made it!" Julian's voice boomed, echoing off the walls. He was the epitome of affluence, wearing tailored clothes that hugged his body like a second skin, exuding confidence that was both magnetic and unnerving.

"Wouldn't miss it," I replied, forcing a smile. The room felt suffocating, the air thick with the scent of expensive cologne and something else—discontent, perhaps, though it was masked by the allure of opulence.

We shared small talk, the kind that bounced off the surface without ever breaking through. Julian boasted about his latest acquisitions—the new car gleaming in the garage and the exotic vacations planned for the coming months. I nodded along, feeling like an imposter in a world built on illusions.

"Come on, let's get a drink," Julian said, leading me to the bar. The shelves glistened with bottles of every hue, each one a promise of escape. I opted for a beer, something grounded and familiar, while Julian poured himself a whiskey neat—a choice that seemed to echo his polished lifestyle.

As we settled into plush leather chairs, I glanced around. The walls were adorned with photographs of laughter and lavish gatherings, snapshots of a life bursting with joy. Yet beneath the smiles, I sensed a hollowness that resonated with my own struggles. The laughter felt rehearsed, the joy curated like the art on the walls.

"Life's good, right?" Julian asked, his gaze fixed on me, seeking affirmation.

"Sure," I replied, but the word felt like sandpaper on my tongue. "You look... happy."

"Happy?" Julian laughed, a sound that was more hollow than hearty. "This? It's just the show. You know how it is."

My heart sank. I had known Julian long enough to see through the layers of bravado. Beneath the façade was a man wrestling with expectations, with a life constructed of glass that felt ready to shatter at any moment.

"Is it enough?" I asked suddenly, surprising myself with the intensity of my question. "All this?" I gestured to the opulence surrounding us—the extravagant furniture, the flickering flames of a designer fireplace, the wealth that filled the room yet felt so empty.

Julian's smile faltered, just for a heartbeat. "What do you mean?"

"Do you ever feel like it's just... not real? Like you're living in someone else's dream?" My voice trembled slightly, the truth of my own discontent spilling over the edges of my carefully constructed walls.

Julian's eyes hardened for a moment before softening. "I guess. Sometimes. But what's the alternative? Living in a shack by the beach? Eating baked beans?"

My stomach twisted at the mention of a simpler life. A shack by the beach, with waves crashing outside and sunsets painting the sky in hues of orange and pink. It somehow felt right; somehow felt preferable to being overshadowed by the relentless pursuit of success. Yet I felt the weight of my choices pressing down; the thought of ambition that might drive me away from authenticity now smothering me.

"Maybe I'd prefer the shack," I muttered, the words slipping out before I could catch them. "At least it's real."

"Come on, Finn. You don't really believe that," Julian scoffed, but there was a hint of uncertainty in his voice.

I met his gaze, searching for something—an understanding, a connection—but all I found was a mirror reflecting back my own insecurities. "I think I'm already lost," I admitted, the confession tasting bitter on my tongue.

The room grew quiet, the laughter outside seeming to fade as the weight of my words settled between us. Julian shifted in his chair, his confidence slipping as he considered my perspective.

"Maybe we're both lost," he finally said, his voice barely above a whisper. "But I can't go back. Not now."

My heart ached for the truth that lay buried beneath the glitter. I realized that the glass house wasn't just a structure; it was a metaphor for the lives we were all living—fragile and transparent, yet so carefully constructed to keep the world at bay.

As the sun began to set, casting long shadows across the room, I felt a deep sense of longing for authenticity—a yearning to reconnect with the simple pleasures that had once filled my life with meaning. I imagined the sounds of the ocean, the warmth of the sun on my skin, the laughter of friends who didn't care about status or wealth.

"Maybe it's time to rethink what's important," I said, my voice steadier now. "What if you stripped away all this and started over?"

Julian stared at me, eyes narrowing as if trying to gauge the seriousness of my suggestion. "You're talking crazy," he laughed, but there was a tremor in his laughter that suggested otherwise.

"Am I?" I replied, feeling a flicker of hope. "Maybe it's time to build something that lasts, not just something that looks good."

In that moment, as the shadows deepened and the lights began to twinkle like stars in the glass walls, I felt a shift within myself. The emptiness that had gnawed at me began to fade, replaced by a burgeoning sense of possibility.

Fleeting Moments

The sun hung low over Byron Bay, casting a warm, golden light that danced on the waves, igniting the ocean in shades of sapphire and jade. I stood at the edge of the shoreline, my feet sinking into the warm sand, my heart heavy with the weight of nostalgia. The sound of the surf was a familiar lullaby, but it felt distant now, almost like a forgotten song.

It was the beginning of the new century, and the town had changed. What had once been a sanctuary of simplicity was now crowded with tourists, their laughter mingling with the screech of gulls, each wave washing away another piece of what I used to know. I scanned the horizon, a mosaic of surfboards and sunburned skin, and wondered if I still belonged to this world.

"Hey, mate!" A voice cut through my reverie. It was a young surfer, brimming with that reckless energy of youth. "You coming out? The waves are perfect today!"

I smiled, the gesture tinged with both warmth and sadness. "Nah, not today. Just watching."

"Suit yourself!" He flashed a grin, turning back to the ocean, a sleek silhouette slicing through the surf like a knife through butter. I felt a pang of longing, an ache for the freedom that the waves offered. But today, I was a spectator in my own life, held captive by choices made long ago.

As I ambled down the beach, I noticed an elderly woman sitting on a weathered blanket, her hands busy with knitting. The yarn slipped through her fingers like memories threading through time. I approached, curious. "What are you making?"

"A scarf for my grandson," she replied, her voice soft but vibrant. "He lives in Melbourne now. I like to keep him warm, even if it's just in spirit."

I nodded, a lump forming in my throat. "That's beautiful. You must miss him."

"Oh, he visits when he can, but life keeps him busy. Just like it keeps us all busy, doesn't it?" She chuckled, her laughter like tinkling glass. "But we need to remember to take moments for ourselves. This," she gestured to the ocean, "is a gift."

I watched her work, the needles clicking rhythmically. It was a simple act, yet there was something profound in it—the way she created warmth from threads, a tangible piece of love wrapped in fabric. "Can I sit with you for a moment?"

"Of course, dear." She patted the blanket beside her, and I lowered myself onto the sand, feeling a strange comfort in her presence.

"I used to surf," I confessed, watching the waves crash. "But life has a way of pulling you under, doesn't it?"

"Like the tide," she said, her gaze steady. "But you can always choose to ride it again. The ocean is always waiting for you, Finn."

Her words lingered like the scent of salt in the air, and I felt a flicker of hope ignite within me. We spoke of life, love, and loss—brief encounters that intertwined our stories, two souls wandering through the tapestry of existence. When I finally rose to leave, she handed me the unfinished scarf, her eyes twinkling with mischief.

"Take it. You never know when you might need warmth."

I accepted it, touched by her kindness, the weight of the yarn in my hands a reminder of the connections we forge, however fleeting. "Thank you. I'll cherish it."

As I walked away, I glanced back at the woman. She was already engrossed in her knitting again, a smile on her lips. I turned toward the water, the sunlight glinting off the waves, and felt a tug at my heart—a whisper of the past that still held sway over me.

Later, I found myself at a local café, the air thick with the aroma of fresh coffee and pastries. It was a bustling hub, filled with people from all walks of life—tourists snapping pictures, locals exchanging laughter. I ordered a flat white, my fingers tracing the rim of the cup, lost in thought.

A young couple sat at the next table, their faces illuminated by the soft light filtering through the windows. They were wrapped up in each other, laughter spilling over as they shared stories, their hands brushing together like fireflies in the twilight. I felt a twinge of envy, a longing for the simplicity of connection. I remembered my own past love, how our laughter had once filled the air like music.

"Isn't it just beautiful?" The woman's voice broke into my thoughts, directed at her partner but loud enough for me to hear. "This moment, the way the sun paints everything gold."

"Yeah," the man replied, his eyes bright with affection. "It's perfect. Just like you."

My heart swelled with both joy and sorrow, the warmth of their connection contrasting sharply with my solitude. I wondered if I would ever find that again—someone who could see the beauty in fleeting moments and hold them close.

Suddenly, the couple turned to me, as if sensing my reverie. "You okay?" the man asked, genuine concern in his eyes.

I smiled, though it felt like a mask. "Just lost in thought, I suppose."

"Don't forget to live in the moment," the woman said softly. "These little things, they're what make life worth it."

"Yeah, it's easy to get swept away," I replied, the truth of her words hitting me like a wave. "Thank you."

With a wave of their hands, they returned to their conversation, and I was left with the remnants of their warmth, a brief encounter that lit up the corners of my heart.

As I stepped outside, the sun dipped lower, painting the sky in vibrant hues of orange and purple. The world felt alive, pulsing with energy and possibility. I walked along the beach, the sand cool beneath my feet, and thought of the encounters I'd shared today—each a fleeting moment, yet woven together like the threads of the woman's scarf.

I reached a secluded spot, where the waves curled gently, whispering secrets only the ocean knew. I closed my eyes, letting the sound wash over me, the salty breeze tangling in my hair. I thought of the choices I had made, the paths I had taken, and the ones left unexplored.

In that moment, I felt a shift within myself, a stirring of something long dormant. The warmth of connection wrapped around me like the scarf, reminding me that even in a changing world, kindness still existed, fleeting yet profound.

I opened my eyes to the horizon, a canvas of endless potential. I would carry these moments with me, reminders of the beauty in impermanence, the fleeting glimpses of kindness that colored my life. Perhaps, just perhaps, there was still a place for me among the waves, a chance to rediscover what it meant to truly live.

And as the sun dipped beneath the horizon, I felt a renewed sense of hope, the promise of tomorrow shimmering like the ocean, infinite and inviting.

I stood there for a long moment, letting the waves curl and crash, the sounds of the ocean filling my ears, as if they were trying to remind me of something—of a time when I wasn't so tangled in my own doubts. The air smelled of salt and possibility. I should have felt free, should have let the weight of my choices dissolve in the mist that hung low over the water. But instead, the optimism that had sparked in me earlier began to feel fragile, like a flickering flame in a windstorm.

I wanted to believe that the connections I had made, the moments of clarity, could be more than just fleeting distractions from the relentless tide of life. I wanted to believe that there was still a place for me in a world that felt so uncertain, so fragmented. The kindness I had glimpsed, the laughter shared with strangers, it all felt so rare, like a precious jewel hiding in plain sight. But what if it was just an illusion? A brief respite in the storm, only to be swallowed up by the same old patterns that had kept me stagnant for so long?

The sun sank lower, painting the sky in hues of red and orange, as if the world was holding its breath. I should have been filled with that same sense of wonder, of rebirth. But a quiet voice, the one I'd been trying to drown out for so long, whispered doubts in the back of my mind.

What if you can't change? What if all these moments of clarity are just moments, fleeting and ungraspable? What if you're too far gone, too entrenched in your own fears and routines to ever break free?

I clenched my jaw, trying to silence the voice. I could feel it, though, gnawing at the edges of my resolve. The reality was always just beneath the surface, waiting to pull me back into its grip. What if I was too old for this kind of reinvention? What if all this talk of rediscovery was just another round of self-delusion? I had spent years convincing myself that I was lost, that the past was a series of missed opportunities. And now, here I was, grasping at straws, hoping for something that might not even exist.

The horizon before me seemed endless, full of possibility, yet I couldn't shake the feeling that it was also indifferent. The waves didn't care about my doubts, they just kept coming, relentless, eroding everything in their path. Maybe that's how life was supposed to be—constantly shifting, constantly moving forward, no matter what.

But what if I'm not ready?

I shook my head, a quiet frustration bubbling inside me. I had a choice, I knew that much. I could choose to lean into the fear, to listen to that voice telling me I wasn't good enough, that I wasn't strong enough to fight against the current. Or I could push past it, take a step, even a small one, toward something different, something better. The problem was, every time I thought I might take that step, the weight of my own doubts pulled me back.

The sun finally dipped beneath the horizon, leaving a bruise of color in the sky. The night seemed to settle in around me, and for the first time, the darkness didn't feel like a blanket of comfort. It felt suffocating, a reminder of how much I had yet to face.

I let out a long breath, trying to quiet the storm in my chest. Maybe tomorrow, I thought. Maybe tomorrow I would find the courage to take a leap, to make the changes I had been longing for. But tonight, the uncertainty felt too big, too overwhelming.

Maybe tomorrow.

The waves kept crashing, indifferent to my inner turmoil, as if they had already moved on, long past the doubts that clung to me. As I turned to walk away, I realized that the ocean would keep coming, whether I was ready for it or not. And maybe that was the lesson—the world would continue to shift, to grow, to challenge me. But whether or not I chose to face it was up to me.

Maybe tomorrow, I thought again, as the stars began to pierce the sky, their light just a distant glimmer, like the hope I was still holding on to. For now, I would walk back to my life, carrying the weight of my choices—but also the possibility of something more, something better, even if it was still too far out of reach.

Chasing Shadows

The sun hung heavy in the late afternoon sky, a molten orb sinking toward the horizon, casting long shadows across the sun-drenched streets of Byron Bay. I leaned against a weathered lamppost, its peeling paint and rusted metal a testament to time's relentless march. I watched the tourists with their sun-kissed skin and designer sunglasses, the air thick with laughter and the tang of coconut oil, as they glided past like glittering fish in a shimmering sea.

It was a new century, and the town felt different—an uncanny blend of vibrant life and stark alienation. The locals had begun to feel like ghosts in their own home, outnumbered by an influx of wealth and superficiality that crowded the beaches and cafés. I found myself an unwitting spectator, drawn to the lives of the affluent, those who floated through life with an ease I could only envy.

A group of young men strolled by, their laughter echoing like music, their bodies adorned with designer swim trunks and shades that glinted in the fading light. They tossed a football between them, their carefree camaraderie a stark contrast to the solitude that wrapped around me like a second skin. I envied their ease, the effortless way they inhabited their world, while I felt like an outsider, marooned on a distant shore.

I stepped into a nearby café, the air thick with the smell of brewing coffee and baked goods, and ordered my usual—a white coffee. As I waited, I caught sight of a couple at a corner table, their conversation animated, fingers brushing against each other with every laugh. They were cocooned in their own universe, the outside world blurring into a distant hum. My heart twisted—a visceral pang of longing, a desire for that intimacy that felt perpetually out of reach.

"Here you go, mate," the barista said, placing the steaming cup in front of me, snapping me back to reality. I nodded, wrapping my fingers around the warm porcelain, its heat a fleeting comfort. I took a sip, the bitter taste grounding me, and turned to observe the world outside.

Through the glass, I spotted a woman draped in a flowing sundress, her hair cascading in sunlit waves, a sun hat perched jauntily on her head. She walked with purpose, yet her eyes sparkled with a kind of joy that I found mesmerizing. I wondered about her story, what dreams swirled behind those bright eyes. She paused by a stall selling handmade jewelry, lifting a delicate silver necklace to the light, the gemstones catching the sun like captured stars.

"Hey, do you think it's worth it?" a voice interrupted my thoughts. It was a man sitting at the table beside me, his expression one of bemused curiosity.

"Worth what?" I asked, momentarily startled.

"The necklace. Looks pretty, but you never know." He chuckled, a hint of cynicism in his tone. "Could be just a piece of crap."

"Maybe it's more about the moment," I replied, surprising myself. "Not everything has to have a price tag."

The man raised an eyebrow, intrigued. "Well said. But it's a tough world out there. People chase shiny things and forget about the weight of the simple."

I nodded, the truth of those words resonating deep within me. It felt like a mantra, a whisper echoing through the corridors of my mind, stirring something long dormant. I glanced back at the woman as she purchased the necklace, her face lighting up with delight. For her, perhaps, that necklace was a moment worth chasing.

After finishing my coffee, I stepped outside, the world vibrating with energy as the sun began its descent, painting the sky in hues of orange and violet. I followed the path of the woman, trailing her from a distance, an uninvited shadow on her journey. It felt strange, yet oddly liberating—watching her interact with the world, unencumbered by doubt or regret.

She entered a gallery, and I hesitated before following her inside. The walls were adorned with vibrant paintings, each stroke a testament to the artist's soul laid bare. I lingered near the entrance, watching as she admired a piece—a chaotic swirl of colors that seemed to pulse with life. It reminded me of my own turbulent emotions, the inner turmoil that often went unseen.

"Isn't it stunning?" the woman said to a friend who had joined her, her eyes wide with wonder. "It's like it captures everything we can't say."

I felt a pang of recognition. There was something hauntingly beautiful about the chaos, the rawness that lay beneath the surface. I turned to leave, feeling like an intruder, but the woman caught my eye, her gaze holding me for a moment longer than necessary. A flicker of understanding passed between us, a silent acknowledgment of shared humanity amidst the cacophony of our lives.

As I stepped back into the street, I felt the weight of the world pressing against me, yet something within me had shifted. The vibrant life around me pulsed with possibility, and for a brief moment, I felt connected to it—a thread woven into the larger tapestry of existence. I caught a glimpse of my reflection in a shop window, an outsider looking in, yet somehow no longer alone.

I wandered down the beach, the sand cool against my feet, and reflected on the fleeting moments I had witnessed—the laughter of strangers, the warmth of a shared smile, the beauty in imperfection. The evening breeze tousled my hair, carrying with it the scent of salt and adventure. I felt a renewed sense of purpose; I had been chasing shadows, but perhaps that was where the light lingered, illuminating the hidden corners of life.

As the sun dipped below the horizon, painting the sky in rich strokes of purple and gold, I sat on the sand and watched the waves roll in, each one a reminder of the ebb and flow of existence. The shadows lengthened, but they did not frighten me. Instead, they whispered secrets of hope and connection, urging me to embrace the transient beauty of it all.

In that moment, I understood that chasing shadows was not a futile endeavor. It was an invitation to explore the depths of humanity, to find solace in the unpolished edges of life, and to celebrate the fleeting moments that shaped my world. And as the stars began to twinkle overhead, I felt a quiet promise—life would continue to unfold, and I would be there to witness it, fully present in the beautiful, chaotic dance of existence.

The Unraveling

I stood at the edge of Byron Bay, where the ocean met the land with a ferocity that mirrored the turmoil inside me. The sun hung low, its last rays glimmering on the waves, turning the surf into molten gold. For a moment, I could almost pretend that life was still as beautiful as it had been in my youth, when the town breathed authenticity and promise.

But now, the landscape felt foreign. The streets, once alive with the laughter of local surfers and artists, had become a parade of high-end boutiques and flashy cafés. Tourists swarmed the bay, demanding pristine experiences that felt increasingly out of reach. The vibrancy that had once characterized the town felt like a mirage, fading under the weight of polished veneers. My heart ached as I watched it all unfold, the town I loved unraveling before my eyes.

I turned from the beach, shoving my hands deep into the pockets of my frayed cargo shorts. Nearby, a group of teenagers laughed, their joy sharp and bright, slicing through the air like shards of glass. They were beautiful and radiant in their youth, oblivious to the weight of the world looming just beneath the surface. I envied their freedom, their ability to revel in moments without a shadow of doubt clouding their minds.

"Hey, man! You coming to the party tonight?" one of the boys shouted, his voice a casual invitation wrapped in youthful exuberance.

I hesitated. Parties had once been the lifeblood of my existence, the pulsing heart of the community. But now, they felt hollow, perfumed with superficiality, each laugh echoing the same emptiness I felt within. "Nah, I think I'll pass," I called back, my voice barely carrying over the crashing waves.

"Suit yourself, old man!" the boy laughed, nudging his friend. I smiled weakly, but that laughter felt like a distant echo in a cavernous space. Old man. How had I become that figure, the one on the fringes of the joy I once embraced?

I wandered into town, the streets lined with trendy shops selling overpriced surfboards and artisan soaps. The scent of fresh bread wafted from a nearby bakery, momentarily breaking through the cloying aroma of sunblock and cheap cologne. I stepped inside, the doorbell tinkling softly, a quaint sound that felt out of place amidst the bustling chaos outside.

"Morning, Finn!" called out Tanya, the barista, a young woman with a pixie haircut and a smile that seemed to light up the dim interior. "The usual?"

"Yeah, thanks." I leaned against the counter, watching her expertly craft my coffee. The steam rose in delicate spirals, a moment of beauty amidst the ordinary. Yet, as I observed her, a gnawing sense of alienation settled in my chest. Tanya embodied the change—the youthfulness and vibrancy I once felt, now bottled up in someone else's hands.

"Got big plans for the weekend?" she asked, pouring the rich brown liquid into a chipped mug.

I shrugged. "Just the usual. Probably just going to take a long walk, think about life. You know how it is."

She raised an eyebrow, concern etching her features. "You need to get out more. There's a lot happening. You should come with us tonight. You might have fun."

"Fun," I echoed, the word heavy on my tongue. Fun had turned into a distant concept, a ghost that slipped through my fingers no matter how tightly I grasped it. "Maybe. We'll see."

I took my coffee and stepped back into the world, the heat wrapping around me like a suffocating blanket. As I strolled along the beach path, memories assaulted me—each grain of sand a reminder of what once was. I remembered the laughter, the bonfires under the stars, the feeling of camaraderie as we surfed the perfect waves, our lives intertwined like the roots of the ancient trees standing sentinel over the shore.

Now, I felt adrift, a ship anchored in a harbor that had long since lost its charm. I could see the changing tides in the faces around me, the superficial connections forming and breaking like waves crashing on the rocks. I longed for substance, for depth, but the town's identity had begun to fray, unraveling like an old sweater pulled at the seams.

I stopped at a lookout point, where the cliffs dropped sharply into the sea, and the sky was a riot of colors. I leaned against the railing, watching the waves churn and crash, a violent dance that mirrored the chaos within. It was beautiful yet heartbreaking—a reminder of the life I felt slipping away.

"Everything's changing, Finn. You're just stuck," a voice whispered in the recesses of my mind. Ella. I knew it was true. The laughter and joy I once shared had faded, leaving behind echoes of regret and longing.

"Hey, mate!" A voice interrupted my thoughts, pulling me back to the present. It was an older man, scruffy and sun-kissed, with deep lines etched into his weathered face. "You alright? You look like you've seen a ghost."

"Just thinking," I replied, the truth hanging heavy between us.

"Thinking ain't going to change a damn thing," he said, taking a swig from a battered thermos. "You either dive in or you don't. Life's too short to be a spectator."

I considered his words, feeling the truth resonate within me. "Yeah, but what if you dive in and it's just... empty?"

"Then you learn to swim, or you float," he shrugged. "Either way, you've got to get wet."

I nodded, the simplicity of that advice settling in my heart. I could choose to dive into the chaos of life, to embrace the uncertainty rather than stand at the edge, afraid of what lay beneath the surface. Perhaps it was time to let go of the past and confront the shadows that had loomed for too long.

As the sun dipped below the horizon, the sky ablaze with fiery hues, I felt a spark of hope igniting within me. I could unravel the threads that bound me, piece by piece, until I found something worth stitching together again. The town, with its shifting character, could be both a canvas and a battlefield—a space for creation amidst destruction.

"Thanks, mate," I said, genuinely this time. The old man nodded, his eyes crinkling in a smile before wandering off, leaving me alone with my thoughts once more.

I took a deep breath, the salt air filling my lungs, and made my way back to the heart of Byron Bay. The night pulsed with potential, laughter and music spilling from open doors, inviting me in. For the first time in a long while, I felt the stirrings of possibility. The unraveling didn't have to mean an end; it could be the beginning of something new.

With each step, I shed the weight of expectation and conformity. Tonight, I would chase the shadows, allowing them to dance around me as I embraced the chaotic beauty of existence. As I walked toward the flickering lights, I knew I would finally step into the fray, ready to discover who I could be amidst the unraveling threads of life.

I could feel the pulse of the town pulling me back in, its heartbeat syncopated with the laughter, the music, the hum of a thousand conversations. For a moment, it was easy to believe that tonight might be different, that I could slip into the flow, shed the weight of the past, and find something new in the chaos of it all. There was potential in the night, a freedom that called to me like the waves beckoning the lost.

But then doubt crept in, just as it always did. What makes you think tonight will be any different?

I pushed the thought away, trying to focus on the energy around me. This is it. This is the moment to step out, to shed the old layers. The streets of Byron Bay had always been a place of possibility, a wild mix of free spirits and tourists, of dreams made real and crushed just as easily. I had watched it all for years, never quite diving in myself, always standing on the edge, peering into the mess of it all but never quite touching it.

I paused, just outside a bar where the sounds of a live band drifted into the cool night air. The place was packed, people spilling out onto the sidewalk, their faces flushed with the thrill of the night. It's all an illusion, the voice inside whispered. They're all just pretending, just like you.

I couldn't help but listen. They don't feel what you feel, Finn. You're just an outsider, always on the fringe, never part of it. You don't belong here.

I shook my head, trying to quiet the voice. No. Not tonight. Not this time. But the doubt clung to me like a shadow, following me, whispering about all the ways I was unworthy of the life I wanted to step into. The expectations I'd carried for so long, the silent judgments, the constant questioning of my own place in it all—they had built up over the years, brick by brick, until they were almost impenetrable.

What if I walked in there, and nothing changed? What if I tried to chase that fleeting sense of freedom, only to find it as hollow as all the other attempts I'd made?

You're just going to disappoint yourself again, the voice sneered. You don't even know who you are anymore, let alone who you want to be.

I felt my feet frozen, just outside that threshold of possibility. The noise inside, the laughter, the warmth—It's all fake, the voice whispered again. Everyone's pretending to be someone they're not. You won't find anything real in there. Not for you.

I closed my eyes for a moment, the weight of it all pressing down on me. The world seemed to spin, full of noise and life, but I felt stuck, as though I were still standing in the same place I had been for years, unable to move forward, always waiting for the perfect moment that never came.

And yet, something inside me resisted, just a little. Maybe the voice was wrong. Maybe tonight could be the beginning of something, a crack in the armor I'd built for myself over the years. Maybe I was wrong to assume it would all fall apart.

But what if I wasn't? What if I was setting myself up for failure, setting myself up to face the truth I didn't want to acknowledge—that I was still too afraid to let go of what had kept me safe for so long? That I was still too trapped by my own expectations, my own fear of rejection, of exposure.

You can't change, the voice insisted. You can't rewrite your story at this point. You're too old, too set in your ways.

I clenched my fists, standing there at the edge of the crowd, feeling the weight of the night pressing in. But what if I'm not? What if I could still choose something different?

The doubt lingered, but the question kept echoing in my mind: What if I could choose differently tonight? Maybe the unraveling didn't have to mean failure. Maybe it didn't have to mean the end. Maybe the threads could tangle together to create something new, something unexpected.

I took a step forward, the sound of my feet on the pavement loud in the silence between my thoughts. Just one step. That's all it took to move past the doubt. And maybe, just maybe, that step would lead to another, and another, until I was no longer standing on the edge of my own life, but fully present in it.

As I reached for the door, my heart thudded in my chest. I'm here, I thought. I'm doing it.

I pushed it open, the noise from inside rushing out to meet me. The world beyond that door was loud, full of life, full of people chasing whatever it was they were looking for. And for the first time, I didn't feel quite as alone.

Maybe this wasn't the end of the unraveling, after all. Maybe it was the beginning.

Lessons in Solitude

I sat on the weathered timber of a tiny secluded Byron Bay pier, the boards creaking beneath me like an old man's bones. It was late afternoon, the sun's rays slicing through jagged clouds, creating pockets of warmth that kissed my skin. The ocean stretched before me, a vast canvas of shifting blues and greens, reflecting the tumult of my own heart.

Here, away from the bustling cafés and the incessant laughter of tourists, I found a rare moment of stillness. The air was thick with salt and the scent of damp earth, mingling with the distant sound of waves crashing against the shore—an unending rhythm, like a heartbeat echoing through the years. I closed my eyes, allowing the sound to wash over me, a baptism of solitude that both terrified and soothed me.

As I sat in silence, the weight of the world pressed down on me. Memories flickered like shadows in the corners of my mind—moments of love lost, friends drifted away, dreams buried beneath the relentless tide of expectation. Each wave that lapped at the pier seemed to pull me deeper into contemplation, each crest a reminder of choices made and paths not taken.

"Just you and me, huh?" I murmured to the ocean, a grin tugging at my lips despite the heaviness in my chest. The water responded with a gentle swell that brushed against the pilings, and for a moment, I felt a flicker of connection, as if the ocean understood my silent struggles.

"Hey!" A voice broke through my reverie, bright and unwelcome. A couple of teenagers sauntered past the pier, boisterous laughter trailing behind them like the scent of cheap cologne. I opened my eyes, irritation mingling with envy as they snapped photos, capturing the fleeting moments of their youth.

"Check it out!" one of them shouted, pointing to the horizon. "Dude, that's like a perfect wave!"

I watched them, my heart aching for the freedom they embodied, the unblemished joy that dripped from their lips like honey. They were like birds, flitting from branch to branch, while I felt like a rock, anchored to the spot. I knew I could join them, dive headfirst into the laughter and chaos, but something held me back—a ghost of past conversations, the echoes of a life that felt increasingly foreign.

"You okay, old man?" one of them teased as they passed. The laughter faded behind them, but their words lingered, heavy and accusatory. I was old. Not in years, but in weariness—a weathered soul lost amidst a sea of youth.

I turned my gaze back to the water, the rolling waves whispering secrets I longed to understand. There was a lesson hidden in this solitude, I felt it deep within. The stillness offered a mirror, reflecting not just my despair but also the possibility of acceptance—of learning to live within my own skin.

"Life's a mess," I muttered to the ocean, "and I'm just trying to make sense of it."

I remembered the advice of my old friend Tom, a surfer who had found peace in the solitude of the waves. "Embrace it, Finn. Solitude's not the enemy. It's a chance to really see yourself, to find the strength you didn't know you had." Those words echoed now, urging me to strip away the layers of doubt and fear.

The sun dipped lower, casting long shadows across the water, and I felt a stirring in my chest. Perhaps this was the moment to confront the truth buried beneath the surface—the truth of my choices, of the life I had constructed and the solitude I feared. I was not just a spectator in my own life; I could be the author, rewriting the narrative.

With renewed determination, I stood up, the old timber creaking beneath me. The ocean stretched out, inviting and vast, and I took a deep breath, feeling the salt air fill my lungs like a promise. I walked to the edge of the pier, toes curling over the wooden edge, the water shimmering below like a mirror reflecting both light and darkness.

I closed my eyes and dreamt.

"Here goes nothing," I whispered, and with that, I jumped. The water embraced me, cool and invigorating, pulling me under, wrapping around me like a lover's arms.

DOWN AND OUT IN BYRON BAY

For a moment, I was suspended in the depths, weightless, freed from the burdens that had tethered me. I surfaced, gasping for air, the world above suddenly bright and alive. The laughter of the teenagers echoed in the distance, but now it felt distant—a fading melody that couldn't touch me here.

The cool water enveloped me, swallowing me whole, pushing me farther from the noise, farther from the expectations. I kicked my legs, swimming further out, feeling the rhythm of the ocean beneath me, the pull of the tides, the sway of the waves. My breath was steady, my body moving with a grace I hadn't felt in years, as if the sea had unlocked something within me, a forgotten freedom.

But then, just as the waves calmed, as I was beginning to feel the flow, I heard it.

A soft, panicked voice, barely more than a whisper, curling through the water like smoke.

"Finn... Finn..."

I froze, my heart suddenly pounding in my chest. The voice was unmistakable. It was hers.

My breath caught in my throat, and for a split second, I thought I had imagined it. Ella? The name hung in the air, thick with something I couldn't define.

"Finn, no... you have to go back. Please..."

The voice trembled this time, a desperate plea, a cry from the deep. My eyes darted around the water, but there was nothing—only the vast expanse of the ocean, its surface glittering beneath the late afternoon sun. I'm hearing things, I told myself, trying to shake off the mounting dread. I'm just tired. It's the water playing tricks on me.

But then, the water shifted beneath me, an unsettling chill sweeping through the waves. No, the voice came again, louder now, frantic. You have to go back. You can't keep going, Finn. It's not safe... not like this...

A cold shiver ran down my spine, and the weight of the words hit me like a punch to the gut. I turned in the water, my pulse quickening as I searched for her, for any sign that this wasn't just my mind playing games.

But there was nothing. The ocean stretched before me, infinite and cold, its surface unbroken. Yet I knew—I knew—that she was there, somewhere beneath, her presence a silent weight beneath the waves.

Ella...

"Why now?" I whispered into the ocean, my voice lost in the rhythm of the waves. The panic rose, clawing at me, but I couldn't make sense of it. The sea was vast, its depths hiding untold secrets, and Ella—my Ella—had long ago been lost to the water, and now, her voice, her presence, had returned in some form I couldn't comprehend.

"You have to leave... please." Her voice quivered with fear, a fear I hadn't heard from her in years. It wasn't just a warning. It was a cry for help.

You need to go back, she repeated, the words cutting through my chest like a knife.

I looked back toward the shore, where the faint outline of the pier was just visible in the distance. But my limbs felt heavy, rooted to the spot, as if the water itself had a grip on me, pulling me deeper. The wind shifted, and the air felt thick with something unspoken—an unresolved ache, a wound that never healed.

"Ella... I can't," I whispered to the open sea. "I'm here... I'm finally here. I need to let go. I need to find some peace."

Her voice cracked, raw and unrestrained. "You can't find peace like this, Finn. Not in the water. Not like I did."

"The water..." The words hit me like a jolt of electricity. Ella. Ella's leaving had never been something I completely faced. Every time I tried, the memories came flooding back—her face, pale and cold, her desperate struggle, the way the ocean had taken her so quickly, so suddenly. I had never understood it. Never forgiven myself for not saving her.

But I need to let go, I repeated to myself. I have to move on. I have to find something real...

"Please," Ella begged, her voice now laced with terror. "Don't make the same mistake I did... don't lose yourself here."

I swallowed hard, choking on the fear that gripped my chest. Am I losing myself? Had I been so desperate for a release from the weight of the past that I had forgotten the lessons learned from it? Was I trying to escape—to run from the very thing I had yet to heal?

DOWN AND OUT IN BYRON BAY

With a final, pained cry, Ella's voice vanished into the swell of the ocean. Silence fell over me, broken only by the sound of my own heartbeat, pounding in my ears.

Then I opened my eyes. I floated there in my dream for a moment longer.

I closed my eyes; then opened them again. The ocean stretched out in all directions, endless, like the weight of the world pressing down on me.

In the end, it wasn't just the voice that shook me. It was the realization that I wasn't done yet. There was still more to face.

Ella's voice would stay with me. Maybe forever.

Ella

Just a memory. Teenagers. So long ago.

The sun hung low in the sky, casting a warm golden hue over Byron Bay as the waves lapped rhythmically against the shore. I sat on the sand, the coarse grains sticking to my skin like memories I could never quite shake. I closed my eyes, letting the salty breeze wash over me, but all I could feel was the weight of her absence, a specter hovering just beyond reach.

Ella. Her name was a melody that danced through my mind, a haunting refrain that played over and over, echoing with both sweetness and despair. I could still see her, a burst of life and laughter, her long hair cascading around her shoulders like sunlit waves. It was a late afternoon, much like this one, when we first tasted the freedom of youth—two teenagers, a couple of drinks, the world stretching out before us like an uncharted sea.

"Come on, Finn! Dive in with me!" she had shouted, her voice lilting above the crashing surf, teasing me with that mischievous sparkle in her eyes. I remembered how effortlessly she glided through the water, the sun reflecting off her skin, making her seem almost otherworldly. I'd sat on the shore, content to watch her, entranced by her beauty. I could never have imagined that this moment, so innocent and playful, would be the last memory I would hold of her.

As the sun dipped lower, I recalled how the light had shifted that day—the warmth turning into a chill as the shadows grew long. Ella had dived into the waves, and then, in an instant, she vanished. The laughter faded, replaced by a cacophony of confusion and fear as I called her name, my voice swallowed by the relentless roar of the ocean. Panic surged through me, a tide of terror I had never felt before. I remembered the frantic search, the lifeguards yelling orders, the other beachgoers falling silent as they realized something was wrong.

DOWN AND OUT IN BYRON BAY

I never saw her again.

Her body was never recovered, leaving behind a void that felt impossibly large. It was a weight I carried alone, a burden that wrapped itself around my heart like a vine, choking off the light. The beach transformed from a place of joy into a graveyard of memories, a constant reminder of what I lost. I never drank again, afraid of losing control, of letting the darkness creep in, just as it had on that fateful day.

I opened my eyes, staring at the horizon where the sky met the sea. The world moved on, but I was anchored in that moment—forever 17, forever heartbroken. I could still feel Ella's laughter, the way it danced through the air like a butterfly, flitting just out of reach. It had become a ghostly whisper, one that taunted me with the beauty of what could have been.

I missed her fiercely—the way she challenged me to be brave, to embrace life with both hands. We had shared dreams of escaping, of traveling the world, finding adventure in every corner. I had once believed in those dreams, in our love that felt so invincible. But as I sat there, I understood that love could be as fleeting as the tide, washing away the footprints of the past.

"Why didn't I dive in?" I whispered to the waves, the question hanging heavy in the air. It felt like a betrayal, that I had stayed behind, watching as she slipped away into the depths. Guilt washed over me, a tide that never receded, mingling with the grief that had become my constant companion.

As the sun sank lower, painting the sky in shades of orange and purple, I allowed the tears to fall, blending with the ocean's salt. I mourned not just Ella but the life we would never share—the unfulfilled promises, the dreams lost to the waves. Each tear was a fragment of my heart, scattered like shells upon the shore, reminders of a love that was both beautiful and tragic.

In that moment, I felt the weight of the world around me—the joy of the sunset, the laughter of children playing in the distance, the warmth of life moving forward. But I also felt the shadows creeping in, the ghosts of the past lingering just out of sight. I was a survivor, yes, but also a prisoner of what once was.

And so I sat, trapped between the past and the present, forever changed by a single moment, forever mourning the girl who had dived into the water and never returned.

Haunted by Hope

I stood at the edge of Byron Bay, the late afternoon sun casting long shadows across the golden sands, weaving a rich tapestry of memories and lost dreams. The air was heavy with the scent of salt and the remnants of summer, a bittersweet perfume that clung to my skin like an old lover's embrace. I could hear the distant laughter of children and the joyous cries of tourists enjoying the last rays of sun before dusk, yet I felt an aching solitude that cut deeper than the horizon itself.

"Hey, Finn!" A voice jolted me from my reverie. It was Colin, an old friend whose laughter still echoed like a familiar song, full of life and careless abandon. We had spent countless afternoons surfing the waves, two wild spirits riding the tide of youth. "You coming or what? The waves are perfect today!"

I forced a smile, but it felt like a mask slipping over my true self. "Yeah, in a minute," I replied, my voice wavering like the flickering shadows around me.

Colin shrugged and paddled out, his silhouette melding with the crashing waves, a bright figure against the darkening sky. I watched him, envy bubbling within me—envy for the freedom that eluded me, for the lightness that seemed to slip through my fingers like water. Once, I had been a part of that world, a creature of the sea, unafraid and unbound. But the years had worn me down, each wave of responsibility crashing over me, eroding the dreams I had once clung to like lifebuoys in a storm.

I turned away from the beach, letting my feet guide me along the worn path that snaked through the dunes. The sun dipped lower, the horizon bleeding hues of orange and pink—a sunset painted with the kind of beauty that stung my heart. As I walked, memories washed over me, sharp and vivid—like the time Colin and I had raced toward the shore, adrenaline coursing through our veins, laughter echoing above the roar of the ocean.

"Finn, we're going to be legends!" Colin had shouted, eyes bright with possibility.

But the dreams of youth had faded, replaced by the mundane drudgery of adulthood. Bills, responsibilities, a fading relationship with Lily—each one a weight tethering me to the earth, preventing me from soaring. I ran a hand through my hair, the salty breeze tugging at my thoughts, a cruel reminder of everything I had lost.

I stopped at a small café, the kind where the walls were plastered with surfboards and photographs of sun-kissed faces. Inside, the chatter blended into a comforting hum, the air thick with the aroma of coffee and freshly baked pastries. I took a seat in the corner, a place where I could observe without being seen. The barista, a young woman with bright pink hair and an infectious smile, took my order.

"Coffee?" she asked, her eyes twinkling.

"Yeah, thanks," I replied, my voice barely above a whisper.

As I waited, I let my gaze wander around the room, landing on a family seated nearby. They were laughing, sharing stories, their joy spilling over like the froth of their cappuccinos. A pang of longing twisted in my chest, the familiar ache of seeing happiness reflected in others—a happiness that felt like a distant shore, forever out of reach.

"Here you go!" the barista chimed, placing a steaming cup in front of me. "Enjoy!"

"Thanks," I murmured, forcing another smile. The warmth of the mug seeped into my palms, grounding me in that moment. Yet beneath the surface, despair swirled like the steam rising from my drink. I thought of Ella—of the way we had once shared dreams over coffee, our words tumbling out in excitement, mapping out a future that felt as if it were already ours. We'd talk for hours, imagining where we'd go, what we'd build, as if the world was waiting for us to claim it. It wasn't just idle chatter; it was a blueprint of possibility. We were explorers, ready to chart new territories, side by side.

Now, those dreams felt like distant echoes, fading with each passing day, slipping through my fingers like sand. I could still hear her laugh, see the way her eyes would light up when she spoke of the life we would create, but the reality of that future felt more and more like a story that someone else had written. She was gone, and with her, the plans we had woven so carefully. What remained now was the ache of unfinished promises, and the question that haunted me: how could I move forward when everything I had imagined was now lost?

Outside, the sun kissed the horizon, casting the world in shades of gold. I stood, feeling restless, and stepped back into the dusk. The beach was quieter now, the laughter fading like the light. I wandered toward the water, where the waves lapped at the shore with a rhythmic sigh, whispering secrets only the ocean could know.

As I stood there, the moon began to rise, casting a silvery glow on the surface of the water. I felt drawn to it, as if the light were a beacon guiding me home. I stepped closer, the coolness of the sand beneath my feet a reminder of the earth's solidity, grounding me in a moment that felt both fleeting and eternal.

"Hey, old man!" Colin's voice broke through the silence again. I turned, and there he was, emerging from the water, droplets sparkling on his tanned skin like jewels. "You're missing the best waves!"

I chuckled, though it felt more like a defense than a connection. "Yeah, I don't think I'm ready for that yet."

Colin's smile faded slightly, concern etching lines across his forehead. "What's going on, man? You seem... off."

I shrugged, the weight of unspoken truths heavy on my shoulders. "Just thinking," I replied, my voice softer now. "About how everything changes."

"Life's like the ocean, Finn. It's always shifting. You just gotta learn to ride the waves."

His words hung between us, a lifeline tossed into turbulent waters. I felt the familiar tug of hope, a flicker of possibility. But I also felt the shadows lurking at the edges of that hope, the fear of embracing the very uncertainty that made life both beautiful and terrifying.

"Maybe," I finally said, looking out at the waves that shimmered under the moonlight. "But what if I can't ride anymore?"

"You can," Colin insisted, his voice firm. "You just have to believe you can."

My heart raced, the weight of despair giving way to something lighter—a whisper of resilience. I stepped closer to the water's edge, feeling the cool surf caress my ankles, a gentle reminder of the life pulsing beneath the surface. The moon lit up the ocean like a silver pathway, and I felt the call of the waves beckoning me back into the fold, back to the joy that had once defined me.

I stood there, feet sinking into the wet sand, the cool ocean foam curling around my ankles. The water was alive, its rhythm steady and relentless, like the pulse of a heart that refused to stop beating. A part of me wanted to step deeper, to feel the weightlessness again, the freedom of being at one with the ocean. But the shadows of Ella's memory were thick, clinging to me like a second skin.

I could hear her voice again, faint but clear, a reminder of everything I had lost. The way she had drowned—so sudden, so raw. The day I watched the waves take her.

I can't go back in, I thought, the cold knot of fear tightening in my chest.

"Colin," I said, my voice quieter now, almost lost in the sound of the waves. "I'm not sure I can. You don't know what it's like... what happened back then."

He tilted his head, his expression softening with understanding, though there was still that underlying spark of challenge in his eyes. "I know it's hard, man. But you can't let the past drown you. The ocean won't stop calling, and neither will you."

I laughed hollowly, shaking my head. "You don't get it. You weren't there, Colin. You didn't see... you didn't feel it. You can't just—" I paused, feeling the words slip away from me as my chest tightened with the weight of memories.

The ocean stretched out before me, its surface dark and endless under the moonlight, an invitation to something I was terrified to face. Ella's voice echoed in my mind, that panic in her plea. "Don't... Don't make the same mistake I did." The words slid into my thoughts, sharp like a blade, cutting through the fragile thread of hope Colin was offering.

He stepped closer, the soft crunch of his feet against the sand grounding me, but I still felt light, suspended between the past and the present, unable to fully connect with either. "Finn, I don't know what it was like for you, and

I can't pretend to. But you can't live like this. You have to let go of whatever keeps you stuck."

I turned my gaze back to the water, its surface glittering with a silver sheen under the night sky. It looked so peaceful, so inviting. But beneath it, I could still see the swirling, chaotic depths where Ella had vanished. "I don't think I can let go," I admitted, my voice barely above a whisper. "Not when the past is still here, every time I close my eyes. Every time I'm near the water."

Colin stood silently beside me for a long moment. I could feel him weighing my words, taking them in with the kind of patience that only a surfer could have, someone who knew the rhythm of life wasn't always predictable, that there were days when the waves just weren't in sync.

"Maybe you don't have to let go all at once, Finn," he finally said, his tone softer now, less insistent. "You don't have to face the whole ocean today. Just... one wave at a time. Take it slow. Let the water have you, piece by piece. When you're ready."

I looked at him then, really looked at him, and saw the sincerity in his eyes. He wasn't pushing me. He wasn't trying to erase my pain. He was just offering a way forward, one that didn't require forgetting the past, but accepting that the future still had room for me in it.

It felt like a lifeline, fragile but real. Maybe one wave at a time.

I stared out at the water again, letting the idea settle in, the edges of the panic easing just enough to let a sliver of possibility creep in. Maybe I wasn't as lost as I thought. Maybe the waves didn't have to be enemies. Maybe they could be my companions again.

"I'll try," I said, finally. The words felt heavy, but they also felt like the first step. "I don't know if I can do it. But I'll try."

Colin gave me a quick smile, a reassuring nod. "That's all anyone can ask. Just try."

The water beckoned—so familiar, so wild—stretching out before me like an invitation I couldn't ignore. I stood at the edge, my toes digging into the soft sand, feeling the pull of the tide, the rush of the waves as they crashed with a force I used to welcome.

But my fear had a weight to it, settling in my chest like a stone. I wanted to dive in. I wanted to lose myself in the saltwater, to let it cleanse me, pull me under and wash away the years of uncertainty that clung to me. I could almost taste the cool embrace, hear the rhythmic rush of the sea filling my lungs, feel the release, the freedom of surrender.

But I couldn't move.

I took a step forward, then froze. My heart raced, my body rigid, my feet rooted to the ground. The waves kept coming, relentless and impatient, but I stayed where I was, caught between the desire to dive and the terror of what it might mean. The fear wasn't of the water—it was of the letting go, of the leap I couldn't bring myself to take.

I exhaled slowly, retreating back to the dry sand. The waves continued their eternal dance with the shore, as if nothing had changed, as if nothing had ever been different. And I... I just stood there, watching, wondering if I would ever find the courage to dive in again.

Silent Screams

The night hung heavy over Byron Bay, a thick blanket of darkness woven with whispers of wind and the distant crash of waves. I lay awake in my small, cluttered cottage, the walls adorned with fading posters of surf legends and abstract art that spoke of dreams long pursued. A ceiling fan whirred lazily overhead, but the heat clung to me, a sticky reminder of my restless thoughts. I tossed and turned, a fish caught in the net of my own mind.

Outside, the world moved on without me—cars hummed by, their headlights slicing through the night like knives through fog. I could hear laughter in the distance, the sounds of a bonfire gathering; it felt like a melody of joy that mocked my solitude. I buried my face in my pillow, willing the noise to fade, wishing for sleep to wrap me in its embrace. Yet, sleep eluded me, a wraith slipping through my fingers.

Swinging my legs over the edge of the bed, my feet hit the cool floor. The air was thick with the scent of salt and something bittersweet, a reminder of the ocean's pull. I dressed quickly, slipping into well-worn jeans and a faded tee, before stepping out into the night, drawn to the pulse of the town, to the people who thrived in the moonlight.

As I wandered the familiar streets, the soft glow of streetlamps illuminated the faces of passersby, each one a chapter in a story I had yet to uncover. I paused at a small café, its patio filled with a haphazard collection of tables and mismatched chairs. A couple sat at the far end, their laughter rising and falling like the tide, but their eyes told another story—flickers of pain hidden behind smiles, the silent screams of two souls adrift in the currents of life.

I lingered, feeling like an intruder in their intimacy. Their words, though light, were laced with something deeper—a desperation that resonated in my own chest. I turned away, pushing deeper into the night, my heart heavy with empathy for those I barely knew but understood all too well.

I found myself at the beach, the moon casting a silver path across the water. The waves rolled in with a soft, rhythmic sigh, each one a reminder of the relentless march of time, the way it washed away both beauty and sorrow. I settled onto the sand, letting the cool grains slip through my fingers, grounding me in this moment of solitude. Here, beneath the vastness of the sky, I felt both insignificant and profoundly connected to everything.

My mind wandered to the shadows I had seen—the stories behind the eyes of strangers. There was the barista with the ink-stained hands, always a smile on her lips, yet the way she clenched her jaw suggested battles fought beneath the surface. The tattooed man who skated by every morning was a fleeting specter, perpetually lost in thought, carrying the weight of unspoken fears. Then there was Lenny, the old fisherman, whose hands were rough as bark, his eyes distant like he'd seen too much, yet still wandered the pier every day at dawn. He never spoke much, but there was something in his silence that held more weight than any words could.

And in the corner of my mind, there was Marley, the young woman who ran the vintage record shop down the road. She was a burst of color in a town that sometimes felt too grey. Her laughter was the kind that made you believe in joy, even when it seemed impossible. But when she thought no one was watching, there was that flicker in her eyes—the way her shoulders slumped just slightly when she thought she was alone. I knew she carried something, too, something she hadn't shared.

They were all wrestling with their demons, silent screams echoing in the caverns of their minds. Each of them was fighting their own war, some more visible than others, but I saw it in the way they moved, in the way their eyes darted or lingered too long, like they were waiting for someone to notice. I'd been one of them once, carrying my own burdens with a quiet rage, keeping them hidden behind the veil of everyday life. But now, here I was, just another face in the crowd, wondering how many others were just as lost, just as tangled up in their pasts.

The more I thought about it, the more I realized that maybe none of us ever truly understood each other. We were all just a collection of broken pieces, trying to make sense of the world in our own way.

"Hey, you okay?" A voice broke through my reverie. It was Jess, her silhouette framed by the moonlight, hair tousled by the wind. She slid down beside me, pulling her knees to her chest, her presence a soothing balm against the chaos of my thoughts.

"Couldn't sleep," I admitted, running a hand through my hair. "Just thinking about... everything."

"Yeah? Like what?" She looked at me, those bright eyes searching for honesty.

I hesitated, the weight of my thoughts pressing against my chest. "Just people, I guess. Everyone's carrying something, you know? It's like we're all walking around with silent screams, and no one talks about it."

Jess nodded, the corners of her mouth turning down slightly. "I've felt that too. Sometimes I think we're all just trying to fit pieces together, like a jigsaw puzzle with missing parts."

I sighed, letting the words hang in the air like a heavy fog. "Do you ever feel like you're just... fading away? Like the more you try to connect, the more you become invisible?"

"Every day," she said softly. "Especially in a place like this, where everyone's chasing the next wave of happiness. Sometimes I wonder if I'm just a ghost in my own life."

"Yeah. It's like, no matter how hard you try to reach out, you're still not really seen. Not truly. Like everything you say, everything you do, just gets lost in the noise."

Jess shifted beside me, her eyes reflecting something deep and familiar. "I get it. But, at least I have Ricky. I can always count on him. No matter what's going on, he's there. And we get through it together."

The words hit me harder than I expected. I felt a sudden emptiness that spread across my chest like cold water. I hadn't realized how much I'd taken it for granted—the idea that someone could always be there, a steady anchor in the storm. Jess had Ricky. She had someone to share the weight with, someone to lean on when the world felt too much.

I didn't have that. I hadn't had that in a long time.

I swallowed hard, the tightness in my throat threatening to choke me. "Yeah... you're lucky. To have someone to rely on."

Jess looked at me, her expression softening as she took in the shift in my tone. "You're not alone, Finn," she said, her voice gentle but firm. "You've got people who care about you. You've got me. And I know you're carrying a lot, but you don't have to do it all by yourself."

I wanted to believe her. I really did. But the hollow ache inside me told me otherwise. The truth was, I wasn't sure who I could rely on anymore. Not really. Not like Jess and Ricky. There were people I had once counted on, but now they were either too far away or too tangled up in their own lives to even notice I was drowning.

I let out a breath, the weight of my own isolation pressing harder now. "I don't know, Jess. Sometimes I wonder if it's all just... too late. Too late for me to make things right, to make any real connections. I feel like I've already missed my chance."

She frowned, her gaze holding mine, searching for something in my eyes. "It's never too late, Finn. You've got time. We all have time, as long as we're breathing. But you have to make the choice. You have to step forward."

The thing was, I wasn't sure if I could anymore. The thought of opening up, of trying again, felt like standing on the edge of a cliff, knowing that the fall could be just as terrifying as staying on solid ground.

Our conversation lingered, a fragile web of shared vulnerabilities. The night felt alive around us, the sound of the ocean a constant reminder of our own ebb and flow. I thought of the way each wave was unique, just like each person I encountered—beautiful and flawed, crashing against the shore only to retreat into the depths.

"Do you think people will ever really understand each other?" I asked, my voice barely above a whisper.

"I hope so," Jess replied, her gaze drifting toward the horizon. "But understanding takes time. It takes... bravery."

I felt the weight of her words, like a stone settling in my gut. There was a strength in vulnerability, an honesty that could bridge the chasms between people. I thought about the moments I had let myself be seen, the times I had shared my own struggles. It was terrifying but necessary, a way to break the cycle of silence that suffocated us all.

As the waves continued their dance, I took a deep breath, inhaling the salty air mixed with the scent of sand and night. "Maybe we should start talking about it—about our struggles, our fears. Not just to each other, but to everyone."

"...understanding takes time. It takes... bravery." Jess's words lingered in the air like a distant echo, calling me back to something I hadn't allowed myself to believe in for a long time. Time. It felt like a foreign concept now, something I had all but given up on. But as I sat there, feeling the weight of her gaze, there was something about the way she said it—you've got time—that made me pause.

Maybe she's right.

The thought was fragile, like a flicker of light in a dark room. But it was there. A spark.

I looked out at the horizon, watching the last remnants of the sun dip below the trees, the colors of the sky reflecting a world of possibility. Could I really step forward? Could I allow myself to trust again, to reach for something more than just survival?

For so long, I'd been living in a holding pattern. Waiting. Waiting for something to change, for someone else to fix things, or for a moment of clarity to suddenly strike. But maybe the change needed to come from me. Maybe I needed to stop hiding from what scared me and start looking for the connections I thought were lost.

I don't have to have it all figured out right now. That was the other thing Jess had said. I've got time.

I felt the tightening in my chest loosen a fraction. Time. It was something I had been measuring against my own failure, thinking there was some cutoff point where I would be too old, too broken, too far gone. But what if that wasn't true? What if the only real barrier was the one I'd put up in my mind?

Maybe, just maybe, this wasn't the end. Maybe I wasn't meant to simply fade into the background, swallowed by the noise of everything I couldn't control. Maybe I could still choose to fight, to connect, to be seen.

But the fear was still there, coiling in the pit of my stomach. I could feel it—the weight of years of missed opportunities, of buried emotions, of things I had let go that I could never get back. How can I make up for all the time I've wasted?

Yet, as I stood there beside Jess, the world around me buzzing with life, something new began to take root. That spark, small and fragile, started to grow. Not in the way a flame rages to life, but more like a slow-burning ember that found its place deep inside me.

Maybe I could make a different choice tomorrow. Maybe I could reach out. Maybe I could build the connections I thought were beyond me.

I glanced over at Jess. "You're right, you know," I said quietly. "Maybe it's not too late. Maybe... maybe I can try again."

She smiled softly, her eyes lighting up with the kind of warmth that made me feel like I wasn't as far gone as I'd believed. "You don't have to do it all at once. Just take one step at a time. The rest will follow."

For the first time in a long while, I felt a sense of possibility that wasn't overshadowed by doubt. It wasn't a grand, sweeping revelation, but it was enough. Enough to remind me that even in the midst of all the uncertainty, there was still room for hope.

Maybe it wasn't too late for me after all.

The Quiet Before the Storm

Byron Bay wore an unsettling calm, the kind of silence that draped itself over the world just before chaos erupted. I stood on the balcony of my small flat, a weathered structure that had seen better days, just like me. The air felt thick and electric, charged with an unseen tension that crawled beneath my skin. I squinted at the horizon where the ocean met the sky, the colors swirling like an artist's palette smeared by a careless hand—gray clouds rolling in, heavy with unspoken promises.

I took a deep breath, the scent of salt and impending rain mingling in the air. It was intoxicating, reminding me of summers spent chasing waves, but today it felt more like a warning. The ocean, once a lover's embrace, now seemed a ravenous beast waiting to unleash its fury. I could hear the distant rumble of thunder, a low growl that sent a shiver down my spine.

Turning away from the view, I stepped back into the cramped living space that bore the remnants of a life half-lived. An old couch, its fabric threadbare and stained, faced a television that rarely played anything worthwhile. Scattered around were remnants of a creative spark—a half-finished painting, brushes caked in dried paint, and a notebook filled with fragmented thoughts. My dreams felt like ghosts, whispering from the shadows, taunting me with their elusiveness.

As the clouds thickened outside, so too did the weight of my thoughts. I could feel my own life swirling in a tempest, each decision an anchor dragging me deeper into uncertainty. Memories washed over me like the tide—my father's disappointed gaze, my mother's quiet resignation, the love that slipped through my fingers like sand. I had always sought solace in the ocean, yet here I was, feeling more isolated than ever.

I poured myself a glass of cheap wine, the kind that burned the throat but dulled the mind. Sinking into the couch, I stared blankly at the peeling walls, their roughness mirroring the turmoil inside me. Each thundering heartbeat echoed the storm brewing beyond, a reminder that change was on the horizon. The fear of the unknown tightened around me like a noose, and for a moment, I questioned whether I would ever escape the cycle of my life.

My phone buzzed, cutting through the haze. It was Jess, her text simple yet inviting: "Storm's coming. Let's meet at the beach?" I hesitated, the allure of the storm pulling at me like an undertow. I could stay here, in the quiet, hiding from the storm brewing within and without, or I could venture out, face the chaos head-on.

With a resigned sigh, I grabbed a worn hoodie and stepped outside. The air crackled with energy, as if the world held its breath. I walked through the narrow streets of Byron, feeling the first raindrops kiss my skin, each one a fleeting reminder of nature's unpredictability. As I approached the beach, the wind picked up, tangling my hair and stripping away the remnants of my hesitation.

Jess was already there, her silhouette framed against the darkening sky. She was an anchor in the storm, her presence a balm for the chaos inside me. "Hey," she said, a smile breaking through the gathering gloom. "Thought I'd find you here."

I smiled back, though it felt strained. "I wasn't sure if I'd come. Just felt… heavy."

"Yeah," she replied, her voice soft yet steady. "It's a weird kind of calm, isn't it? Like everything's about to change."

I nodded, my gaze drifting to the horizon where the sea met the sky, a violent dance brewing beneath the surface. The waves surged higher, crashing against the shore with an intensity that mirrored my own turmoil. "Sometimes I feel like I'm just waiting for something to happen," I confessed, the words tumbling out before I could second-guess them.

Jess took a step closer, her eyes searching mine. "What are you waiting for, Finn?"

I sighed, running a hand through my hair, the wind whipping around us like a tempest. "I don't know. Maybe for the storm to pass. Or for something to change. But I feel stuck, like I'm treading water and the shore keeps drifting further away."

"You're not alone in that," she said gently. "We all have storms to weather. It's what we do with them that matters."

Her words settled over me, a soothing balm against the brewing chaos. I glanced at her, really looked at her, and saw the same fears reflected in her eyes—the weight of expectations, the burden of dreams unrealized. We were two ships navigating a turbulent sea, both yearning for a safe harbor.

As the first real gust of wind swept through the beach, I felt a jolt of energy course through me. The storm was no longer just an external threat; it was a catalyst for change, a reckoning that demanded I confront my fears. "Maybe it's time to stop waiting," I murmured, the realization crystallizing in my mind.

Jess smiled knowingly, a spark igniting in her gaze. "What do you want to do then? What's the first step?"

I pondered her question, the weight of possibility hanging in the air. "I think... I think I need to start writing again. Really writing. Not just letting it sit and collect dust." The thought felt liberating, like a surge of electricity sparking through me.

"Then let's do it. Let's make a plan," Jess urged, her enthusiasm infectious. "You can't control the storm, but you can control how you respond to it."

I felt a flicker of excitement as Jess's words bounced around in my mind, but just as quickly, a shadow of doubt crept in. Writing again. Really writing. It felt like stepping onto an old, familiar path, one I had walked many times before—except this time, the road seemed overgrown, distant, a place I had almost forgotten. Could I really do it? Could I face the blank paper again without the heavy weight of failure pressing down on me? Could I succeed on my own...?

The thought of success hung in the air, but it was a murky thing. What does success even mean anymore? The question lingered in my chest, twisting like a knot. I had spent years thinking of writing as something I would do, but never be. It was always a side project, something to escape into, to soothe myself when the world felt too loud. But now—could it be more? Could it be me, my life, my future?

The idea of writing for the sake of writing, of expressing what lived inside me, felt like a reclamation of something pure. But then the practical side of me—the one that had been buried under years of doubt—whispered, You can't just do that. You need money. You need to survive.

I closed my eyes for a moment, taking in the weight of that internal tug-of-war. Selling my writing... that would be success, right? But that brought its own brand of anxiety. What happens if I sell out? What if my work turned into a product? What if it lost its heart, its soul, just to appeal to the market? I thought of Mark going into advertising in Sydney. I thought of Marla painting pretty pictures for tourists. I remembered the pressure of trying to fit into boxes, the creative world's demand for something polished, for something that could be sold. Is that what I really want? Or do I want to remain authentic, even if it meant barely scraping by?

The contrast was suffocating: authenticity versus making a living. If I stayed true to myself, would I be okay with being poor, with never truly 'making it'? Can I handle that kind of failure for my entire life?

But then, a darker thought slithered in: What happens if I don't try at all? The pit in my stomach deepened as the weight of inaction pressed against my chest. What was worse—selling out and living a lie, or doing nothing and letting the years slip by in the quiet agony of missed chances? In the end, isn't doing nothing the real failure?

I leaned against the wooden railing, my fingers gripping it tighter than necessary, feeling the cool of the breeze against my skin. I'm already in the storm, I thought. Maybe the question isn't whether I can control it, but whether I can live with the consequences of not doing anything.

I opened my eyes again, looking out at the ocean. The waves rolled in, relentless, never stopping. The world keeps moving, no matter what we decide.

A part of me knew that, if I didn't take that first step—if I didn't push through the fear of failure, of judgment—then I would always be trapped in this cycle of uncertainty. At least if I try, I can say I did something.

I looked at Jess. "I guess the first step is letting go of the idea of perfection. Just... doing."

Her smile widened. "Exactly. No more waiting for the perfect moment. You've got all the time you need, but you have to make it count."

I nodded slowly, the weight in my chest lifting just a little. Maybe it won't be perfect, I thought. Maybe I'll fail, maybe I won't make a living from it, but at least I'll be living the way I want to.

For the first time in a long while, the idea of painting didn't feel like a burden or a fantasy. It felt like a choice—an imperfect, uncertain, but very real choice.

Maybe that was enough to start with. Maybe that's all I needed.

But as the sky darkened and the first heavy drops of rain began to fall, doubt crept in like a quiet shadow, reminding me how fragile this new resolve might be. Could I really embrace this path, knowing how easily I had turned away from it before? What if the weight of it all—the uncertainty, the vulnerability—was more than I could bear?

Still, there was a shift within me—a recognition of the power I held over my own life. I was no longer a passive observer, waiting for the storm to pass; I was a participant in my own life, ready to embrace the chaos.

Yet as the wind howled around us and the ocean roared in response, that creeping doubt lingered. I stood tall, yes, but part of me couldn't shake the feeling that maybe the tempest had already begun, and I wasn't sure if I was ready for what came next.

The quiet before the storm had given way to a tumultuous embrace, but beneath the surge of excitement, a faint whisper of fear reminded me: Life was a series of waves, and maybe, just maybe, I wasn't as ready to ride them as I'd hoped.

Tides of Change

I stood on the windswept beach of Byron Bay, the sand gritty beneath my bare feet, each grain a remnant of the past, a whisper of stories buried deep. The ocean stretched out before me, a restless entity, the waves rolling in like a symphony of sighs. I watched as they crashed against the rocks, sending sprays of saltwater into the air—a stark reminder that nothing remained unchanged, that everything was in constant flux.

The sun hung low, casting a golden hue over the water, and for a moment, I felt the warmth seep into my bones, washing over me like a long-forgotten embrace. But beneath that warmth lay an undercurrent of anxiety, a tightening in my chest that mirrored the tide's relentless pull. 1998 Byron Bay was a place once steeped in community spirit, now slowly morphing under the weight of development and change.

I turned my gaze towards the beach, where families sprawled on colorful towels, laughter ringing out like chimes in the wind. But the laughter felt different now, a symphony out of tune, notes clashing with the distant cries of seagulls and the rhythm of the ocean. Newcomers flocked to the area, their presence marking the shore with a distinct divide between the old and the new. The locals, faces weathered by sun and salt, watched from the fringes, their expressions a blend of pride and sorrow.

"Hey, mate! You coming in or what?" A voice pulled me from my reverie. It was Dave, an old friend with a mane of salt-and-pepper hair, his skin bronzed and leathery from years in the sun.

"Yeah, just thinking," I replied, forcing a smile, but the words felt hollow, echoing in the emptiness that lingered just below the surface.

"Thinking too much'll get you in trouble," Dave chuckled, but there was a seriousness in his eyes, a shared understanding of the disquiet that hung in the air. "Come on, let's catch some waves before the light goes."

I nodded, though a part of me hesitated. The ocean called to me, but the sense of belonging that once accompanied such invitations felt frayed. I waded into the surf, the cool water invigorating yet chilling, a stark contrast to the heat of the sun above. As I paddled out, the waves crested and fell, each one a reminder of the fleeting nature of life—here one moment, gone the next.

"Look at 'em," Dave shouted, pointing to a group of surfers who were clearly outsiders, their boards sleek and polished, their laughter loud and carefree. "They don't even know the rules of the break. Just paddling in like they own the place."

A pang of resentment rose within me. It wasn't just the surfers; it was the cafés that had morphed into trendy spots for brunch, the art galleries filled with sterile strokes from newcomers who painted without knowing the land. The town was changing, and with it, the very fabric of our community was being pulled apart. I felt like a relic, clinging to memories while the world moved on without me.

As I sat at the edge of the water, its power surged through me, a momentary escape from the turmoil within. The water roared around me, a wild, untamed force, yet here I was, a part of it, if only for a moment. I glanced back at the shore, where the old-timers lingered, their expressions a mixture of nostalgia and resignation. They understood the tides of change, had lived through seasons of loss, yet here they remained, a quiet strength in a world that seemed to be forgetting them.

Dave came and sat beside me, the warmth of his presence grounding me as the noise of the younger surfers continued to churn behind us. The sound of boards clashing, boards scraping against the waves, the constant calls and whoops as they fought for their next ride—it all seemed so loud, so frantic, compared to the stillness I craved.

He followed my gaze, his eyes narrowing as he watched the group of tourists. "It's like they're just rushing through it all," he said quietly. "Trying to get to the next big thing, not really feeling the wave, you know?"

I nodded, the weight of my thoughts pressing down on me. "Yeah. It's all about the ride. Not about the ocean or the other people out there." I shook my head, frustrated. "It used to be different, Dave. There used to be this understanding, this shared respect for the waves, for the space. Now... it's like everyone's just out for themselves."

He sighed, rubbing a hand over his face. "Yeah, I see it too. It's not just the surfing, though. It's everything. The way people treat each other, the way the world is moving, faster and faster. It's all about what you can grab for yourself before it's gone."

I felt a tightness in my chest at his words. It was the truth, and it was the truth that hurt the most. The world had shifted, and somewhere along the way, I had missed it. Or maybe I hadn't tried hard enough to keep up. Either way, it didn't matter. The change was here, and it was glaring, impossible to ignore.

"It's hard, isn't it?" I said, my voice quieter now. "To feel like you're just... a bystander in your own life. Like everything is moving forward, and you're stuck in the past."

Dave looked over at me, his expression softening. "I get it, man. Trust me, I do. But you can't keep waiting for things to go back to what they were. We've gotta figure out how to live in this new world, even if it doesn't feel like our world anymore."

His words hung there between us, a mixture of understanding and truth. I wasn't sure I was ready for that. Ready to accept that things couldn't be the same. But I also knew that if I didn't, I'd stay stuck, stuck in a memory of what was instead of being present for what could be.

I stared out at the waves, feeling the salt in the air. The tourists, the chaos—they were all part of the changing tide. But the ocean itself? The ocean had a rhythm, something steady, something eternal. And maybe, just maybe, if I focused on that, I could find my own rhythm again too.

"Maybe I don't have to fight the change," I said slowly, more to myself than to Dave. "Maybe I can just... flow with it. Like the ocean does."

Dave didn't respond right away. He just sat beside me, his gaze on the water. For a while, we didn't need words. The sound of the waves crashing, the distant laughter, the birds calling—it all felt like it was part of the same song. And maybe, for a moment, I was starting to understand it.

Dave pointed to a young surfer, obviously a tourist getting his first taste of riding a wave in Byron. With a mop of sun-bleached hair and too much enthusiasm, he dropped into a wave just as another surfer, a girl with a bright pink board, paddled out to catch the same one. She didn't see him coming, and by the time she did, he was already halfway down the face of the wave, carving it with a reckless abandon that didn't care about the others around him. She swerved, her board wobbling under the sudden shift, barely avoiding a collision.

I watched as the girl yelled something at him, but the guy just laughed it off, hooting into the wind as if the whole world was his to dominate. It wasn't an act of aggression, but an act of ignorance, as if the others in the water were just obstacles in the way of his fun. And he wasn't the only one. Another surfer, a girl with a messy bun and a neon rash vest, dropped in on a wave without checking if anyone else was in the line-up. She cut across another guy's path, forcing him to kick out early. He didn't even look at her as she paddled past, too busy scanning the horizon for the next set to come in.

I shook my head, feeling a sharp pang in my chest. They're just kids, I reminded myself. But there was something about the way they moved, the way they claimed the water without acknowledging the space they shared with each other, that rubbed me the wrong way. It wasn't just the competition—it was the lack of respect, the feeling that they were only in it for themselves, oblivious to the others around them.

It wasn't always like this. I'd seen the surf scene shift in the last few years, the more aggressive attitude taking over, the sense of community that used to be so central to this place slowly fading. In the past, there had been unspoken rules—a mutual understanding that the ocean was bigger than any of us, that we were all just guests in its domain. Respect the wave, respect each other. But now, it felt like people were just looking for the next thrill, the next ride, without considering the impact it had on those around them.

I looked at Dave, who seemed lost in his own thoughts, his eyes fixed on the water. I knew he had seen it too.

"You notice that?" I asked, my voice quiet but edged with frustration.

He glanced over at me, his gaze following the group of surfers. "Yeah," he said, nodding slowly. "It's like everyone's in their own world. Not really sharing the waves, you know? It's more like a competition. It wasn't always like this."

I exhaled, frustrated by how the scene had changed. "It's all about getting that next ride, without thinking about who's in the way. It's like they're treating it like a race, not a shared experience."

Dave was silent for a beat, then shook his head. "Yeah, it's weird. They don't get it. Surfing was about the rhythm, the connection—being with the ocean, not just conquering it."

I leaned back on my hands, staring out at the horizon. The waves still rolled in, steady and timeless, indifferent to the chaos on the surface. I didn't want to be that guy—the one who complained about the younger generation, who longed for the past. But damn, I missed it. I missed the simplicity of just being out there with people who understood.

Maybe that's part of it, I thought. Maybe it's not about being perfect, or always catching the biggest wave. Maybe it's about finding that connection again—whether it's with the ocean or with each other.

I stood up, brushing sand from my hands. "I think I'm gonna head out. I don't know, Dave, I just... I need a minute."

He looked up at me, a knowing smile playing at the corner of his mouth. "Yeah, man. I get it. Go clear your head."

I walked along the water's edge, the coolness of it seeping into my feet as the waves lapped at the shore. The energy around me was still buzzing, young, wild, chaotic. But I didn't have to be a part of it. Not today. Today, I just wanted to feel the ocean again, the way it used to feel—calm, familiar, steady. Maybe the world was changing, maybe it was growing faster than I could keep up with, but the sea? The sea would always be the same. And I needed that.

My heart was heavy. Ella's voice came to me: "It's like they've come to take without understanding what it means to be part of something. It used to be about the connection, you know? The locals, the stories...it feels different. Like we're losing something."

I whispered: "But I don't know how to fight it. I'm just trying to get by, trying to keep the memories alive."

"Memories..." Her voice trailed off as I stared out at the horizon, where the sky kissed the sea. "It's like we're the ghosts of a place that doesn't recognize us anymore."

Silence hung between us, thick and palpable. I could feel the weight of unspoken words, the grief of a community unraveling at the seams. The tide continued its relentless march, a reminder that change was both inevitable and cruel.

As the sun dipped lower, painting the sky in hues of orange and purple, I felt a sense of urgency swell within me. "Maybe it's time we start telling our stories," I said, my voice steadier. "Not just to each other but to them. The newcomers. Show them what Byron was and still can be."

Ella's voice rose. "You think they'd listen?"

"Maybe." I replied, feeling the embers of hope flicker to life within me.

As we watched the last rays of sunlight disappear into the horizon, I felt a shift within myself. The tides were changing, yes, but they didn't have to wash away everything I loved. With every story shared, every memory reclaimed, we could weave a new narrative—one that honored the past while embracing the future.

The Artist's Dilemma

The air in Byron Bay had grown thick with anticipation, like the moment before a storm breaks—a tension humming beneath the surface, crackling in the sunlight. I leaned against the peeling paint of the old surf shack, the salty breeze ruffling my hair, carrying the scent of fried fish and sunscreen. The beach stretched out before me, a golden expanse dotted with sunbathers and surfers, but today, the usual vibrancy felt muted, as if the world was holding its breath.

It was here that I met Maya, an artist with wild curls that danced in the wind like seaweed caught in the tide. She sat cross-legged on a blanket, her fingers stained with paint, her eyes focused on a canvas that captured not the beauty of the bay but its undercurrents—the encroaching development, the changing faces, the shadows looming over our once close-knit community.

"Isn't it beautiful?" I asked, nodding toward the water.

Maya looked up, her expression a mixture of amusement and disdain. "Beautiful? Sure. But look closer. It's all changing. The buildings rise like tombstones, marking the death of what we once had."

Her words struck a chord deep within me. "I get that. It feels like the town's losing itself."

She nodded, returning her gaze to the canvas. "I try to capture that loss, but no one wants to buy it. They want the postcard views, the idyllic sunsets. It's frustrating. I want to scream."

"Maybe you should," I suggested, half-joking. "Art's supposed to be an expression, right?"

"It is. But when you're drowning in bills and the rent's due, you find yourself painting what sells. It's a choice between integrity and survival." Her voice trembled slightly, revealing the vulnerability beneath her defiance.

I felt the weight of her words. I knew too well the struggles of balancing passion with reality. The bittersweet dance of dreams and the mundane was a song I had heard all my life. I had watched friends sacrifice their authenticity for comfort, trading creativity for a paycheck, and the cost was etched in the lines on their faces, in the way they spoke of their aspirations as if they were ghosts.

Maya's canvas was a raw portrayal of a world caught in limbo—a half-constructed luxury hotel loomed in the background, its sterile lines contrasting sharply with the chaotic beauty of the ocean. The waves crashed against the rocks with a fury that echoed her frustration, a primal scream against the tide of commercialization threatening to wash away everything we cherished.

"What if you turned your frustration into something more?" I suggested, a spark igniting in my chest. "What if you painted a series, each one telling a part of the story? Maybe people would connect with that."

She tilted her head, her eyes narrowing in thought. "You think so? People want pretty pictures, not a reminder of what they're losing."

"Maybe that's exactly what they need. To feel something real, to confront the change rather than just accept it," I urged, feeling a surge of hope.

As the sun began its descent, casting long shadows across the sand, Maya's face softened. "You make it sound easy, Finn. But every stroke on the canvas feels like a gamble. I risk everything by exposing my truth."

"It's a gamble worth taking," I insisted, leaning closer. "Your voice matters. If you don't tell your story, who will?"

Maya paused, her brush hovering over the canvas. The colors blended like the emotions swirling within her—a riot of anger, sadness, and hope. I could see it, the battle she waged not just against the tides of change but within herself. I understood that feeling all too well, the ache of wanting to belong while fearing the loss of oneself.

"Okay," she said finally, determination threading her voice. "I'll do it. I'll paint my truth, no matter the cost. I want to scream about the beauty and the destruction. Let's see if anyone cares."

As we talked, the shadows lengthened, and the first stars began to flicker in the sky, fragile pinpricks of light against the darkening canvas of night. I felt the warmth of camaraderie blooming between us, a connection forged in shared struggles and unspoken fears. In Maya's art, I saw a reflection of my own journey, the desire to create meaning amidst chaos.

"Have you ever felt like you're losing touch with your roots?" I asked, my voice low. "Like the ground beneath you is shifting?"

"All the time," Maya replied, her gaze drifting toward the horizon. "It's like the town is changing so fast, and I'm just... lost in it. Sometimes I think I'm fighting a battle I can't win."

I nodded, the weight of her words settling in my chest. "It's scary to feel like you don't belong anymore. I see it in the faces of the locals, the ones who've lived here forever. We're all clinging to something that's slipping away."

In that moment, as the waves whispered secrets to the shore, I felt an unshakable bond with Maya—a shared understanding of the existential dread lurking just beneath the surface of our lives. It was a reminder that amidst the noise and chaos, there existed a deeper truth, a thread connecting us to the past and the future.

As night enveloped us, I watched Maya paint, her movements fluid, the colors vibrant and alive. She poured her heart onto the canvas, each stroke a testament to the struggle, the beauty, and the despair echoing through our lives. I marveled at how she transformed her pain into something tangible, something that could provoke thought, ignite conversations, and perhaps even inspire change.

"Your work will speak," I murmured, more to myself than to her. "It will remind people of what's at stake."

"I hope so," she replied, glancing at me with a flicker of vulnerability. "But the world's loud, Finn. Sometimes it feels like we're just echoes in an echo chamber."

"Then let's make our voices louder," I said, the words spilling from my heart. "Together."

In that instant, as the stars shimmered above, I understood the power of connection—not just between people, but between art and life. The struggles we faced were not ours alone; they were shared threads woven into the tapestry of existence. As Maya painted her truth, I felt a resolve solidify within me—a determination to embrace the chaos, to fight for authenticity amidst the noise, to create meaning in a world that often felt devoid of it.

ALEX TELMAN

And as the waves crashed relentlessly against the shore, I knew that even in the face of transformation, the heart of Byron Bay beat on, vibrant and alive, waiting for those willing to listen, to connect, and to create.

Lost in Translation

The sun hung low over Byron Bay, a bruised orange glow spilling across the sky like spilled paint on an artist's palette. I stood at the water's edge, the sand cool beneath my feet, watching the waves curl and crash—each one a whisper of the stories I could never fully tell. I took a deep breath, filling my lungs with the salty air that tasted of freedom and regret, and turned to face the beach.

Around me, tourists mingled—brightly colored shorts and loud laughter punctuating the air like jarring notes in a melancholic symphony. They were creatures of sunlight, eager to capture the essence of the place through snapshots and idle chatter, oblivious to the undercurrents running deeper than the tides.

"Hey! You're a local, right?" a voice called out. I turned to find a couple, arms draped around each other, their skin sun-kissed and gleaming. The man was lanky with a baseball cap turned backward, and the woman sported oversized sunglasses that shielded her from more than just the sun.

"Yeah," I replied, a hint of wariness creeping into my tone. "What's up?"

"Can you tell us the best spot to catch the sunset?" The woman's voice dripped with enthusiasm, a sugary sweetness that felt foreign in my throat. "We heard it's amazing here!"

"Sure," I said, nodding toward the headland. "Go to the lighthouse. It's popular for a reason."

"Great! What else should we see?" The man leaned closer, curiosity barely masking a desire to possess the local knowledge I held.

I hesitated. "It depends on what you're after. This place isn't just beaches and sunsets." I paused, a bitter laugh escaping me. "It's... more complicated than that."

"Complicated?" The woman furrowed her brow, clearly not grasping the nuance. "But it's so beautiful! How can it be complicated?"

I felt the familiar weight of frustration settle in my chest, the desire to shake them and make them see. "Beauty can hide the cracks, you know? This town—once a tight-knit community—is caught in the crosshairs of gentrification and tourism. It's becoming something it never was."

They exchanged glances, unsure how to respond. The man shrugged, his smile faltering. "But it's paradise, right? How can you complain?"

My jaw clenched. "Paradise comes with a price. The locals are getting pushed out, and the character of the place is fading. It's like a postcard that doesn't quite capture the heart of it." I gestured toward the bustling café across the street, where the barista, tattooed and weary, served lattes to tourists with hollow smiles. "Look around. People are just here for a weekend escape, not for the stories, the struggles."

"Wow, I didn't realize." The woman's excitement dimmed, and I could almost see her perspective shifting like the tide. "That's really sad."

"Yeah, it is," I said, feeling a pang of sadness wash over me. "It's like watching a friend drown while everyone else cheers them on, thinking they're just enjoying a swim."

I turned away, watching the horizon where the sky kissed the sea, the boundary between reality and dream blurring in the fading light. I longed for the moments when I could step back from it all, when the weight of the world could lift, even if just for a moment.

"What's your name?" the man asked, breaking into my reverie.

"Finn."

"Nice to meet you, Finn. I'm James, and this is my girlfriend, Sarah." He extended a hand, and I shook it, feeling the warmth of their optimism and naivety.

"Listen, if you're around tomorrow, we're doing a beach bonfire. You should come. Meet some people!" Sarah chirped, her voice a sweet melody against the harshness of reality.

I forced a smile, the prospect of socializing gnawing at me. "Maybe. I'll think about it."

"Come on, it'll be fun!" she pressed, her enthusiasm almost infectious. "You've got to show us the real Byron Bay!"

DOWN AND OUT IN BYRON BAY

But I felt an ache in my chest, a dissonance that wouldn't be soothed by beach bonfires or laughter. "The real Byron Bay isn't just fun and games. It's also the quiet desperation of those who can't afford to live here anymore."

They blinked at me, the reality of my words hanging in the air like an uninvited guest. "What do you mean?" James asked, his brow furrowed.

"It means there's more to this place than meets the eye. The tourists come and go, but the locals are left to pick up the pieces, to watch their home transform into a playground for the rich. It's a silent scream beneath the surface."

As I spoke, I could see understanding flicker in their eyes, a crack in their bubble of ignorance. For a moment, I felt a swell of hope. Maybe the tourists could learn, could see beyond the sunsets and surfboards.

"What can we do?" Sarah asked, her voice softer now, stripped of earlier bravado.

I shrugged, the heaviness of the conversation weighing me down. "Just be aware. Share the stories. Ask questions. Don't just consume the place; engage with it."

"Like, how?" James leaned in, curiosity piqued.

"Talk to people. Listen to their stories. The old fisherman at the end of the pier, the barista, even the artists. They're all part of this place, and they'll tell you things you won't find in any guidebook."

"Wow, I never thought of it that way," Sarah said, her gaze drifting toward the surf, where a group of locals laughed and splashed in the water. "Maybe we're the ones who need to learn."

"Exactly," I said, feeling a rush of connection. "It's not about just taking pictures and leaving. It's about understanding what you're part of."

As the sun dipped lower, casting shadows that elongated and danced, the three of us stood together, gazing out at the ocean. In that moment, I felt a flicker of something bright within—a sense of purpose, a fragile hope. Maybe, just maybe, we could bridge the gap between the locals and the tourists, between the stories and the snapshots.

"Thanks, Finn," Sarah said softly, her voice warm with gratitude. "We'll try to see more than just the surface."

"Good," I replied, a tentative smile breaking across my face. "That's all I can ask."

As they parted, I felt the weight of the conversation linger, a quiet echo that accompanied me as I walked along the shore. The waves whispered their secrets, and in the distance, the lighthouse stood tall, a sentinel against the changing tides.

I understood that Byron Bay was not just a place on a map; it was a living, breathing entity, pulsing with life and energy, shaped by the people who called it home. It wasn't the glitzy cafes, the sprawling boutique shops, or the crowded beaches lined with sun-kissed tourists; it was the quiet moments tucked into the corners of the town, the spaces between the waves, the spaces between people. It was in the slow rhythm of the day, the quiet exchanges in the farmers' markets, the surfboards leaning against fences, the faded graffiti on hidden walls.

Byron Bay had always been a place of reinvention, a town that attracted dreamers, wanderers, and seekers. The air itself seemed to hum with possibility, with the energy of people trying to escape the constraints of their pasts, chasing the idea of freedom in the sound of the ocean and the expanse of the sky. But somewhere in the tension between the tourists seeking their own slice of paradise and the locals trying to hold on to what made this place special, a certain kind of raw authenticity had been lost—or at least, it felt like it had.

In the space between the tourists and the locals, in the heart of the shifting sands, lay the essence of what it truly meant to belong. It wasn't about being born here or having a deep ancestral tie to the land. It wasn't about how long you'd lived in the town or whether your surfboard had the right brand logo on it. It was something more subtle, something more intrinsic. It was about understanding the rhythm of the place, about becoming a part of the landscape in a way that felt both humble and powerful.

It was in the shared smile of someone who had just finished a long surf, their body salt-worn and tired, yet their eyes alight with the joy of being fully immersed in the present moment. It was in the knowing nod of the barista, who, despite her busy morning, still found the time to listen when you asked how her day was. It was in the stories passed between strangers, in the warmth of the sun on the back of your neck, in the wild wind that rattled the palm trees and whispered secrets only the truly attuned could hear.

DOWN AND OUT IN BYRON BAY

And perhaps, I thought, that's what I had been searching for all along—not just a place to exist, but a place to be. Not a place that conformed to what I thought it should be, but a place that allowed me to be myself, even in the chaos, even in the uncertainty. I realized that belonging wasn't about fitting in—it was about being seen. It was about existing alongside others who were doing the same, even if their paths were different. We all had our own stories, our own wounds, our own light. And that was the beauty of it.

As I stood there, watching the tide roll in and out, I felt a quiet sense of peace wash over me. Byron wasn't perfect. It wasn't the same as it had been, and it never would be. But that was the truth of life—it was always changing, always shifting. There would always be new faces, new struggles, and new triumphs. But at its core, there would always be that spirit, that pulse, that sense of belonging—if I was willing to open myself up to it.

I wasn't sure what the future held for me here, but for the first time in a long time, I felt like I was ready to find out.

Dancing with Shadows

The night settled over Byron Bay like a thick quilt, heavy with the scent of salt and the promise of rain. I stood outside the community hall, where laughter and music spilled into the streets, beckoning the restless souls within. A rickety sign painted in fading colors announced the "Monthly Dance"—words that whispered of connection amidst the chaos of life. I adjusted my collar, feeling the fabric scratch against my skin, a reminder of the confines that held me tight.

Inside, the atmosphere pulsed with energy, the kind that thumped in time with the heartbeats of the crowd. Strings of fairy lights hung like stars caught in the web of night, illuminating faces flushed with joy and laughter. I felt the pull of the music, a siren's call promising liberation. The sounds swirled around me—laughter mingled with rhythm, a cacophony that felt both alien and familiar.

I lingered at the periphery, a ghost among the living. The dancers moved with abandon, bodies swaying like reeds in the wind, casting shadows that danced along the walls. Each twirl, each spin, was a rebellion against the mundane, an escape from the weight of their lives. But for me, the shadows felt more like a shroud—reminders of the disappointments, the regrets, the memories that haunted me like old lovers.

Leaning against the wall, arms crossed, I observed as if through a pane of glass. My heart ached with longing, not just to join them but to understand the freedom that ignited their spirits. The lights pulsed, each beat resonating in my chest, a rhythm I longed to embody. I thought of the past—how art had once been my refuge, how each brushstroke on canvas had allowed me to lose myself in the chaos of creation. But those days felt like a distant echo, drowned beneath layers of silence.

DOWN AND OUT IN BYRON BAY

A movement caught my eye—a woman with wild hair cascading down her back, her dress swirling like the ocean, all bright blues and greens. She spun with a ferocity that drew the gaze of everyone around her. I felt an unfamiliar tug in my chest, a yearning to break free of my self-imposed cage. The music shifted, taking on a haunting quality, and for a moment, the world around me blurred into a haze of color and sound.

"Hey, why are you just standing there?" A voice broke through, sharp and vibrant. I turned to see a young man, all energy and smiles, a living embodiment of the rhythm that pulsed through the hall. "You look like you need to dance."

"I can't," I replied, the words slipping from my lips like a confession. "I don't know how."

"Neither do I," the young man said with a laugh, stepping closer, his eyes bright. "But that's not the point. It's about losing yourself, letting go. Come on!"

I hesitated, but the music surged, a swell of sound that seemed to demand my presence. I could feel the weight of the crowd behind me, a collective energy urging me to step forward. It was a simple invitation, yet it resonated deep within me, a call to shake off the shadows that clung to my soul.

With a deep breath, I stepped into the open space, feeling the eyes of strangers upon me. My heart raced, but the rhythm enveloped me, pulling me into the dance. At first, I stumbled, awkward and unsure, but then I let the music guide me, allowing my body to sway with the melody. Each movement began to dissolve the remnants of my hesitations, the shadows that whispered doubt began to fade.

I found myself alongside the woman with the wild hair. She moved with grace and abandon, her laughter a balm that soothed my frayed edges. Heat rose in my cheeks as we danced in tandem, our movements synchronizing into a wild, chaotic harmony. For the first time in a long while, I felt seen, like a brushstroke finally finding its place on the canvas of existence.

"See?" she shouted over the music, her eyes sparkling. "It's not about how you dance; it's about how it makes you feel!"

Her words sunk deep, resonating with an undeniable truth. I closed my eyes, letting the music wash over me, feeling it seep into my bones. I danced not just with her, but with the shadows of my past—each step a defiance, each twirl a release. The ghosts of regret, of missed opportunities, started to dissipate, replaced by a burgeoning sense of liberation. In that moment, I was not just Finn Sullivan; I was a part of something greater, a collective heartbeat that pulsed through the room.

The night unfolded like a story, each song a chapter filled with laughter and life. I danced until sweat clung to my skin and exhaustion threatened to pull me under. I watched as couples spun and swayed, their joy radiating like sunlight cutting through clouds. The hall became a refuge, a sanctuary where art manifested in movement, a testament to the resilience of the human spirit.

As the music slowed and the tempo softened, I found myself standing still, breathless. The woman with the wild hair joined me, both of us panting, smiles plastered across our faces. "What's your name?" she asked, her voice tinged with warmth.

"Finn," I replied, my heart still racing. "And you?"

"Lila." She extended her hand, and I took it, feeling the spark of connection ignite between us.

"You danced like you were born to it," she said, her eyes locking onto mine with a fierceness that made me feel seen in a way I hadn't in years. "It's about letting go, right?"

"Yeah," I said, a grin breaking across my face. "Maybe I've been holding on too tight."

The night began to wind down, but the air remained thick with possibility. Lila and I slipped outside, the cool night air brushing against our flushed skin. The world was alive with sound—waves crashing against the shore, laughter echoing through the streets. We stood beneath the vast expanse of stars, a canvas painted with dreams, and I felt a stirring deep within.

"Do you want to go for a walk?" I asked, the words tumbling out before I could second-guess myself.

"Absolutely," she replied, her smile a beacon in the dark. As we walked side by side, I felt the shadows that had loomed so heavily begin to shift, revealing a path forward illuminated by newfound connection and understanding.

DOWN AND OUT IN BYRON BAY

We walked in comfortable silence for a few moments, the night stretching around us like a vast, open invitation. The moonlight cast long shadows on the path as we meandered along the beach, our feet sinking slightly into the sand with each step.

"I'm surprised I haven't seen you around before," I said, breaking the quiet. "Are you new here?"

Lila shrugged, her wild hair swaying in the cool breeze. "Not exactly," she said, her voice playful. "I guess I've been coming and going for a while. Byron has a way of pulling you in, doesn't it?"

I nodded, understanding exactly what she meant. The pull of this place had always been magnetic, like a promise of freedom in its most raw form. But it was also a place that could swallow you whole, if you weren't careful.

"Yeah, it's... complicated," I said, unsure how to explain. "Feels like there's a version of me here that I can't quite grasp."

She glanced at me with a knowing smile, as if she understood more than I'd said. "I get that. It's like the place changes, but it also makes you face parts of yourself you'd rather leave behind."

I didn't respond right away. There was truth in her words, and something in the way she said them—like she knew the struggle of not quite fitting into the world around you—struck a chord deep within me. I looked at the horizon, where the sea met the sky in an infinite expanse, a metaphor for the way my own thoughts seemed to stretch endlessly, never quite touching the shore.

"You ever feel like you're running from something?" I asked before I could stop myself. It was the first time I'd voiced it, and it felt like the kind of question that could either open the floodgates or close them for good.

Lila was quiet for a moment, her eyes on the path ahead, and I wondered if I'd gone too far. But then, she answered, her voice softer than before.

"Yeah. I think we all do," she said, her words weighted with something I couldn't quite place. "But running doesn't really get you anywhere, does it? At some point, you have to face it. Whatever it is."

I glanced at her, surprised by the depth of her response. "That's easier said than done," I muttered, the cynical edge creeping into my tone without invitation.

She laughed, the sound light and free. "Yeah, I know. But maybe it's not about making the demons disappear. Maybe it's about learning how to live with them, to make peace with them." She paused, glancing at me. "I'm a musician. And in a way I think that's what music is for me. You don't try to 'outrun' it. You use it, you make it part of your story."

Her words hung in the air like a quiet revelation. Use it, she said. Make it part of the story.

It made sense, and yet it felt radical. The idea that pain, doubt, and fear could be woven into the fabric of who I was, rather than pushed into corners to be ignored or avoided. Maybe that was what I had been missing all this time—the acceptance of all the pieces of myself, not just the shiny, acceptable parts.

We reached the end of the path, where the beach curved and the sound of the waves grew louder. The world felt both vast and intimate in that moment, the ocean's whispers pulling me in.

"You really think it's that simple?" I asked, my voice quieter now, uncertain.

Lila stopped, turning to face me, her eyes searching mine. "No," she said with a smile that was more knowing than anything else. "I don't think it's simple. But I think it's worth trying." She paused again, and then, with a softness that caught me off guard, added, "We don't have to do it alone, either. Sometimes we forget that."

I felt a lump form in my throat. For a moment, I had forgotten how much I craved connection, how much I needed it. It was like I had been walking through the world with my hands tied, unable to reach out for what I truly wanted, too afraid of what it might cost me.

"But who do you lean on?" I asked, the question slipping out before I could stop it. "Who do you turn to when it gets too much?"

Lila considered this for a moment, the light breeze playing with her hair as she looked out at the water. "My music. And I guess I've learned to turn inward a lot," she said quietly, "but there are always people who will show up when you need them. You just have to trust that they will." Her gaze met mine again. "And you have to be open enough to let them in."

Her words landed with a thud, deep in my chest. I realized then that I'd been building walls around myself for so long that I had forgotten how to let people in. The isolation wasn't because no one cared—it was because I hadn't allowed anyone to care.

"Maybe I've been too scared to open up," I confessed, the vulnerability in my voice raw, unfiltered. "I've been afraid of getting too close to anyone, even though I crave it."

Lila stepped closer, her presence grounding and steady. "It's scary," she said softly. "But there's something beautiful on the other side of that fear. We all have our walls, Finn. But sometimes it's the cracks that let the light in."

I looked at her, feeling the weight of the truth in her words settle inside me. For the first time in a long time, I felt the tightness in my chest loosen just a little. It wasn't much, but it was something. Something I could hold onto.

"Maybe we all need a little light," I said, my voice thick with the raw honesty of the moment.

Lila smiled, that spark of understanding in her eyes again. "We do. And sometimes, we find it in the most unexpected places."

As we stood there, the world around us felt both overwhelming and comforting in its vastness. The ocean, the stars, the night itself—it all seemed to whisper that there was always room for more. Room for connection, for change, for growth. And maybe, just maybe, it was time for me to let go of the things I'd been holding onto so tightly and let the light in.

With Lila by my side, I felt like I was taking the first steps toward something I didn't fully understand yet, but something that felt right. Something that wasn't about perfection or control, but about the messy, beautiful dance of living.

Reflections in the Water

I stood at the edge of the beach, the sun casting long, lazy fingers over the sand as if reluctant to let go of the day. The waves lapped at my feet, the cold water a sharp reminder that I was still alive, still breathing. Each crash of the surf felt like a heartbeat—rhythmic and insistent—echoing the turmoil within me. The beach was alive, vibrant with tourists and locals alike, their laughter rising and falling like the tide, but I felt like an outsider peering into a world that danced beyond my reach.

I kicked off my worn sandals, the gritty sand squishing between my toes, grounding me in this moment. The air was thick with the scent of salt and sun, mingled with the faint trace of coconut oil, a reminder of summers spent as a carefree child, days that felt endless and warm. Yet now, as I watched the waves curl and break, I felt the weight of years pressing down like the oppressive heat of midday sun. Each wave crashed against the shore, a reminder of all the changes I'd faced, the relentless ebb and flow of time pulling me further from who I once was.

Taking a deep breath, I filled my lungs with the salty air and stepped closer to the water. It kissed my ankles, sending chills up my spine, and for a moment, I closed my eyes, letting the sensation wash over me. It was here, in this liminal space between land and sea, that I felt the most myself—and yet, also the most lost.

I thought of the young man I used to be, all dreams and wide-eyed wonder, as buoyant as the surf that now ebbed and flowed before me. Back then, the world had seemed ripe with possibilities, each moment a blank canvas waiting to be filled. But time had a way of creeping in, tainting that canvas with shades of gray and the harsh lines of regret. The memories washed over me like the tide, and I felt myself sinking beneath the weight of them.

DOWN AND OUT IN BYRON BAY

"Hey, Finn!" A voice broke through my reverie, pulling me back to the present. It was Lila, her laughter ringing like wind chimes, carefree and bright. She approached with arms open wide, her golden hair catching the light. "What are you doing all alone out here? You're missing the party!"

I blinked, momentarily disoriented, as the sound of her voice cut through the fog of my thoughts. Lila. It had been weeks since that night—since the dance—and yet here she was, as if she had stepped right out of one of those fleeting memories. I hadn't seen her since that night under the stars, when we'd walked along the beach, sharing secrets and dreams, the world feeling bigger and smaller at the same time.

For weeks, I'd replayed that evening in my head, the way we'd danced, the way she'd looked at me with those wide, understanding eyes. I'd wondered if it had meant something to her too, or if it was just one of those moments, easily forgotten once the night was over. I'd kept it close to me, though, like a secret I wasn't ready to let go of—her laughter, her smile, the way she made everything feel lighter, more possible.

But there she was, standing in front of me now, pulling me from the heavy weight of my thoughts like a lifeline.

"I didn't realize I was missing anything," I said, a small laugh escaping my lips. "Just needed some time to think."

Lila cocked her head, a playful grin tugging at the corners of her mouth. "Thinking? At the beach? You should be out there, soaking in the chaos. Besides, you looked like you needed a distraction."

I smiled, unsure how much to reveal. "I suppose I could use a distraction. Haven't seen you in a while."

She took a few steps closer, dropping down beside me, brushing sand off her legs as she settled next to me. Her presence felt like a jolt of energy. "I know. I've been... around," she said, her voice trailing off as if unsure of how to explain herself. "But I thought about that night too. The dance, the walk... I've been wondering if you ever really let go of it. Or if it was just a one-time thing for you."

I didn't know what to say at first. The words I'd been holding onto for so long felt tangled in my chest, unspoken and unacknowledged.

"I didn't think I'd see you again, to be honest," I said quietly. "It's funny how life takes you in all these different directions, and sometimes you just... let things slip away."

Lila nodded, her eyes softening as she watched me. "I get it. It's easy to let things slip by when you're afraid to reach out for them. Or when you're not sure if they're worth reaching for. But sometimes, you just have to take the chance, right?"

Her words landed heavy in the space between us, and I felt something in me stir, like an ember waiting to catch fire. Maybe it was the years of doubt and self-imposed isolation that had kept me from reaching out to anyone, but there was something about her—about how she seemed to always be looking for the light in things, even when they seemed lost in the shadows—that made me feel like it was okay to hope again.

"I've been trying to figure things out," I admitted. "For a long time, it felt like everything I touched was slipping through my fingers. Like no matter what I did, I couldn't get a grip on anything. But..."

I trailed off, unsure how to finish the thought.

"But?" she prodded gently, her eyes never leaving mine. "What's holding you back?"

I hesitated. What was holding me back? Was it fear? Was it that deep-rooted feeling of not being worthy of connection, of not knowing how to let someone in again? Or was it something else?

"The fear that maybe it's too late," I said finally, the words surprising even me. "Too late to reconnect with myself, with the person I used to be. Too late to reach for what I want and actually hold onto it. I don't even know what that would look like anymore."

Lila looked at me intently, her gaze steady. "It's never too late, Finn. You've got this whole ocean in front of you, and all you've got to do is learn to ride the waves again. Don't worry about whether you've missed your chance. Start now. No one says you've got to have it all figured out."

Her voice was calm, but there was an undeniable strength in it. She was right. It wasn't too late. Maybe I had been so focused on the mistakes and missed opportunities that I'd forgotten there was always room for more, always a chance to start over.

"I think that's the hardest part for me," I said, the words coming slowly, like a confession. "Not knowing how to start. Not knowing if I'm going to fail again."

"You will fail. And it's okay," Lila said, shrugging casually. "Failure isn't a bad thing. It's just part of the process. But the real failure is in never trying at all."

I looked at her, really looked at her, for the first time in a long while, and realized how much I'd been avoiding that very truth. Maybe the reason I hadn't moved forward wasn't because I couldn't, but because I hadn't allowed myself to. Fear of failure, fear of being disappointed, had kept me stagnant.

"You're right," I said, a flicker of something new stirring inside me. "Maybe I've been afraid to try because I didn't want to face what I might lose. But what if what I gain is more important?"

Lila smiled softly, the glow from the moonlight making her look almost ethereal. "Exactly. Sometimes, it's the things we're afraid of that turn out to be the ones that shape us most."

I sat back against the sand, feeling the cool breeze sweep across my skin. For the first time in a long while, I didn't feel so alone in my thoughts. The weight of doubt wasn't completely gone, but it had lessened, pushed aside by the warmth of connection, of someone who understood that fear and failure were only part of the story.

"Maybe it's not too late," I said again, this time with more conviction. "Maybe I'm just getting started."

Lila nudged me playfully. "I think you're more than ready, Finn. Let's see where that takes you."

And for the first time in a long time, I believed her.

"Come join our party?"

I chuckled, but my heart wasn't in it. The laughter of the group behind her bubbled up like champagne, light and effervescent, while I felt like a stone sinking to the ocean floor. "I don't know, Lila. I'm not really in the mood for a party."

"Come on! You can't just stand here like a sad sack," she pressed, stepping closer, her energy almost palpable. "You need to break free from all that thinking. Just dive into the chaos!"

"Maybe that's the problem," I said, my voice barely a whisper against the sound of the crashing waves. "I've been diving into chaos for too long."

Her expression softened, and for a moment, I saw the concern etched in the lines of her face. "What's really going on, Finn? You know you can talk to me."

I looked out at the horizon, the endless expanse of water merging with the sky, a perfect blend of blue that felt like a cruel joke against my gray thoughts. "It's just... I'm changing, you know? Everything feels different now. I feel different."

"Different how?" she asked, her tone gentle, like the waves that rolled softly against the shore.

"I don't recognize myself anymore," I admitted, my voice trembling as I fought against the tide of vulnerability rising within me. "I used to feel like I belonged here, like Byron was home. Now, I feel like a ghost haunting familiar places."

She reached for my hand, grounding me in the moment. "You're still you, Finn. Just because things change doesn't mean you have to lose yourself. You've got to embrace the new."

I nodded, the truth of her words echoing in the depths of my mind. Yet, the struggle to accept change felt like wrestling with the ocean itself—relentless and vast. "I guess I just miss the simplicity of it all," I confessed. "Back when life didn't feel so complicated. When I could run into the ocean without thinking twice."

"Life is complicated," Lila said, squeezing my hand. "But that doesn't mean you have to face it alone. Come back with me. Join us. Dance in the chaos."

I watched the waves crashing against the shore, the foam curling and receding like the thoughts swirling in my mind. The ocean was both soothing and chaotic, a reflection of the duality within me. I longed to dive into it, to lose myself in the depths and find something raw and real, something untouched by the weight of expectation.

"Okay," I finally said, a flicker of determination igniting within me. "Let's do it. Let's dance in the chaos."

As we walked back toward the group, I felt the cool water brush against my calves, each step a reaffirmation of my decision to engage with life, to embrace the unknown. The laughter and music grew louder, wrapping around me like a warm blanket, a reminder of the joy that still existed in the world.

The sun dipped lower in the sky, casting golden rays that danced over the surface of the water. As we joined the others, I allowed myself to surrender to the moment. Laughter spilled from my lips, mingling with the sound of crashing waves and the thumping bass of the music. I felt alive again, a flicker of the old me igniting within.

And in that moment, standing on the edge of the world, surrounded by people and the beauty of the ocean, I realized that change was inevitable, but it didn't have to be feared. Instead, it could be embraced—a reflection in the water that revealed both the chaos and the beauty of life.

As the sun finally slipped beneath the horizon, I took a deep breath, feeling the cool air brush against my skin. There was a moment of quiet before the weight of it all settled in—the uncertainty that had been growing inside me like a slow tide. For all the strength I thought I had, for all the resolve I had convinced myself I possessed, a gnawing doubt remained.

Was I really ready to face whatever lay ahead? Was I strong enough to leave behind everything I had known, everything that had shaped me? The idea of change, of stepping out of the only life I had ever known, filled me with a deep unease, like standing on the edge of something I couldn't yet see but knew would demand everything from me.

I wanted to believe that within me was the strength to dance through the storms, but the truth was, I wasn't sure I had learned how to navigate them. And the calm—could I find joy in it, or would I simply feel lost, adrift in a new rhythm I wasn't sure how to follow?

The waves lapped at the shore, a steady reminder that change was inevitable, but I couldn't shake the feeling that the calm I craved might never come, or that when it did, it wouldn't be enough to ease the weight of what I was about to lose.

The Feast of Excess

I stepped through the heavy oak door of a sprawling mansion, the scent of truffle oil and roasted garlic wafting through the air like a siren's call. The space was opulent, a stark contrast to the modest surroundings I'd grown up in—a small, weather-beaten cottage where meals were often a patchwork of leftover rice and wilted vegetables. Here, chandeliers dripped with crystals that refracted the soft candlelight, creating a kaleidoscope of warmth that danced over a long table set for a feast.

Standing at the threshold, I felt the weight of the world outside the golden glow. A gentle breeze stirred, carrying the sound of laughter and clinking glasses from within. The invitation had felt like a cruel joke, a slip of paper that read, "Join us for an evening of indulgence," as if I, with my rumpled clothes and unkempt hair, could ever belong among these polished silhouettes.

"Finn! You made it!" A voice broke through the haze of my thoughts. It was Claire, the host, her smile wide and welcoming, the kind that could light up a room—or blind someone with its brightness. She swept me into a hug that felt both warm and suffocating. "Come, let me show you around!"

Claire was an old friend, someone who had once been a steady presence in my life. We'd shared a kind of quiet intimacy in the years before I retreated into myself, a bond that had once felt so natural, so unbreakable. I'd always had feelings for her, though I never really knew what to do with them. There were moments when I thought she felt the same way, but time and circumstances never aligned for us to act on it. Now, seeing her again, those old feelings resurfaced with the same intensity, though tempered by the distance that time had created.

I followed her deeper into the mansion, past the gleaming kitchen where a team of chefs bustled about like busy bees, their white jackets pristine against the chaotic beauty of the culinary symphony they were orchestrating. Each clang of metal on metal echoed in my mind, a reminder of the clamor of my own life—simple, raw, and often overwhelming.

"This place is incredible," I managed to say, though the words felt inadequate. My voice was small compared to the opulence surrounding me.

Claire laughed, a bright sound that cut through my hesitations. "It's just a house, Finn. It's what we do in it that matters." She led me to the dining room, where the table was adorned with fine china, golden cutlery, and a massive bouquet of exotic flowers, vibrant and almost garish in their extravagance.

"Take a seat!" Claire gestured to the table, and I hesitated, feeling like a stray dog invited into a palace. But before I could protest, I was pushed into a chair between a woman in an expensive silk dress and a man in a tailored suit, their laughter rippling like champagne bubbles, light and ephemeral.

The meal began, and I found myself surrounded by stories—tales of travels to distant lands, high-stakes business deals, and the latest art exhibits. Each story was gilded with a sheen of excess, as if the very act of living had become a competition for the most flamboyant experiences. I listened, nodding along, but inside I felt like a ghost haunting their revelry.

When the food arrived—plates of roasted duck with figs, buttery lobster tails, and an array of desserts that looked like they'd been crafted by angels—my stomach growled. As I took a bite, the flavors exploded in my mouth, rich and overwhelming. It was delicious, but there was a hollowness to it, as if the extravagance masked something deeper, something I couldn't quite grasp.

"What do you do, Finn?" a voice interrupted my reverie. It was the man to my left, his eyes sharp and appraising, as if I were just another piece of art on display.

"Uh, I write," I said, surprised by the admission. "Mostly poetry and some articles."

"Poetry?" The man raised an eyebrow, skepticism flickering across his face. "How quaint."

I felt a flush rise to my cheeks. "I mean, it's not much compared to what you all do, but—"

"Not much?" the man scoffed. "What's that even mean? Do you live in a cardboard box? You can't pay the bills with sonnets and haikus, can you?"

I wanted to retort, to defend the sanctity of my art, but the words caught in my throat. I felt small, as if I'd been plucked from my world and dropped into this one of shimmering excess, where every conversation was a measurement of wealth and status.

As the night wore on, the laughter became louder, the toasts more extravagant. My heart sank further, an anchor pulling me down to depths I didn't want to explore. I recalled the simplicity of my childhood—meals shared with my mother, the taste of fresh bread and the smell of herbs from our small garden, the warmth of conversation that had nothing to do with power or prestige.

"Hey, don't let him get to you," Claire leaned in, her voice a soothing balm against my rising anxiety. "He's just a blowhard."

"Yeah," I replied, forcing a smile. But even her words couldn't shake the feeling that I was lost in a world that celebrated everything I didn't understand.

When the dessert arrived—a towering chocolate mousse that looked as if it could topple over at any moment—I felt a surge of rebellion. With each bite, I savored the decadence but thought of the simplicity of a slice of fruit pie shared on a sun-drenched porch.

"Finn!" Claire's voice cut through my thoughts again. "What's your favorite thing about Byron? You know, besides the beaches and surf?"

I hesitated, the question hanging in the air like a dare. "The sunsets," I said finally, the truth spilling out unbidden. "They remind me that beauty can exist in simplicity. They don't need to be adorned with gold."

The table fell silent, the laughter replaced by an uneasy stillness. I felt their eyes on me, a mixture of confusion and curiosity. "That's... poetic," Claire finally said, though her smile was tight, as if she didn't quite know what to make of my words.

"Maybe it is," I replied, surprising myself with the conviction in my voice. "But sometimes, the most profound moments happen when we strip everything away."

A silence settled, and for the first time, I felt a crack in the facade of their gathering. I could see the flicker of recognition in some eyes—an understanding that perhaps they, too, felt the weight of expectation, the longing for something genuine amidst the clamor of their lives.

As the evening wound down and guests drifted away into the night, I lingered, allowing the stillness to envelop me. I stepped outside onto the balcony, the cool air brushing against my skin. The stars above shimmered like scattered diamonds, vast and unyielding against the backdrop of the darkened sky.

I exhaled, a breath I hadn't realized I was holding, feeling the weight of the evening's contradictions settle into clarity. This world of excess was dazzling, yes, but it was also a mask, a shield that protected the fragility beneath.

Glancing back at the house, where laughter echoed faintly, I felt a sense of peace. The feast had been overwhelming, but it had also revealed something precious: the importance of authenticity amidst the noise, the beauty of a life lived in truth rather than in excess.

As I turned to leave, I realized that while I may never fit neatly into the boxes of wealth and status, I didn't need to. My identity was shaped not by the opulence around me, but by the simple moments that filled my life with meaning—moments like sunsets, laughter shared among friends, and the quiet reflection of a poet searching for truth in a world of chaos.

Moments of Clarity

I sat at a table in a dimly lit café in Byron Bay, the familiar hum of conversation and the clinking of cups forming a chaotic symphony around me. The air was thick with the aroma of coffee—a bittersweet blend that mirrored my own life, half-formed and overflowing with potential yet tinged with a sense of loss. Sunlight streamed through the window, casting a warm glow that softened the sharp edges of the world outside, but inside me, turmoil raged on like a tempest.

I took a sip of my cold latte, the chill biting at my lips. It was an ordinary afternoon, yet clarity felt particularly elusive today, as if it were hiding just beyond my reach, teasing me like a memory just out of grasp.

Across the room, a couple laughed—a genuine, unfiltered joy that reverberated through the space, forcing me to confront the emptiness swirling within. I turned my gaze to the window, watching as tourists strolled by, their sun-kissed skin and carefree laughter igniting a pang of jealousy deep in my chest. They were here to escape, to indulge in the wild beauty of the coast, while I felt shackled by my own routines, entangled in a web of regrets and unfulfilled dreams.

"Lost in thought again?" Lila's voice broke through my reverie. She slid into the seat across from me, her presence a burst of sunlight. She wore a flowy sundress that danced with the breeze, the colors vibrant against the muted backdrop of the café.

"Just thinking about how I seem to be stuck in this endless loop," I replied, attempting to smile but feeling it falter. "Same cafés, same coffee, same worries."

"Maybe it's time to break the cycle, then," she said, her tone light, but her eyes held a depth that matched my own despair. "What do you really want, Finn?"

DOWN AND OUT IN BYRON BAY

I hesitated, the question swirling in the air like smoke. What did I want? I opened my mouth, ready to respond, but the truth felt too raw, too tangled in my heart. Instead, I let the silence stretch between us, a chasm filled with unspoken words.

"Life is too short for half-truths," Lila finally said, breaking the tension. "You know that. You've always known."

I looked down at the table, the grain of the wood seeming to twist and turn like my thoughts. "I want to feel something again. I want to be alive, not just existing."

She leaned in closer, her voice dropping to a conspiratorial whisper. "Then stop waiting for clarity to come to you. Go out and find it. Make it happen."

The conviction in her words echoed inside me, rattling loose fragments of my own buried desires. I felt a flicker of hope ignite, a fragile flame amidst the shadows. But before I could respond, the café door swung open, and a gust of wind swept in, carrying with it the sounds of the outside world.

My gaze snapped to the door as a young girl rushed in, her hair wild like a storm, cheeks flushed from the heat of the sun. She clutched a handful of seashells, her eyes sparkling with a joy that seemed untainted by the weight of the world. She paused, her gaze sweeping over the room before she spotted a woman sitting alone in the corner—her mother, perhaps—looking weary and distant. The girl rushed over, her exuberance crashing against the heavy atmosphere like a wave against the shore.

"Look what I found!" she shouted, plopping down beside her mother, shells spilling across the table like treasures unearthed from a pirate's chest. I watched, captivated by the moment—a vivid reminder of the beauty in simple joys.

"Those are beautiful, honey," the mother replied, distracted, her voice tinged with exhaustion. The girl's enthusiasm dimmed slightly, but she continued to hold up each shell as if it were a rare gem, her excitement undeterred.

"Can't you see how special they are?" she urged, her voice rising with passion. "We can make something amazing with them!"

I felt a sharp ache in my chest. This child, so vibrant, so full of life—she saw beauty where others might overlook it. In her innocent excitement, I recognized a part of myself that had been dormant for too long, a part that had once found wonder in the world.

"Hey, Finn!" Lila's voice pulled me back from the brink of nostalgia. "Are you with me?"

"Yeah, sorry," I said, shaking my head as if to clear the fog. "I was just thinking..."

"About what?" Lila pressed, her expression a mixture of curiosity and concern.

"That little girl," I said, nodding toward the corner. "She's got something special—this ability to find beauty in everything. It's... inspiring."

Lila followed my gaze and smiled softly. "Children have a way of reminding us of what's important. They haven't yet learned to hide their joy behind layers of cynicism."

"I wish I could see the world through her eyes," I mused, the desire swelling in my chest like a tide rising to meet the shore. "To feel that kind of freedom."

"Then go find it," Lila urged again. "Life is messy, but it can also be beautiful. You just have to allow yourself to feel it."

I nodded slowly, as if awakening from a long slumber. I had spent too long wrapped in the cocoon of my own despair, waiting for clarity to drop into my lap like an unwanted package. It was time to break free, to let the wildness of life seep in.

"Let's go to the beach," I said suddenly, the words bursting forth like a long-dormant wave crashing to shore. "Let's make the most of this day."

Lila's eyes lit up. "Now you're talking!"

As we rose from the table, the café buzzed with life, but it felt different now—less chaotic and more vibrant, a tapestry woven from the threads of our shared experiences. We stepped outside, the sun embracing us, and the laughter of the girl echoed in my mind, a song of hope.

The beach stretched out before us, a canvas of blues and golds, shimmering with possibility. The waves danced, crashing with a wild abandon that resonated deep within my soul. I took a deep breath, the salty air filling my lungs, invigorating me.

DOWN AND OUT IN BYRON BAY

Together, we walked toward the water, the sand warm beneath our feet, grounding me in the present moment. Each step felt like a reclaiming of my spirit, a return to the wild heart that had been buried under layers of doubt.

As the waves lapped at my toes, I felt a surge of clarity—a momentary glimpse into the beauty of life's chaos, the interconnectedness of all things. I was not just a spectator; I was part of the rhythm, part of the dance.

And in that moment, I understood: clarity doesn't come from waiting—it's found in the act of living, in the moments of joy and connection that weave the fabric of existence. With Lila by my side, I felt ready to embrace it all, ready to find beauty in the wild, chaotic world that stretched before me.

"Let's collect some shells," I said, grinning as we approached the shoreline, the sun casting long shadows behind us. Lila laughed, her voice bright against the backdrop of crashing waves, and together we stepped into the rhythm of the sea, ready to discover the treasures hidden beneath its surface.

We walked along the water's edge, the rhythmic sound of the waves crashing against the shore matching the restless pulse inside me. The cool evening breeze tugged at my clothes, a gentle reminder of how much I had been letting slip through my fingers.

"You know, I feel like I've been stuck in these endless loops," I admitted, my voice low, almost as if saying it out loud would somehow make it more real. "I get caught in my head, replaying the same negative conversations over and over. The same doubts. Same insecurities. It's like I can't escape them. Every thought just circles back to the same old fears."

Lila looked at me, her gaze soft but steady. "I know that feeling. It's like being trapped in a room with no doors. The only way out is to make a choice, even if it's a scary one."

I let out a frustrated breath, kicking at a stray stone on the sand. "It's hard. I've been so entrenched in Byron, in the way things are, I'm not sure if I can really break out of it. I mean, what's outside of here? What if it's just more of the same?"

Lila gave a small, knowing smile. "I get that. I've felt that too. But sometimes, you've got to step outside the story you've been telling yourself to see what else is out there."

There was a long pause between us.

"You know, I'm actually leaving Byron soon. Going to keep traveling, see more of Australia. My friends and I are headed up the coast—there's a whole new world waiting to be explored... You coming?"

I felt a pang in my chest at the mention of leaving. It wasn't that I didn't want to experience more, but the thought of stepping away from everything I knew—everything I had built, or perhaps, everything that had built me—made my stomach tighten. "Sounds amazing," I said, trying to hide the hesitation in my voice. "But... I don't know. I've been here so long, and I've always wondered if leaving was the answer. But what if I just end up running from everything? What if it's just another way of avoiding the mess I'm in?"

She stopped walking, turning to face me, her eyes calm but intense. "You're not running, Finn. You're searching. And sometimes, to find what's next, you've got to leave behind what's comfortable, even if it's scary. You might just find a piece of yourself out there you never knew existed."

I looked at her, unsure of what to say. The idea of stepping into the unknown—of leaving Byron behind—felt like standing on the edge of a cliff, with the ocean far below. Part of me was terrified of the fall, terrified of what I'd lose. But there was something in her words, something in her energy that made me wonder if I was more afraid of staying than I was of going.

"What if I don't know how to leave?" I asked, my voice barely more than a whisper.

"You don't have to have all the answers right now," Lila said, her voice light but full of assurance. "Just take the first step. Come with us. We'll figure it out together."

I stared out at the ocean, the waves rolling in with a steady persistence that made me feel small, yet somehow more alive. For a moment, the possibility of leaving—of stepping into something new—felt less like a threat and more like an invitation. But the fear was still there, gnawing at the edges of my thoughts.

"I don't know," I muttered, my doubts creeping in again. "I've got so many things tying me here. It's not that simple."

Lila was quiet for a moment, her gaze searching mine. "It never is simple. But maybe it's worth making things a little complicated if it means you get to live, really live, instead of just existing."

I swallowed, the weight of her words sinking in. Maybe she was right. Maybe it wasn't about having it all figured out, but about being brave enough to try something new, to take a chance on myself.

"Alright," I said finally, the words tasting strange on my tongue. "I'll think about it."

Lila grinned, her face lighting up with a mix of excitement and understanding. "That's all I'm asking. No pressure. Just... think about it. And when you're ready, you know where to find me."

As we continued walking along the shore, the night stretching before us, I felt a faint stirring of hope. It wasn't much yet, but it was something. A whisper in the wind, the possibility of change. And for the first time in a long time, I wondered if maybe, just maybe, I was ready to chase it.

The Last of the Hippies

I strolled through the streets of Byron Bay, the sun casting long shadows that danced on the pavement. The air was thick with the scent of salt and eucalyptus, a mix that comforted me while reminding me of days when the town pulsed with raw, unrefined energy. Now, the surf shops and trendy cafés felt like a veneer—glossy and artificial, concealing the gritty truth of the land beneath.

As I passed a mural of a dreamcatcher, its vibrant colors faded against the harshness of time, I recalled how once, I felt a part of this place, a cog in the wheel of its free-spirited charm. But as the years rolled on, the authenticity slipped through my fingers like sand. The hippies, the rebels, the artists—where were they now? It was as if the soul of Byron had been bottled and sold off, leaving behind a hollow echo of what had once been a sanctuary for the wild-hearted.

"Oi, mate! You look like you've lost your way," a voice called out, pulling me from my thoughts.

I turned to see an older man, his hair a wild tangle of gray and white, dressed in a patchwork vest that seemed to capture the spirit of the sun and sea. He was seated on a crumbling wooden bench outside a dilapidated shop—a relic from another era, one that hadn't yet surrendered to the encroaching tide of consumerism.

"Just wandering," I replied, a hint of resignation in my voice.

The old man chuckled, a sound like gravel rolling down a hill. "Wandering's good, but don't forget to look around. You might find what you're missing."

Intrigued, I sat down on the edge of the bench. "What's that?"

"Authenticity," he said, his eyes twinkling like stars struggling to shine through the city's glare. "It's the spirit of this place. Once, we danced barefoot on the grass, sang to the ocean, and shared everything. Now, look around." He gestured to the bustling street filled with tourists and flashy signs. "It's all a show, mate. All glitter, no gold."

"Do you remember the old days?" I asked, leaning in closer, desperate to grasp a piece of the past.

"Ah, the late sixties," he sighed, his voice laced with nostalgia. "We lived like the wind—free and unbound. No one cared about the size of their bank accounts or the labels on their clothes. We cared about the earth, the waves, each other." His eyes glimmered with unspoken memories. "But you see, mate, authenticity and stability are fragile. It's easy to lose sight of them, especially when the world tries to wrap you in plastic."

I had always thought stability meant accumulating things, making safe, sensible choices like buying a nicer car, moving into a bigger house with a better view, convinced that these tangible improvements would somehow make the restlessness inside fade. Society told me this was the way to be happy—financial security, material comfort, a well-curated life—and although I rebelled against those, I believed it.

But I saw that the more people gathered, the more I realized it wasn't working for them. They were missing something deeper, something that couldn't be filled with possessions or achievements. They had neglected the kind of stability that comes from within—the kind that comes from self-awareness, emotional peace, and living authentically.

But I built walls around myself and allowed the noise of daily life to drown out everything else. I had gotten so caught up in proving my worth to myself that I lost touch with who I truly was. I felt like an empty shell, carried by the tide. The harder I grasped at my inner self, the further I drifted from myself. I had created a life that no longer felt like mine. And yet, the fear of letting go of what was familiar kept me tied to it, as if somehow if I just stuck with it long enough, it would all make sense. But deep down, I knew it wouldn't.

"What happened to the others?" I asked, my voice barely above a whisper. "The ones who lived that way?"

"Some got lost in the hustle, others just faded away," he said with a shrug. "But a few remain—still fighting the good fight, still singing the songs that remind us who we are. You just have to look for them. They're the ones still barefoot in the grass, looking for the magic in the mundane."

I looked out at the street, my heart heavy with a yearning for connection. "Do you think it's possible to find that spirit again?"

The man studied me, his expression turning serious. "It's within you, mate. And it's there every generation. You just have to choose to live it. Let go of the fear that binds you. The world is a messy place, but it's also beautiful. You can't chase authenticity in a place; it has to come from within."

As the sun dipped lower in the sky, casting a warm golden light over the town, I felt a stirring in my chest—a flicker of hope mingled with a hint of rebellion. "How do I start?"

"Start small," he replied. "Dare to be honest with yourself. Share your truth. Create without boundaries. Seek out those who still dance in the light. And don't be afraid to get a little messy."

I smiled, the weight of uncertainty lifting, if only just a little. "Sounds like a plan."

The man reached out and clasped my hand, a gesture of camaraderie, a bridge connecting two souls from different times. "Good. Now go on, mate. The sunset's waiting, and the ocean is always calling."

As I stood up and made my way toward the beach, I felt a renewed sense of purpose, a whisper of the wildness that had once thrived within me. The waves lapped at the shore, each crash a reminder of the world's ebb and flow, of life's relentless pursuit of authenticity.

With each step, I felt the burden of expectation begin to lift, replaced by the warmth of possibility. I glanced back at the old man, who waved goodbye—a guardian of memories, a keeper of the flame.

I reached the water's edge, the cool waves washing over my feet, grounding me in the present. The horizon stretched infinitely before me, a canvas yet to be painted, and for the first time in a long while, I felt the stirrings of joy rise within—a desire to reconnect, to create, to truly live.

In that moment, as the sun sank into the ocean, I understood the beauty of impermanence and the power of choice. I was ready to embrace the chaos, to dive headfirst into the mess of life, to seek out the wild spirit that still flickered within me, and to honor the legacy of those who had come before.

DOWN AND OUT IN BYRON BAY

Byron Bay was changing, but so was I. And perhaps, just perhaps, that was enough.

Songs of the Sea

The sun hung low over Byron Bay, casting golden rays that danced on the waves like the laughter of children. I strolled along the boardwalk, the salty breeze tugging at my shirt, ruffling my hair as if nature itself were trying to wake me from a slumber that had lasted far too long. The scent of sunscreen mixed with the tang of ocean spray—a fragrant reminder of the life pulsing around me, vibrant yet distant.

As I wandered, I caught sight of Lila, standing by the water's edge with her friends, laughing as they joked around. We had known each other for a while now, long enough that there was a familiarity between us—an easy kind of connection that came with time. She had that magnetic energy about her, always drawing people in, yet when our eyes met, it was as though the rest of the world faded away. We shared a silent understanding, an unspoken bond.

I watched as she excused herself from her group, making her way over to me. "What are you doing out here all by yourself?" she asked with that playful smile of hers, her eyes bright and full of life.

"Just clearing my head," I replied, feeling the weight of the day's thoughts pressing against my chest. "Needed a break from everything."

She nodded knowingly, her expression softening. "I get it. Things have a way of piling up, don't they?"

I smiled, appreciating the comfort in her presence. "Yeah. Sometimes it feels like I'm stuck in an endless loop, you know? Like I'm always having the same negative conversations in my head, over and over, just spinning in circles."

Lila tilted her head, her brow furrowed in thought. "I hear you," she said after a moment, her voice gentle but firm. "I think everyone gets caught in those loops at some point. But you can choose to step out of it, Finn. You don't have to keep listening to those voices."

I didn't answer immediately, just let her words settle inside me. There was truth there, but it felt so far away, like something I couldn't quite reach.

"You ever feel like you're just... going through the motions?" I asked, my voice quieter now. "Like, no matter what you do, you're still waiting for something that'll make it all... make sense?"

Lila's expression softened. "All the time," she said, her voice laced with an honesty I admired. "But sometimes, you have to make your own sense of things. You can't wait for life to hand it to you. You have to take the reins, even if it's scary."

I paused, feeling the weight of her words. "Maybe you're right," I said slowly, trying to digest the idea of it all. "But it's hard to shake the fear. Fear of failure. Fear of not living up to... whatever it is I'm supposed to be."

"You've got more in you than you think," Lila said softly, her gaze steady. "I've seen it in you before. Your writing, your ideas—there's something real there. It just takes time to get through the clutter and make space for it again."

Her words cut through the fog that had clouded my thoughts. A flicker of hope stirred in me, but it was fragile, like a candle flame caught in a draft.

Lila took a step closer, a playful glint in her eyes. "Actually, I've been thinking," she said, almost mischievously. "What do you think about collaborating on something? You write, I play music—we could create something together. It's been on my mind for a while."

I blinked, taken aback. The idea was intriguing, but also intimidating. "Collaborate?" I repeated, a nervous laugh escaping me. "You're asking me to actually put myself out there again?"

Lila's smile widened. "Yeah, why not? It's a chance to get out of your head and do something that matters. We both know how easy it is to keep waiting for the 'right' moment, but that moment might never come unless we make it happen."

I looked at her, and for the first time in a while, I felt that spark—like maybe, just maybe, I could start stepping out of the shadows I'd been hiding in. "Okay," I said, my voice a little steadier. "Let's do it. Let's see what happens."

Her eyes lit up with excitement, and I could feel the change stirring within me, a sense of purpose returning, piece by piece. "Great," she said. "We'll start simple. Write something, record a few rough ideas—whatever flows. Let's do it soon."

"yeah, soon." Perhaps I could have sounded more enthusiastic.

" Finn, you do remember that I'm leaving Byron soon? We should get something going before I go, if you're in."

The reminder of her leaving hit me harder than I expected. Lila was someone I had come to rely on—her energy, her creativity, her ability to ground me when I needed it most. The idea of her leaving made a knot form in my stomach, and I couldn't quite shake the unease that settled in.

"So you're definitely leaving?" I asked, trying to keep my voice even.

She nodded, her expression softening. "Yeah, it's time. A few friends and I are heading up the coast. I want to see more of Australia, and maybe... maybe I'll find some new inspiration for my music."

I swallowed the sudden rush of disappointment. "That sounds amazing," I said, though my tone betrayed a tinge of regret. "When are you leaving?"

"Soon," she replied, a wistful smile on her face.

I tried to mask the wave of disappointment that hit me, but I could feel it settling in my chest like a weight I couldn't shake. It wasn't just that Lila was leaving—it was the idea that something I had come to rely on, something that had grounded me when everything else felt unsteady, was suddenly about to vanish. The fear of change felt like it was closing in, tightening its grip on me.

"Right," I said, trying to keep my voice steady, though the unease was creeping in. "You did mention it, didn't you?" I almost laughed, the sound tight and forced. "I guess I just... didn't think it would be so soon."

Lila gave me a soft smile, reading my reaction with ease. "Yeah, I know. It's a bit abrupt. But you knew it was coming, Finn. It's just time. I've been here a while, and there's more to see, more to experience. It's all part of the journey, right?"

I nodded, but something in me felt off, like I was watching a chapter of my life close before I was ready for it to end. She'd been a steady presence—someone who encouraged me to step out of my comfort zone, to push past the doubts that had kept me stagnant. The thought of her leaving felt like an anchor being pulled from the shore, leaving me with nothing but an expanse of open sea ahead.

"I get it," I said finally, though it wasn't really that simple. "But it's just... it's hard to imagine Byron without you around. You've kind of become a part of this place, you know?"

Lila's eyes softened, and for a moment, I saw something in her—something quiet, but powerful. She stepped closer, her presence warm and grounding. "I understand," she said gently. "But Byron will still be here when I'm gone. It's not about the place; it's about what you make of it. What you do with it."

I couldn't help but let out a quiet sigh, my mind racing. "Yeah, I guess," I murmured, my gaze dropping to the sand beneath my feet. "But it's easier to stay where you're comfortable. You know that, right?"

Lila chuckled softly, but there was an edge to it—something almost tender in the way she spoke. "I do. But you can't stay in one place forever, Finn. Eventually, you have to move. Even if it scares the hell out of you." She paused for a beat, then added, "And maybe that's exactly what you need. To move. To shake things up. To stop letting your fear keep you locked in this mental loop of what-ifs."

I opened my mouth, but the words didn't come right away. She was right. I knew she was right. My entire life had been about trying to play it safe, trying to stay comfortable, trying to avoid the risk of failing. But the more I thought about it, the more I realized—comfort wasn't getting me anywhere. It was just keeping me stuck.

Lila studied me for a moment, her gaze steady and thoughtful. "You don't have to come with me, Finn. I'm not asking you to drop everything and follow me. But if you want to shake off that rust, maybe you should think about it. A change of scenery. A different pace. It might just wake you up in a way Byron can't anymore."

I felt a pulse of uncertainty flicker in my chest. Could I really leave? Was I ready for that kind of change? The idea of being somewhere new, away from everything I knew, felt like a leap into the unknown. But a small part of me—an unfamiliar part—wondered if it could be the answer I had been looking for.

Lila gave me a knowing smile, as if reading my thoughts. "Look," she said, "I'm not asking you to decide now. Just think about it. Don't let fear keep you stuck in the same place forever."

I met her gaze and, for the first time in what felt like forever, I didn't feel so alone in my thoughts. Lila had a way of making me believe that maybe—just maybe—there was more to life than the familiar walls I had built around myself.

"Okay," I said quietly, feeling the weight of the decision press against my chest. "I'll think about it." But even as I said it, I knew that thinking about it was the first step to something much bigger than I had imagined.

Lila smiled, a genuine, warm smile. "I'm glad to hear that. Whatever you decide, Finn, you're not stuck. You never have been."

The waves crashed against the shore, rhythmic and endless, and in the distance, I could just make out the golden horizon.

"But hey, we still have time. We can make something happen, right?"

"Yeah," I said, the words feeling real for the first time. "Yeah, we can."

As she turned to rejoin her friends, her laughter floating on the breeze, I watched her go, feeling both the pull to be a part of something bigger and the fear of what her leaving meant. But the idea of collaborating, of creating something real together, sparked something inside me that I hadn't felt in a long time.

The waves crashed softly in the distance, each one echoing the rhythm of my heart. Maybe it was time to stop running from what I was meant to do.

The Spiral Down

The rain fell in sheets that blanketed Byron Bay, a heavy curtain drawn across the sunlit façade that once felt like home to me. I watched it from my cramped cottage, the sound of water slapping against the pavement merging with the muted chaos of my thoughts. The walls, once vibrant with the colors of my youth, now felt like prison bars, closing in around me.

The coffee in my chipped mug had gone cold, forgotten on the table alongside crumpled bills and empty promises. I'd thought about writing, about expressing the turmoil swirling in my mind, but the words had turned to stone in my throat, suffocating beneath the weight of despair. Each day felt like trudging through thick mud, the effort required just to exist becoming a chore I could no longer bear.

My phone buzzed—a message from Lila. "Hey! Hope you're still interested in writing together? Let's catch up!" The brightness of her words pierced through the fog, but that light faded quickly, replaced by a familiar sense of inadequacy. What did I have to offer? The inspiration that once flowed freely was now dammed, a stagnant pool reflecting only the darkest corners of my psyche.

I dragged myself to the window, the gray sky mirroring my mood. Outside, people moved under umbrellas, their laughter muffled like echoes from another world. I felt like a ghost among the living—invisible and untouched, yearning for a connection I could no longer feel.

The spiral began with little things—a missed deadline at work, a fight with a friend over nothing, the realization that I hadn't smiled in days. Each small setback felt like a stone dropped into the depths of a well, rippling through my sense of self until it became a tidal wave of despair. The vibrant, carefree spirit that had once danced through Byron's streets now felt like a relic of a time that belonged to someone else.

I could still hear the laughter, the music, the warmth of those summer nights spent under the stars, strumming my guitar, filled with hope and youthful exuberance. But now, the notes twisted into dissonance, and the memories stung like salt in an open wound. "Get it together," I muttered to myself, the words bitter on my tongue. But what if I couldn't?

A knock at the door jolted me from my thoughts. It was Lila.

The moment she stepped inside, the contrast between her energy and the heaviness that clung to me was stark. Her eyes, bright and full of purpose, scanned the room, the smell of rain still fresh on her clothes. She was wearing that same easy smile I had grown used to—the kind that somehow made everything feel a little less heavy, even when it wasn't.

"Hey," she greeted me, her voice a breath of fresh air in the damp room. "Ready to write?"

I stared at her for a moment, the words sitting on my tongue, but nothing came out. I was struggling with something much bigger than the project we were supposed to be collaborating on. Her presence only intensified the frustration I had been keeping under wraps for days.

"Yeah," I said, my voice flat, despite the internal battle. "I'm ready."

She set her bag and guitar down on the floor and dropped into the chair across from me, the familiarity of her being here almost unbearable now, given the weight of everything else that was unsaid. The silence stretched out between us like a thick fog.

Lila pulled out her notebook, flipping it open to a blank page. "So, what are we thinking? Lyrics, poetry—" She trailed off, her eyes locking onto mine. "Anything's fair game."

But I couldn't focus on her enthusiasm. My mind kept circling back to what she had told me the other day—about leaving. It kept gnawing at me, that sense of impending loss.

"You're really going, huh?" I blurted, unable to hold it in any longer.

Lila paused, a frown creeping onto her face. "Yeah, Finn. I told you. I've been thinking about it for a while now." Her eyes softened, but there was something in them—something guarded, like she knew I wasn't just talking about her leaving. "I need to keep moving, you know? It's what I do."

My chest tightened, the words spilling out before I could stop them. "It's not just that, Lila. It's—" I stopped myself, trying to find the words that didn't sound as bitter as they felt. "You're leaving, and all I can think about is... what does that mean for me? You've been here, and it feels like every time I try to get a grip on something, it slips away."

She leaned back in her chair, staring at me for a moment, her expression unreadable. The air between us crackled, charged with something unspoken. Finally, she spoke, her voice quieter than before, but firm. "Finn, I told you—this isn't about you. It's about me. I need to go. I need to see new things, experience something different." She exhaled sharply, a hint of frustration creeping in. "I can't stay here forever, running on the same treadmill, doing the same things."

"I know," I muttered, but the words tasted like ash in my mouth. "I get it. But you're always moving, Lila. And I'm just stuck. You come in and out of my life like a whirlwind, and I can't even—" I broke off, my voice growing tight with emotion. "I can't even figure out what the hell I'm supposed to be doing here. You don't get it. You don't have to stay still like I do. I don't know how to keep up with you."

Lila's brow furrowed, her lips pressing into a thin line as she studied me, the weight of my words hanging between us like a fog. "Is that really what you think?" she asked, her tone soft but edged with something else now—something I couldn't quite read. "You think I'm moving to escape all of this? To get away from you?"

I shook my head, but the frustration spilled out anyway. "No, I'm not saying that...

"Be quiet for a moment." Lila demanded, as she reached for her guitar and began strumming:

OH, THE WINDS OF THE north they call,
   Where the green hills meet the sea,
   But my heart is lost, my love is gone,
   And it will never come back to me.
   The stars in the sky no longer shine,
   For I miss the glow of your eyes,
   And the lark's song in the morning light,

Sounds like a mournful sigh.
Where the rivers run deep and slow,
I walk in the shadows alone,
For you were the sun that lit my way,
Now I only have the stone.
Oh, sweet was the whisper of your voice,
Like the breeze through the old oak tree,
But now the silence, it fills my soul,
And I ache with this misery.
Through the vale and the meadows wide,
I wander, lost in my thought,
And I search for the warmth we once had,
But you're the love I have sought.
The mountains may crumble, the sea may rise,
But my heart will stay with thee,
For the time we shared, now gone with the tide,
Is the dream I'll forever see.
Oh, love, if you hear me call,
Come back to where you belong,
For this world without you is cold and gray,
And my heart is a broken song.

I SAT ON THE WORN WOODEN floor, my back against the wall, my eyes fixed on Lila as she sang. The soft, haunting melody filled the room, wrapping around me like a ghost, pulling me deeper into an ache I hadn't known I was carrying. Her voice was like velvet, smooth and tender, but it cut through me, unraveling the parts of me that I'd been trying so hard to hold together.

As the last notes faded into silence, I wiped my eyes quickly, embarrassed by the tears I hadn't been able to hold back. I cleared my throat, trying to steady myself, but my voice still shook when I spoke.

"You—Lila, you're... you're something else, you know that?" My words came out rough, laden with emotion I hadn't expected. "The way you sing, the way you 'feel' the music—there's this depth to it, like you're not just playing... it's like 'giving' something. It's... it's special. It's not just your voice, it's you. You make me feel things. Things I didn't even know I need to feel."

I looked up at her, the weight of my words sinking in. "You make the world feel bigger, Lila. And I don't think you even realize how much that matters. But you are leaving, and I'm here. Stuck here, just like I've always been. You... you're out there living your life, and I'm just..." I ran a hand through my hair, the panicked words coming faster now. "I don't even know why I'm still in Byron. I don't know why I'm still here, doing the same shit over and over."

Lila stood up, her hands on her hips, and for a moment, I thought she was going to walk out. But she didn't. Instead, she took a deep breath and said, "Finn, it's not about being stuck. It's about choosing to be here. You're so caught up in your own head that you can't even see what's in front of you. I'm not leaving because I'm trying to escape—I'm leaving because I need to find something, something that I can't find here anymore. And I can't keep waiting around for you to figure it out."

Her words hit me like a punch to the gut. "You can't just leave without me, Lila," I said, almost pleading, my voice breaking. "I can't keep doing this alone. You... you're the only person who's really here for me, now!. You can't just—"

I stopped myself, feeling the weight of everything I hadn't said crash down on me. I was suffocating under the realization that, maybe, I wasn't just afraid of her leaving. I was terrified of what would happen if I didn't change, if I didn't do something.

Lila's face softened, her anger subsiding into something quieter, more resigned. "I have to, Finn," she said, her voice quieter now, a hint of sadness lacing her words. "I can't live for both of us. You have to find your own way. It's not fair to either of us if I stay just because you don't want to be alone."

There was a finality to her words that hit me harder than I expected. It was the truth. She was right. She couldn't stay to fix me. I had to fix myself, but I didn't know how to do it without her.

"I don't want you to go," I said, my voice barely a whisper.

Lila sighed, her shoulders sagging slightly as she looked down at me. "I know, Finn. But sometimes you have to let go of the things you hold onto so tightly, in order to find the things that are meant for you." She turned to leave, but paused at the door, looking back over her shoulder. "I'll still be here, in a way. But you... you have to find your own way forward. It's time."

And then she was gone.

The door clicked softly behind her, leaving me alone again, but this time it felt different. The air felt heavier, charged with something I couldn't quite place. Maybe it was the reality of her leaving, or maybe it was the weight of the conversation that still hung in the air. But as I sat there, I realized something that I hadn't been able to admit before: maybe it wasn't just her that I was afraid of losing. It was myself.

A New Dawn

I awoke to the relentless sound of waves crashing against the rocky shore, their rhythm a constant companion in my life here in Byron Bay. The early morning light seeped through the gaps in my curtains, a hesitant glow spilling into the room, washing over the disarray of clothes, dirty dishes, and the remnants of last night's confrontation with Lila.. A new day was breaking, yet I felt the weight of yesterday clinging to me like a thick fog.

Sitting up, I ran a hand through my tousled hair, feeling the sun warm my skin even before it fully emerged from the horizon. The scent of salt and earth mingled in the air, a promise of possibility that felt just out of reach. As I stared out the window, the world beyond my cramped cottage stirred with life. Surfers bobbed on the ocean's surface, silhouetted against the rising sun, their bodies gliding with a grace I had long forgotten.

"Today," I muttered to myself; as if saying the word aloud could summon the courage buried deep within me. "Today is the day."

I stumbled into the bathroom, my reflection greeting me with the familiar gaze of someone who had spent too long lost in a haze of disillusionment. The mirror framed my weary eyes, dark circles beneath them telling stories of sleepless nights and regret. I splashed cold water on my face, the shock pulling me momentarily from the numbness that had wrapped around me like a shroud.

Dressing quickly, I threw on a faded T-shirt and a pair of board shorts that hung loose on my frame. As I stepped outside, the ocean breeze whipped around me, tousling my hair and pulling me into the day like an old friend. The salty air filled my lungs, reminding me of the vitality that once coursed through me.

I walked along the beach, the sand soft and warm beneath my feet, each step feeling like a declaration of intent. There was something sacred about the early hours, a stillness that lingered before the chaos of the day began. As I wandered, the colors of dawn splashed across the sky—pinks, oranges, and yellows bleeding into one another, creating a canvas of beauty that took my breath away.

Pausing, I gazed at the horizon where the sun dipped low, painting a fiery orb that promised rebirth. It struck me then—transformation didn't come from grand gestures or sweeping changes. It was the small decisions, the choice to wake up and embrace the day, to let go of the past and step into the light of new beginnings.

I spotted an elderly man sitting on a rock, his weathered face lined with the marks of a life well-lived. He was sketching in a tattered notebook, his hand moving with a fluid grace that spoke of a passion untouched by time. I hesitated, feeling the urge to approach but tethered by the fear of vulnerability.

"Beautiful, isn't it?" the old man said without looking up, his voice warm and inviting.

"Yeah," I replied, the word barely escaping my lips. "It really is."

The man turned his gaze from the page, his eyes sharp and bright. "You're young. Don't waste the moments. Each day is a gift, wrapped in the chaos of life."

I felt a lump form in my throat, the old man's words cutting through the fog of my thoughts. "I'm trying," I admitted, the truth spilling out before I could catch it. "I don't even know where to start."

The man smiled, a knowing smile that held decades of wisdom. "Start by letting go of the fear. It's the weight that holds you down."

I nodded, feeling the flicker of something—hope, perhaps—begin to stir within me. "What if I fall again?"

"Then you get back up," the man replied, his tone steady. "Life is a series of ups and downs. Embrace the falls; they'll teach you how to rise."

With those words echoing in my mind, I walked away from the man, a lightness in my step that hadn't been there before. I was still grappling with the shadows of my past, but now there was a thread of resolve weaving through me. I found myself craving connection, a desire to reach out to those I had lost along the way.

DOWN AND OUT IN BYRON BAY

I headed to the local café, the scent of freshly brewed coffee mingling with the salty air. As I entered, the familiar sounds of clinking cups and laughter enveloped me, but there was also an emptiness that lingered in my heart. I scanned the room, spotting a group of friends laughing together, their joy a sharp reminder of my solitude.

"Hey, Finn!" A voice broke through the din. It was Maya, her face lighting up with recognition. "Come join us!"

I hesitated, a flicker of anxiety rising within me. But then I remembered the old man's words—about the importance of connection. With a deep breath, I walked over to the table, the warmth of their smiles wrapping around me like a soft blanket.

"Thought you were lost in your own world," Sam joked, patting the empty seat beside him.

"Not anymore," I replied, feeling the corners of my mouth lift in a genuine smile.

As we shared stories, laughter bubbled up, a cathartic release that felt as though it were cleansing me of the years spent in isolation. Each moment spent with them reignited the embers of belonging that had dimmed over time. I felt seen, understood—a reminder that I was not alone in this chaotic dance of life.

With every laugh, every shared glance, I began to shed the layers of despair that had cloaked me for too long. The world outside faded into the background as I realized I was part of something larger than myself—a tapestry woven with the threads of friendship, love, and hope.

The sun rose higher in the sky, casting a golden hue over the café, illuminating the faces of those who surrounded me. In that moment, I understood that change begins within. It's a choice to embrace vulnerability, to reach out for connection, and to take each day as it comes.

As I left the café, the wind tousling my hair, I felt a sense of renewal coursing through me. The shadows of yesterday were still there, but they no longer defined me. A new dawn had arrived, and with it, a chance to write my story anew—one filled with the beauty of existence and the hope of every tomorrow.

Navigating the Grey

The early morning light crept into my cottage like a thief, stealing away the last remnants of sleep. The air was thick with the scent of stale cigarettes and unwashed sheets, a stark reminder of the nights spent lost in a haze. I sat on the edge of my bed, the wooden slats creaking beneath me as I stared at the wall, blank except for a few faded posters peeling at the corners. Outside, the surf rolled in, the waves crashing against the shore like an urgent whisper, beckoning me to join the world beyond my closed doors.

I ran a hand over my face, feeling the scruff of my unshaven jaw, the weight of indecision heavy in my chest. I'd always been drawn to the raw, messy edges of life—the dive bars, the unfiltered conversations, the moments of gritty honesty. But lately, I felt like I was teetering on the edge of a moral abyss, where right and wrong blurred into a haze of grey.

"Get it together, Finn," I muttered, my voice hoarse and echoing in the silence. But I didn't know if I could.

The dilemma gnawed at me. I'd seen it in the eyes of my friends, those nights when laughter turned brittle, when the truth behind the façade threatened to crack open their carefully constructed lives. It was in the way Maya's smile faltered when she spoke about her mother's illness, the way Sam deflected his own insecurities with bravado. They were all navigating their own storms, and I felt like I was drowning in my own uncertainty.

I forced myself up, dressed in a faded T-shirt and board shorts, and stepped outside. The sun was bright, the sky a brilliant blue, but the colors felt dulled by the weight in my chest. I headed toward the beach, where the sand was warm beneath my feet, each grain a reminder of the passage of time. As I walked, I noticed the locals setting up for the day: surfboards propped against the dunes, families laying out their towels, the smell of coffee wafting from the nearby café.

My gaze fell upon an older couple, their hands intertwined as they strolled along the water's edge, laughter spilling from their lips like music. They were a snapshot of joy, an embodiment of love's simplicity, but even that image felt tinged with bittersweet nostalgia. I wished for connection, yet the weight of my choices felt like chains wrapped around my ankles.

"Hey, Finn!" a voice called, breaking my reverie. It was Jess, waving as she approached, her sun-kissed hair dancing in the breeze. "You look like you've seen a ghost."

"More like a bad decision," I replied, forcing a grin. "What's up?"

"Just soaking in the sun before work. You should join me for a swim." Her eyes sparkled with mischief, but I saw the concern lurking just beneath the surface.

"I don't know," I hesitated, glancing at the waves. "I'm not really in the mood."

"Why do we always have to make choices, Finn?" she had asked, her voice barely above a whisper, as if admitting the question made it too real. "Sometimes it feels like there's no right answer."

I had wanted to tell her that I understood, that life was a series of grey choices painted with shades of regret and hope. But I hadn't known how to articulate that, trapped in my own confusion.

"Yeah," I replied, the tension in my chest loosening, if only for a moment. But the grey thoughts returned, swirling in the back of my mind like an impending storm. I could see it now: every choice a ripple, every action a consequence, creating waves in the lives of those around me.

We sat on the beach sipping from cold coconuts and the conversation drifted. I felt the warmth of camaraderie, the laughter ebbing and flowing like the tide, but a shadow loomed over me.

"What's eating you, Finn?" Jess asked, her tone turning serious. "You've been distant lately."

"It's just...life, you know?" I rubbed the back of my neck, feeling the tension return. "Everything feels so tangled, like there's no clear path. I don't want to hurt anyone, but sometimes it feels inevitable."

She nodded, her expression softening. "That's the thing about life. It's messy. We're all just trying to navigate through the grey."

"Yeah," I said, a heaviness settling back in. "But what if I make the wrong choice?"

"Wrong? Right? They're just labels we put on things." Her gaze held mine, steady and unwavering. "Sometimes the best we can do is be honest with ourselves and with others. It's okay to feel lost.. But come on Finn! What's the real problem?"

"Can I ask you something?" I finally broke the silence, my voice rough, uncertain.

Jess raised an eyebrow, her fingers lightly tapping the rim of her cup. "Always."

I hesitated, looking down at the clear water. "Lila... she's leaving," I said, the words tasting heavier than I expected. "And I'm... I don't know what to do about it. I'm not sure how to feel. I mean, part of me wants her to stay, but I'm also scared of... well, of everything. Her leaving, me being left behind. It's like I'm stuck in this endless spiral where nothing feels real, but also nothing feels like it's mine anymore."

Jess and I walked back to the shore. "You're not stuck," she said softly, but firmly. "You're just afraid. You've been living for everyone else's expectations for so long that now that something—someone—is challenging that... it feels like you're losing control."

I felt a knot form in my chest, and I nodded slowly, though I didn't know how to explain it. "I've always thought I had time, you know? Time to figure things out. Time to get it right. But Lila's this force of nature, and now... now it feels like everything's changing too fast. I'm just... I'm scared of what happens if I can't change with it."

Jess's gaze softened, her hand lightly resting on mine. "Finn, change is inevitable. It always is. It doesn't matter if you feel ready or not—it's going to happen. The question is: what are you going to do when it does?"

I bit my lip, wrestling with the truth of her words. "I think... I think I've been waiting for someone to tell me what to do. I've been waiting for someone else to fix things. Maybe it's Lila... maybe it's everyone else around me. But I feel like I'm losing my grip, Jess."

She exhaled slowly, like she had been holding her breath too, and then looked me dead in the eyes. "Finn, you're not going to find yourself by clinging to other people. Not Lila, not anyone else. You've got to start asking yourself what you need, not what you think someone else can give you. What do you want? What do you want out of your life?"

The question hit me like a wave and I didn't know the answer. I had spent so much time thinking about what I was supposed to do, what I was supposed to want, that I had forgotten how to listen to myself.

"I don't know," I admitted, my voice cracking slightly. "I used to think I had it figured out. You know, stability, a career as a writer, a house with a view—what everyone says you should want. But... I don't feel like I'm living my life. I feel like I'm just going through the motions. And now, with Lila... it's like everything's unraveling, and I don't know where to start putting it all back together."

Jess was quiet for a moment, then leaned in a little closer, her voice lowering as if she were telling me a secret. "You've got to stop looking for someone else to fix you, Finn. Not Lila, not anyone else. You've got to fix yourself first. And that's scary. But it's also the only way you'll ever get to the point where you're not chasing after something or someone to feel whole."

I looked at her, feeling the weight of her words settle inside me like a stone in my chest. I knew she was right. I'd been clinging to the idea of Lila, the idea of what she could offer me—hope, direction, inspiration—without realizing that I was the one who had to find those things for myself.

"Yeah," I whispered, more to myself than to her. "I think I've known that for a while now. I guess I was just hoping it wouldn't be so... hard."

Jess gave me a small, understanding smile. "It's always hard, Finn. Life's never going to hand you the answers, not like that. You have to go out there and get them. And, honestly, you've got to be okay with not having it all figured out."

I let out a long breath, the kind of breath that felt like I'd been holding it for too long. "I don't know if I'm ready for that. I don't know if I'm ready to let Lila go. She's become this... this fire in my life, you know? Always so sure of herself. I'm scared if she goes, I'll be... nothing."

"You're not nothing," Jess said, her voice steady and sure. "You're just finding your way. And if Lila's the one to help you see that, then that's good. But you've got to see it for yourself. You can't rely on her, or anyone else, to make you feel whole. You've got to do that for yourself."

I nodded, though the weight of the truth felt heavy on my shoulders. "I know. It's just... it's scary. All of it. I don't even know where to begin."

Jess squeezed my hand. "You've already started. The fact that you're asking the questions is the first step. You'll find your way. But you have to stop waiting for someone else to give you the answers."

"Lila's mentioned me travelling with her. I don't think I can go. I mean I don't think I can leave Byron."

Jess's eyes narrowing slightly as she considered my words. There was a quiet understanding in her gaze, like she could see the conflict swirling inside me.

"I get it," she said, setting her mug down with a soft clink. "Byron's home, right? You've spent so much of your life here, the rhythms, the routines. It's like your anchor. I think a lot of people feel like they can't leave the places that shaped them, even when they're dying to break free."

I shifted uncomfortably, the weight of her words hitting too close to home. "Exactly. It's not that I'm not tempted. Hell, part of me wants to go, to just throw caution to the wind and see something new. But... Byron's the only place that's felt stable for so long. If I leave, I feel like... like I might lose myself."

Jess leaned towards me slightly, her eyes soft but intense. "I'm not going to tell you to just drop everything and go—because that's not for everyone. But... maybe you're not looking at this the right way. Maybe it's not about leaving Byron, it's about where you're going. Sometimes we get so focused on the idea of stability that we forget what we're really searching for."

I frowned, trying to piece her words together. "What do you mean?"

Jess looked at me strangely, as if arranging her thoughts like a puzzle. "Byron isn't just a place, it's a state of mind. It's familiar. It's comfortable. But... you can bring parts of yourself with you anywhere. You're not going to lose who you are just by leaving for a while. Sometimes, stepping out of your comfort zone is the only way to truly see who you are when you're not defined by the same walls, the same faces, the same routines. It's not about abandoning Byron—it's about expanding your world."

I looked at her, unsure of how to process that. "But what if I go and I don't find what I'm looking for? What if I just feel... more lost?"

Jess shrugged, a slight, almost imperceptible smile on her lips. "That's the gamble. But think about it. How many times have you stayed stuck in your head, wondering what's beyond this place, only to talk yourself out of it? If you never take the leap, you'll never know. And maybe that's the real risk—staying exactly where you are, letting life pass you by while you wait for some perfect moment to come along."

I swallowed hard, Jess's words cutting deeper than I'd expected. I felt like I had spent too many years trapped in the comfort of the known, waiting for the right time, the right circumstances to make a move. And now, when I finally had an opportunity—when Lila, of all people, was offering me a chance to break free—I was paralyzed by fear.

"You're saying I should just go with her, then?" I asked, still uncertain, but with a flicker of something stirring inside me.

"No, Finn." Jess's voice was steady, like she was laying out the truth for me, plain and simple. "I'm not saying you should go, but I am saying you should think about it. Think about what you need. Not what Byron needs, not what Lila needs, but you. And, for once, don't let fear be the thing that decides for you."

I stopped, letting her words settle into my chest like stones sinking slowly in water. The doubt that had gripped me so tightly loosened just a little, enough to let in the possibility of something else, something beyond the safety of Byron and the life I'd built here.

"I guess I never really thought of it like that," I admitted, rubbing the back of my neck. "I've been so scared of change, of leaving everything behind... I never stopped to ask if it might be exactly what I need."

Jess smiled, a knowing look crossing her face. "Sometimes, you have to leave to find what's really inside you. And you can always come back to Byron—if you need to. But at least, then, you'll know that you didn't let the chance slip away because you were too scared to step into the unknown."

I took a deep breath, feeling a mix of excitement and dread creeping into my bones. Jess was right. I was scared, but maybe that fear was exactly why I needed to listen. If I stayed here forever, I might end up a shadow of myself.

And maybe that's what I had been avoiding all along—being brave enough to move forward, even when the path wasn't clear.

"I'll think about it," I said finally, my voice steadier now, though my heart was still racing. "I think I need to stop running from things and start seeing them for what they really are."

Jess gave me a small, encouraging nod. "Exactly. Sometimes, the hardest thing is just giving yourself permission to want more."

But then Jess hesitated for a moment, glancing down at her hands before meeting my eyes again. There was something in her expression—shy, almost guilty—as if the question had been on her mind for a while. "Have you, uh… have you spoken to Ricky lately?" she asked, her voice a little softer than usual.

The question caught me off guard. I shifted uncomfortably, my thoughts momentarily drifting to the space between us and the complicated dynamics that lingered. "Not much," I replied, unsure of where this conversation was going. "Why?"

Jess looked away, a faint blush creeping up her neck. "I don't know… I just thought maybe you should."

Her voice trailed off, like she was trying to find the right words without overstepping. I felt the weight of her concern, but it left me wondering if she was more worried about Ricky, or about me.

Embers of Belonging

The sun dipped low over Byron Bay, painting the sky in fiery hues of orange and pink, as if the heavens themselves were igniting in a last gasp of warmth before surrendering to the cool embrace of twilight. I leaned against the weathered wooden railing of my balcony, a half-empty beer in hand, staring out at the ocean. The waves rolled in with a rhythm that echoed the tumult in my heart—crashing and retreating, retreating and crashing—an endless cycle of longing.

Tonight, I was hosting a gathering—an invitation I had sent out in a fleeting moment of optimism, now feeling more like a challenge. The last few years had shredded my connections like the saltwater wears down the coast. Friends had faded, like the glow of a dying fire, and I wasn't sure what would remain when the embers finally cooled.

It was my 30th birthday—though no one knew it— a milestone that felt both weighty and fleeting; a milestone that hung in the air like an unspoken truth, heavy and elusive. I was filled with the soft hum of anticipation, but I couldn't shake the feeling that time, like an unseen tide, was quietly eroding everything I thought I understood.

The doorbell rang, a sound both jarring and welcoming. I wiped my hands on my jeans, brushed back the strands of hair that had fallen over my forehead, and opened the door. There stood Lila, her smile bright enough to pierce through my gloom. She had a guitar slung across her back, its wood polished to a shine, the strings gleaming like silver threads in the fading light.

"Ready to bring the house down?" she teased, stepping inside, her energy filling the space like sunlight after a storm.

"More like bring the house to a gentle simmer," I replied, forcing a grin. I moved aside to let her in, catching the scent of sandalwood from her skin—a fragrance that lingered long after she had left.

Soon, the cottage filled with voices, laughter spilling over like the froth of waves against the shore. Old friends drifted in—Sam, with his unkempt hair and worn-out sneakers, and Maya, her vibrant skirt swirling like a kaleidoscope as she entered. Dan. Tanya. Jess. Ricky. Each hug was a reminder of warmth, each smile a flicker of connection that had been absent for too long.

"Let's get this party started!" Sam declared, flopping onto the couch and grabbing a guitar from the corner. "I can't believe you actually decided to host something, Finn."

"Yeah, it's a big step," Maya chimed in, winking. "Don't get used to it."

I chuckled, but beneath the humor lay an undercurrent of anxiety. I had spent so long in isolation that the thought of vulnerability felt like stepping onto a tightrope stretched high above a chasm. Yet, as the first notes rang out, blending with the chatter and laughter, something inside me began to stir.

We sang songs from our youth, tunes filled with reckless hope and passion, our voices merging into a tapestry of memories. I watched Lila as she strummed, her fingers dancing over the strings, each pluck resonating deep within me—a bittersweet reminder of the creativity I once embraced.

As the night wore on, I found myself drawn to the warmth of their companionship, the way their laughter intertwined with the music, creating a cocoon of safety that felt foreign yet familiar. Each shared glance, each inside joke rekindled the flickering flames of connection. Yet, with each laugh, I felt a twinge of regret, a reminder of the distance I had allowed to grow.

Lila caught me staring, her gaze penetrating. "You okay?" she asked softly, her voice cutting through the noise.

"Yeah, just... thinking." I forced a smile but felt the weight of truth pressing down on me.

"About what?" Her brow furrowed, concern lacing her tone.

"Just how far I've fallen away," I admitted, my voice barely above a whisper. "It's like I've been watching life happen from the sidelines."

"Finn," she said, her gaze steady, "you're here now. That's what matters. Sometimes we just need to find our way back."

Her words hung in the air, heavy with understanding. I looked around at my friends—each face familiar, yet I felt like an outsider in my own life. The laughter felt like a bridge I had yet to cross, and I wondered if I could ever reclaim that sense of belonging I once took for granted.

As the music swelled, I felt the desire to share something raw, something real. "I used to write," I blurted out, surprising even myself. "Poems, songs... It was like breathing. But I stopped. I didn't know how to face it all."

"Why not?" Sam asked, his eyes wide with curiosity. "You still can, you know. We're all here."

A wave of vulnerability washed over me, and I took a deep breath. "Because I was scared. Scared of what it might reveal, of what it might mean. But tonight... it feels different."

Lila nodded, her gaze warm. "Then write again. Share it with us. We want to hear your voice."

I felt a flicker of hope ignite within me. Perhaps this was my chance to reclaim that part of myself that had been lost. I grabbed a notepad from the table, the paper crinkled and faded, but still blank and waiting.

"Okay," I said, my voice steadying. "But I'm not promising anything good."

The others cheered me on, their encouragement wrapping around me like a warm blanket. I started to write, the words flowing out like water from a broken dam—raw, unfiltered, a reflection of the chaos that had been brewing within me.

Time seemed to slip away as I poured my heart onto the page. In those moments, surrounded by friends who believed in me, I felt the chains of isolation begin to loosen, the embers of belonging fanned back into a flickering flame.

As I finished, I looked up, their faces expectant. "Alright," I said, my heart racing. "Here goes nothing."

The room fell silent as I read aloud, my voice trembling but gaining strength with each line. The words spoke of pain, regret, but also of hope and resilience—the struggle to find my place amidst the chaos. With every verse, I could see the emotions reflected back in their eyes, the understanding, the connection forming anew.

ALEX TELMAN

BENEATH THE HOLLOW Sky"
I am not the song that rises
with the morning—
not the breath of fire
or the warmth of light.
I am the shadow caught between
the thunder and the silence,
the stillness that shudders
under the weight of all I cannot name.
I have worn my days like a coat,
threadbare and frayed with wear,
and yet it clings,
too tight against this skin
that no longer remembers
how to break open,
how to spill out
the things that roil beneath
this bone-caged heart.
I listen to the waves crash on the shore,
feel their hunger,
but my feet are heavy in the sand,
frozen by the thought of
what it means to reach
and what it means to fall.
I wanted to love like the ocean—
fierce and untamed,
crashing against the rocks,
pulling the world into my grasp.
But instead, I lie beneath the hollow sky,
a wilted thing,
waiting for the rain
that never falls.
Every night, I sit
with the ghosts of my dreams,
the ones that whispered

once, long ago—
that I could be more
than this—
more than the echo
of something forgotten.
But what if my hands are not enough?
What if I was never meant to speak
in the language of the stars
but in the whispers of the void
that stretches endless,
like the spaces between breaths?
I wanted to run,
but I am too afraid of what I will find
on the other side of this silence—
too afraid of the empty sky
that waits for me,
its vastness a mirror to
my hollow chest.

WHEN I FINISHED, A heavy silence enveloped the room, broken only by the sound of Lila's soft applause. "That was beautiful, Finn," she said, her voice thick with emotion. "You have a gift."

"I don't know about that," I replied, a smile creeping onto my face. "But it feels good to share it."

The night stretched on, laughter and music intertwining with stories of old, each tale bringing us closer. The warmth of connection wrapped around me, a cocoon of acceptance. I realized that even through the darkest moments, there could be light—flickers of hope that reminded me I was never truly alone.

And as the evening wore on, the hum of conversation around me fading into a dull murmur. I sat there, my gaze fixed on Lila, her laughter mingling with the soft clink of glasses, but I couldn't shake the gnawing discomfort settling in my chest. The uncertainty that had been hovering in the back of my mind now loomed like a shadow, stretching across the space between us.

She was talking with Ricky and Jess, her eyes alight with some shared joke, her smile effortless. She always seemed so... alive, like the world had a way of falling into place around her. I envied it, that ease she carried with her, the way she never seemed to be weighed down by the same heavy thoughts that clouded my mind.

But tonight, I felt different. It was like something had shifted. The rhythm of our conversations, the spontaneity that once defined us, felt like it was losing its spark, flickering on the edge of something I couldn't quite name.

I watched her, caught in a loop of my own thoughts. What if she's right? What if I'm just running in circles, stuck in a life that no longer feels like mine? What if I really do need to leave this place, let go of all this, to find some kind of clarity? The thought terrified me, and yet, part of me wanted to reach out and grab onto it, as if it could somehow break the chains I'd wrapped myself in.

"Finn." Her voice cut through the haze, pulling me out of my spiraling thoughts. She was standing in front of me now, her brow furrowed in concern. "You okay? You've been staring at me like I'm some kind of puzzle."

I blinked, feeling my cheeks flush, but I couldn't look away. "Yeah, just... lost in my own head." I smiled weakly, but it felt strained, like the muscles in my face were unfamiliar with the expression.

She tilted her head, a glimmer of something unreadable flashing across her face. "I've noticed you've been a little off lately." She hesitated, her fingers gently brushing the edge of the table. "Is it because I'm leaving? Because I told you, I didn't mean to make you feel..."

I felt a wave of guilt wash over me. She hadn't done anything wrong. She was simply living her life, chasing what inspired her, as she always did. But I couldn't help the pang of unease that spread in my chest at the thought of her leaving, of the space she would leave behind, the part of me that I felt connected to slipping further away.

"It's not that," I said, my voice sounding smaller than I intended. "I just... don't know what I'm doing anymore. I keep thinking about leaving Byron, but then I think about everything I've built here. And... I'm scared. I'm scared that if I leave, I'll just be running away from something I can't face."

Her gaze softened, and for a moment, she was quiet. I could see her weighing her words, like she was trying to choose the right ones to break through whatever wall I'd built around myself.

"You don't have to run, Finn," she said finally, her voice low and steady. "You just need to decide what's worth holding onto and what you need to let go of. It's not about running—it's about moving toward what feels real. The rest of it, the stuff that weighs you down... it'll fall away."

I shook my head, unsure. "It's not that simple. You make it sound so easy."

Lila gave me a gentle smile, one that felt like she understood the depth of my struggle, even if I couldn't fully put it into words. "It never is. But you're never going to find out until you let yourself take that first step." She paused, studying me with a look that was both tender and firm. "I'm leaving, yes. But I'll be around. And I want you to be okay. I want you to find your way, whether that means leaving Byron or staying here and finally seeing what you've been avoiding."

Her words hit me like a punch, leaving a mark I couldn't ignore. The idea of her being gone—of her not being here when I finally got the courage to sort through everything—felt like losing a part of myself. But it also made me realize how much of my life had been spent clinging to things, to the comfort of the known, instead of stepping into the uncertainty that would lead me to something new.

I met her gaze, and for the first time in what felt like forever, I felt something inside me stir—a sense of purpose, however small, beginning to push its way through the confusion. Maybe she's right. Maybe it's time to stop waiting for life to come to me.

"Thanks," I said, my voice steadier now. "For... everything. I'll figure it out. I just need to take it one step at a time."

Lila smiled, her eyes warm with understanding. "That's all any of us can do." She reached over, placing a hand on mine for a moment before standing up. "You'll be okay, Finn. I know you will."

And as she walked away, I felt a little lighter, as if some of the weight that had been pressing down on me for so long had been lifted, if only just a little.

Maybe I wasn't as lost as I thought. Maybe it was time to let go of the fear and embrace the unknown.

Because whatever happened next, I knew I had to choose my own path.

Ricky and Jess

It was just an ordinary evening when Ricky and Jess dropped by. I'd been sitting on my bed, nursing a warm beer, the familiar sound of the trees rustling in the breeze, the faint crash of the waves in the distance—comforting, in its own way. Byron Bay had always felt like home to me, for all its chaos. But lately, even the town I thought I knew so well felt distant, like something I couldn't quite reach anymore.

The knock on the door startled me. For a second, I hesitated. It was rare for Ricky and Jess to just show up—usually they'd message first. But then again, maybe they had something important to tell me. I set the beer down, wiped my hands on my jeans, and went to open the door.

Ricky was the first to step inside, his usual easy smile spread across his face—the one that usually meant trouble, or laughter, or long talks about surfing. Jess stood behind him, her arms crossed, her expression serious, her eyes flicking between the floor and me. It wasn't like her to look so guarded.

"Hey, man," Ricky said, stepping in without waiting for an invitation. "You busy?"

I raised an eyebrow. "Not at all. What's going on?"

Jess didn't answer right away. I could feel the tension in the room, her usual calm replaced by something more uneasy. Ricky looked at her before turning back to me.

"Actually, we've got something to tell you," he said, his tone light, but I could tell it wasn't the usual Ricky. There was something beneath it, something else I couldn't quite put my finger on.

My stomach tightened. "Yeah? What's up?"

Jess finally looked up, meeting my eyes, and sighed. "We're leaving, Finn," she said, the words quiet but heavy, like they were a weight she'd been carrying for a long time.

The room tilted. I blinked, trying to process the words. "What do you mean, leaving? Like... leaving Byron?"

She nodded. "Yeah. Ricky and I... we're moving to Brisbane. We're heading out in the next couple of weeks."

My mind scrambled to catch up. "Brisbane? But—why? You were both born here, Jess. Ricky... hell, you're made of Byron sand. What's going on?"

Ricky shrugged, but it was too practiced, too rehearsed. "It's just time, man. We've been talking about it for a while now. Byron's... it's changed, you know? Things feel different. We need a change of pace."

My chest tightened. "A change of pace? You're just... leaving everything behind?"

Jess stepped forward, as if trying to bridge the distance that had suddenly stretched between us. "Finn, it's not like that. It's not about leaving everything. It's about moving forward. We've been feeling stuck here, like we're trapped in this moving circle that doesn't go anywhere. Byron's not the place we want to be anymore."

My head was spinning. "But—this place is home. You know it, I know it, everyone knows it. How can you just... leave it all behind?"

Ricky sat down on the couch, his usual joking expression replaced by something more serious. "It's not about the place, man. It's about what we need right now. You ever feel like you're stuck? Like you're living in same nightmare every night, doing the same things, and it's... draining? Byron's not giving us what we need anymore."

Frustration hit me, rising up my throat. "So you're just going to give up on Byron? On everything here? Just like that?"

Jess's expression softened. She sat across from me, her gaze filled with something like regret. "We're not giving up on anything, Finn. Things are changing. For us, for everyone. You're the only one who seems stuck. You're not the same person you were all those years ago."

Her words hit harder than I expected. I had spent months trying to figure out what was wrong with me, what had shifted inside me. And now Jess was calling it out, just like that.

Ricky's voice was gentle, almost like he was trying to help me understand. "It's like... we're not the same people anymore, Finn. Things change. People change. You've been holding onto something, but deep down, I think you know it's not going to bring you what you need."

I felt the heat of my face flush. "I'm not holding on to anything. I'm just... I don't know, trying to find some clarity. So don't act like I'm stuck here, like I don't see what's happening. I've been living these cracks for months now."

Jess's face softened, and she leaned forward a bit. "That's not it, Finn. You're not seeing it for what it is. You're stuck in the past, and I think you know it."

The silence hung between us, thick and heavy with everything we hadn't said. I leaned back, my eyes darting between them, searching for something, anything that would make sense of it. Ricky and Jess—they'd always been fixtures in my life, constants in a place that felt like a second skin. Now they were leaving?

It felt like the rug had been pulled out from under me.

"So, what? You think I should just... pack up and leave too?" I asked, bitterness creeping into my voice. "That's your answer? Just leave?"

Jess's face softened further, and she spoke quietly. "We're not saying you have to leave, Finn. We're just saying that sometimes, to move forward, you have to let go of the things that keep you tied to the past. Byron's not going to give you what you need if you're not ready to face it."

Ricky nodded. "We're doing this because it feels right for us. It's what we need. We're not asking you to follow, but maybe... maybe it's time you thought about doing something different, too. You've got so much potential, Finn, but you're stuck in the same nightmare."

I sat there, trying to process their words. I felt like the walls were closing in on me, the weight of their departure pressing down harder with every sentence.

"I don't know, guys," I said, my voice small. "I don't know if I can just... leave."

Jess looked at me with a tenderness that cut through the tension. "You don't have to leave. But you have to start somewhere. Maybe it's time to stop waiting for things to change around you and start changing within you."

I sat in silence, her words echoing in my head. Finally, I exhaled, a long, slow breath. "I'll think about it," I said, barely above a whisper. But deep down, I wasn't sure I could make sense of any of it.

The idea of leaving—of leaving Byron, of leaving everything behind—felt like something too big to grasp. It was easier, almost, to stay where I knew the rhythm, the pulse, even if it was a rhythm that was slowly killing me.

But Ricky and Jess, they were gone. They had moved on in a way I hadn't. And the weight of their departure pressed heavier on me with each passing moment. Maybe it was time for me to move, too. But was I ready to leave?

It seemed like everyone was leaving me. For the first time, my cottage felt claustrophobic. The walls, once a sanctuary, now seemed to close in around me, suffocating with their weight. The familiar sounds of the waves and the rustling trees outside felt distant, muffled, as if they too had abandoned me. Jess and Ricky's words echoed in my head, a relentless rhythm that I couldn't escape. The air felt thick with unspoken things, with the spaces between us that had suddenly grown so wide. I had always found comfort in this place, but now it felt like I was trapped in a story I couldn't rewrite.

The Burden of Dreams

I sat on the weathered porch of my home, where salt and sun intertwined with the remnants of my past. The morning air was thick with humidity, curling around me like an old lover refusing to let go. I watched as the sun clawed its way above the horizon, spilling molten gold over the ocean, each wave reflecting a dream I once dared to chase. Now, those dreams lay scattered like driftwood on the shore—broken, splintered, and forgotten.

Sipping my coffee, the bitter brew grounded me in the present, stark against the sweet aroma of toasted memories wafting through my mind. The café down the street buzzed with locals and tourists, their voices melding into a cacophony of laughter and longing. I could hear snippets of conversation, fragments of lives intertwined, their hopes and disappointments rolling off their tongues like the tide. It was a symphony of existence, yet I felt like a ghost, lingering on the periphery, haunted by my own unrealized aspirations.

As a child, I spun dreams like a spider weaving silk, each one a delicate thread connecting me to a future filled with potential. But somewhere along the way, those threads frayed. The weight of societal expectations pressed down on me like an iron hand, squeezing the breath from my lungs. "Get a real job," they said. "Stop daydreaming." The world wanted me to fit neatly into boxes, to don a suit and tie, to chase stability instead of passion.

But passion was a tempest, a wild beast raging within me, demanding acknowledgment. It clawed at my insides, whispering in the stillness of the night when shadows danced on my walls. I remembered the thrill of scribbling poetry in the margins of my schoolbooks, the electric joy of creating, of pulling words from the depths of my soul. Now, that spark felt distant, dimmed by the encroaching weight of adulthood.

"Hey, Finn!" A familiar voice cut through my reverie. It was Lila, her bright energy a contrast to my pensive gloom. She plopped down beside me, her hair a wild halo in the morning light. "What's got you all broody?"

"Just thinking," I replied, my voice trailing off as I stared at the horizon. "About...everything."

"Everything's a big word. Spill it." She nudged me playfully, her eyes dancing with curiosity.

I hesitated, the words clinging to my throat like smoke. "I don't know, Lila. I feel like I'm supposed to have it all figured out by now, but..." My voice faltered. "I'm lost."

She watched me, her expression shifting from playful to concerned. "You're not the only one, you know. Everyone's fumbling around in the dark, trying to make sense of it all."

I nodded, the weight of her words settling in. "But I'm just tired of pretending to be someone I'm not. I want to create, to write, to be true to myself. But it feels like the world won't let me."

"Stuff the world," she said, her voice fierce and unapologetic. "You're not here to please anyone else. You're here for you. It's your life."

Her words were a balm, soothing the jagged edges of my insecurities, yet I felt the familiar resistance rise within me. "But what if I fail? What if I'm not good enough?"

"Failure is part of the game, Finn. You can't win if you don't play." She leaned in closer, her eyes searching mine. "You've got to stop carrying the weight of everyone else's expectations. Your dreams are yours, not theirs."

As she spoke, I felt the layers of doubt peeling away, exposing the rawness beneath. It was terrifying and exhilarating, like standing at the edge of a cliff, looking down into the unknown. "What if I'm too far gone?" I whispered, vulnerability cracking through.

Lila reached for my hand, her touch grounding. "You're not too far gone. You're right here, right now. And right now, you have the power to choose. Don't let fear dictate your life."

I closed my eyes, allowing her words to wash over me, and envisioned the dreams that had lingered in the back of my mind—stories untold, poems unspoken, the essence of who I was waiting to be unleashed. Each dream shimmered like a beacon, calling me home.

"Maybe I need to start small," I said, an ember of determination igniting within me. "Just write something. Anything. Get the words flowing again."

"Exactly! Just let it out," she encouraged, her enthusiasm infectious. "Don't overthink it. Let the words spill onto the page like the waves crashing on the shore."

My heart raced at the thought. Writing felt like a reclamation, a way to excavate the parts of myself buried under the weight of expectations. The burden of my dreams began to shift, becoming a catalyst for change rather than a ball and chain.

"Or maybe, don't start small. Maybe do something big!"

As we sat together, the sun climbing higher in the sky, I felt a shift within me. The fear that had clung to me like a shadow began to dissipate, replaced by the warmth of possibility. I was no longer merely navigating the currents of life; I was ready to dive in, to embrace the chaos and beauty of my own existence.

"I think I'll do it," I said, a smile breaking through the heaviness. "I'll write. I'll let the words come."

Lila grinned, her eyes sparkling with encouragement. "Yes! And I'll be here cheering you on every step of the way."

Lila's words settled like a gentle breeze in my chest, stirring something I thought I'd lost. The act of writing, once a daunting mountain, now felt like a path I could begin to walk. There was something raw and freeing about her energy, and in that moment, I found myself believing that maybe, just maybe, I could push past the suffocating walls I'd built around myself.

But as the weight of that new possibility settled in, something else she said lingered, pulling at the edges of my thoughts. The simple joy of writing, the spark of inspiration—how much longer would I get to share this moment with her?

Lila was watching me, her gaze warm and expectant. But there was a slight hesitation in her posture now, as if she was about to say something that might change everything.

"Finn," she began softly, her tone more serious than I expected, "I need to tell you something."

I turned toward her, immediately sensing the shift. "What's up?"

She exhaled slowly, glancing out over the ocean, as if gathering her thoughts. "I'm leaving. Next week."

The words hit like a cold wave crashing over me, and for a moment, I couldn't speak. I had braced myself for a lot of things, but this? This wasn't something I was prepared for.

"What?" My voice came out rougher than I intended. "Leaving? But... where are you going?"

She turned her eyes to meet mine, her gaze steady but filled with an almost unreadable sadness. "I'm heading north. My friends and I are traveling up the coast, to explore a bit more of Australia. It's been in the works for a while now, and I think it's time."

I felt a tightness in my chest, the realization hitting harder than I could have expected. For the first time since I'd known her, I felt a sharp, unanticipated sense of loss. It was real.

"But... we were just talking about writing together. You're really leaving?" I could hear the pleading in my voice, the uncertainty I hadn't intended to reveal.

Lila looked away for a moment, as though considering how to respond. "I know. I know we had plans. And I want to keep writing, Finn. But I need this. I've been feeling like I need a change, a new place, a new direction. I'm not sure what I'll find out there, but I think I'll find something important. For myself."

The words stung, but they also made sense in a way I couldn't quite articulate. I had seen her this way before—restless, always seeking something, always searching for meaning. But hearing her say it so plainly, that she was leaving, hit deeper than I had anticipated.

"I get it," I said, though the words felt hollow in my mouth. "But it feels like just when I'm ready to take a step, you're... you're going. And I don't know how to feel about that."

Lila's lips parted, and I could see the internal struggle on her face. "I'm sorry, Finn. I didn't want it to feel like this. But we can't control timing, can we? Maybe it's just the way things are meant to go."

I ran my hand through my hair, my mind spinning. The timing had never been worse, it seemed. Just when I was ready to break through my own hesitation, Lila was preparing to leave. It was real. Wasn't there some cosmic joke at play? Or maybe it was just life, unbothered by the intricacies of my plans and dreams.

"Are we... still going to write?" I asked, my voice uncertain, even a little small. The thought of her leaving didn't just feel like a physical absence—it was as if the anchor that had been keeping me steady was suddenly being yanked out from under me.

She smiled softly, but the sadness lingered in her eyes. "Of course. I'm not disappearing completely. We can still share what we create. We can still work on ideas, even if we're not in the same place. I'll still be here, in a way. And you'll be there, doing your thing."

"Yeah, but... I won't be able to just walk over to you when I hit a block. I won't have you there, reminding me to just write, to just let go. It's not the same." I felt the frustration bubble up—anger at the circumstances, at the universe, for making everything feel like it was always just out of reach. This was real. "I don't know if I can do this without you."

Lila reached across the space between us, her fingers brushing mine in a gesture that felt too brief, too fleeting. "You don't need me to do it, Finn. You've got everything you need inside of you already. I'm just here to remind you of that. But it's your journey. Don't forget that."

Her words felt like a lifeline, but they also felt like a goodbye.

"I'll miss you," I said before I could stop myself, the words heavy with unspoken meaning. I wanted to tell her how much her presence had meant to me, how much I had relied on her, not just for inspiration but for the connection I'd come to crave. But somehow, all I could manage was that simple sentence.

Lila smiled, a wistful, bittersweet curve of her lips. "I'll miss you too, Finn. But you'll be okay. You're stronger than you think."

For a moment, neither of us spoke. We just sat there, watching the waves crash against the shore, feeling the pull of the ocean and the shifting tides of life. A strange sense of finality settled between us, a quiet understanding that things were changing, that we were changing, and there was no stopping it.

"So, when do you leave?" I asked quietly, trying to hold on to some semblance of normality.

"Next week," she said, her voice soft. "I'll still be around for a few more days. We could hang out, maybe write some more before I go. But after that, I'll be gone. It's just... time, you know?"

"Yeah," I muttered, my gaze dropping to the ground. "It's time."

Lila stood, her movements graceful, like she was already preparing to step into a different chapter of her life. "I'll see you before I go, Finn. And when I'm gone, just remember—you're never really alone in what you create. We're always connected, through the words."

I nodded, even though part of me wasn't sure if I believed it. But I wasn't ready to say goodbye yet. Not just yet.

As she walked away, I watched her retreating figure, a strange emptiness blossoming in my chest. The wave of uncertainty hit me again, stronger than before. She was leaving, and I didn't know how to navigate this new reality, but one thing was for sure—her absence was going to be felt deeply, in ways I may not be ready to face.

Ella

I stood on the beach at Byron Bay, the early morning sun casting golden shards across the sand. The tide rolled in, a rhythmic pulse that mirrored the ebb and flow of my thoughts. Each wave crashed against the shore, retreating only to return, a reminder of life's unyielding cycles. I watched as the water licked at my feet, cool and inviting, pulling back to reveal glistening shells—treasures buried in the sands of time.

It was a day like any other, yet today felt different. The air was thick with the scent of salt and promise, a faint whisper of nostalgia curling around me like sea mist. I closed my eyes, letting the sounds of the ocean envelop me—the rush of water, the distant cries of gulls, the laughter of children playing further down the beach. Life thrived in every corner, yet I felt like a spectator, standing at the edge of a world pulsing with energy while I remained suspended in quiet contemplation.

I remembered the highs—those fleeting moments of joy that shimmered like sunlight on water. The thrill of my first published poem, laughter shared with friends under starlit skies, the tender warmth of love that once ignited my heart. But those memories were intertwined with shadows—regrets, failures, and losses that gnawed at me, leaving an ache that refused to fade. The beauty of life felt tainted by its harsh realities, and I grappled with the relentless push and pull of hope and despair.

"Hey, Finn!" A voice jolted me from my reverie. It was Ella, her hair a wild cascade of curls dancing in the wind. She approached, her smile brightening the dullness I had felt. "You look like you're about to drown in your thoughts. Come on, let's go for a swim!"

I hesitated, my heart heavy with uncertainty. "I don't know. What if the waves are too strong? What if—"

"Stop it!" She laughed, cutting me off. "That's exactly what I mean. You're always worrying about what could go wrong. Just jump in! The ocean won't bite. Come on! It's time!"

I looked at her, standing there with her carefree energy, the sunlight catching the tips of her curls, and I felt something stir in me, something familiar, something that had been buried for far too long. Ella's voice was like a gentle wind, coaxing me, reminding me of the wild abandon I used to have. The fear that had wrapped itself around my chest seemed so distant in that moment, though it still lingered at the edges.

"I don't know, Ella," I said again, my voice quieter this time. My mind flashed to the memory of that day, the day she drowned—the way the sea had seemed so calm, so welcoming, and then, in an instant, everything had changed. I could still hear the waves crashing, the air thick with salt and fear. "I haven't swum in years."

Ella's expression softened, the playfulness in her eyes turning to something deeper, something understanding. "I know, Finn. But you've got to stop living like the past is holding you down. You're drowning in your fear, not the ocean. You don't have to swim alone anymore."

Her words hit me harder than I expected. It was as if the weight of the years since her death—the silence, the grief, the self-imposed isolation—had been building, and now, in this strange moment, it all began to crack. I hadn't realized how much I'd allowed that fear, that loss, to become a barrier in my life, how I'd let the memory of her drown me in a way.

The ocean stretched before me, vast and inviting, as if it were waiting for me to make my move, to step back into it. My breath hitched. The pull of the water, the rhythm of the waves, it was all so familiar, so alive, but so distant. What if something happened? What if I couldn't find my way back?

Ella must have sensed the hesitation in my eyes because she stepped closer, her presence almost like a balm, soothing the storm inside me.

"You don't have to do this for anyone but you, Finn. But there's freedom in the water," she said, her voice carrying the same sense of adventure she had always had, the same joy in simply existing. "When I was alive, I never worried about how deep the water was, how far the current could pull. I just... I just swam. The ocean always had a way of bringing me back, no matter how far I went."

DOWN AND OUT IN BYRON BAY

My eyes searched hers, and for a moment, I felt the pull of something I hadn't allowed myself to feel in a long time: hope.

Ella reached out, her hand brushing mine lightly, her fingers warm with a kind of reassurance that made the doubt in me start to loosen. "You never know until you try. And if you do it, you won't be alone. You've never been alone, Finn. You just have to remember that."

I swallowed, tasting the salt in the air, the faint tang of the sea filling my senses. She was right, in a way. I hadn't truly been alone—not really. The people I had loved, the ones who had shaped me, their spirits were still here in ways I hadn't allowed myself to acknowledge. Ella, her laughter, her brightness—they were never gone. Maybe the only thing that had really left was my ability to see them, to feel their presence in the here and now.

"You'll be with me?" I asked, unsure of whether I was asking her or the memory of her.

"I always have been," she whispered, and there was something in her voice that made it feel like she wasn't just a memory anymore, that she was something alive in me, a part of me I had locked away for too long.

A tremor ran through my body, something deep, something I couldn't ignore. Slowly, I began to step forward, my feet sinking into the soft, wet sand. The sound of the waves grew louder in my ears, the pull of the ocean wrapping around me like a song I had forgotten the lyrics to.

Ella's laughter rang out in the air, light and free. "Come on, Finn. Let's see what you're really made of."

I stood at the water's edge for a moment longer, my chest tight, but my heart finally open. Then, with a deep breath, I stepped forward, feeling the coolness of the waves rise around my ankles, the surge of the sea slipping beneath my feet like a familiar embrace.

The first wave hit me, cold and sharp, and I gasped as it rushed over my chest. For a split second, everything inside me froze—the panic, the fear, the memories of that day—but then, just as quickly, they faded, swallowed by the rhythm of the ocean. The water pulled me deeper, and I pushed forward, each stroke feeling more natural than the last, each breath of salt air filling me with a clarity I hadn't known in years.

Ella's voice echoed in my mind, a constant presence, urging me on. "That's it, Finn. You're doing it. Let go."

And for the first time in a long time, I did. I let the water hold me, let it carry me, and for once, I didn't feel like I was drowning. I felt... alive.

"See?" Ella shouted over the roar of the surf. "This is what it's about! Letting go!"

As we floated on our backs, staring up at the endless blue sky, I felt a shift within me. The rhythm of the ocean, the rise and fall of the tides, echoed the rhythms of my own life. Moments of joy mingled with sorrow, each high giving way to a low, and in between, there was a fragile beauty—a transition that shaped who I was.

"It's like life, isn't it?" I mused, gazing at the clouds drifting lazily overhead. "The waves come and go. Sometimes they're gentle, sometimes they crash hard. But they always return."

"Exactly," Ella said, her voice softened by the water. "We can't control the tide, but we can learn to ride it. Embrace the changes. Find beauty in the flow."

The realization washed over me like the sun breaking through the clouds. Life wasn't meant to be a constant state of happiness or despair; it was a series of movements, a dance between light and shadow. I had spent so long clinging to the highs, fearing the lows, that I had forgotten to appreciate the moments in between. The laughter with friends, the quiet solitude of a sunrise, the bittersweet taste of a memory—each was a thread in the tapestry of my existence, adding depth and richness to my story.

Emerging from the water, I felt reborn, cleansed of the heaviness that had clung to me. Ella and I sprawled on the warm sand, the sun kissing our skin as we caught our breath. A gentle breeze rustled through the palm trees, and for a moment, time seemed to stand still.

"Do you ever think about how far we've come?" Ella asked, her eyes reflecting the shimmering sea. "All those moments, both good and bad, have led us here."

I nodded, the weight of her words resonating deep within me. "I think I've spent too much time resisting change. It's like fighting the tide; it just pulls you under."

"Right? And what if instead, we learned to float?" Ella's smile was infectious, her optimism wrapping around me like a warm blanket. "Embrace the shifts, the uncertainty. It's where the magic happens."

I considered this, realizing how often I had chased certainty, only to be met with disappointment. What if, instead, I surrendered to the flow? What if I allowed life to unfold naturally, trusting in its rhythm?

"I want to try," I said slowly, determination growing within me. "To embrace the highs and lows, to accept the changes. To find beauty in all of it."

Ella beamed, a light igniting in her eyes. "That's the spirit! Life is messy and beautiful, just like the ocean. Let it take you where it wants to go. You have to let go, Finn."

"You have to let go!" Ella's voice trembled in the air, but there was no mistaking the finality in it. The wind whispered through the trees, carrying with it the weight of something unspeakable. Her presence, once so vivid, began to dissolve, like the first light of dawn creeping over a dark horizon, pulling the night away, piece by piece.

"I too have to let go," she continued, and her words were soft, as though the very air around us was holding its breath, unwilling to let them escape. She reached out, her hand floating inches from mine, and in that moment, I could feel the space between us widening—no longer the electric connection of shared memories, but the aching distance of what we could never reclaim.

"After today... I'm not coming back." Her voice cracked, and I could feel her struggle against the pull of something greater than either of us. "It's time for me to leave."

Her words hit me like a punch to the gut. The ocean around us, once an embrace, felt like it was pulling away, a thousand miles of emptiness between us, swallowing her up. It was the final, unspoken truth I had been terrified of, the one thing I hadn't allowed myself to believe. That she could really leave. That she had to leave.

The waves crashed louder, a harsh, unforgiving sound, and in that moment, it felt like the world itself was breaking apart, the shoreline slipping through my fingers like sand. I reached for her, desperation clawing at my throat, but my hand passed through her like smoke.

"No, please," I begged, my voice raw, as though the words had been trapped in my chest for years, desperate to escape. "You can't. You—"

Her face, that face I had carried in my heart for so long, was blurry now, fading. She smiled, but it wasn't the bright, reckless smile I remembered. It was soft, bittersweet. She looked at me with the kind of love that wasn't tethered to time or space but had always been there, a constant, lingering like the scent of the ocean itself.

"You have to live, Finn," she whispered, her eyes locking onto mine with a clarity that shattered everything I thought I knew about grief. "You have to stop waiting for me to come back, to fix the broken parts of you. I'm not your anchor anymore."

I wanted to scream. I wanted to hold on to her so tightly that the world couldn't take her away, that the past couldn't rip her from me. But it was already too late. The more I tried to grasp at her, the more she slipped away, fading with the tide, leaving only a hollow space where once she had been.

"Ella, I..." I trailed off, unable to finish the words, my throat closing in on itself. I couldn't breathe, couldn't speak. She was slipping through my hands like water, and no matter how tightly I gripped, I couldn't stop her.

"I know," she said, her voice almost a sigh now. "I know you'll be okay. You'll find your way, Finn. You've always had the strength within you... you just need to believe it again."

And then, before I could even say goodbye, before I could find the words to express the ache in my chest, she was gone. Like a dream fading in the light of day, like a bird flying into the sky, her presence evaporated into nothingness, leaving only the bitter taste of salt and loss in the air.

I stood there, frozen in the vast, empty space that had once been filled with her, feeling like I was unraveling, like a part of me was being buried beneath the waves, never to resurface. The ocean roared louder, as if mocking me, as if telling me to let her go, to let it all go.

And yet, in the silence that followed, I could still feel her—her warmth, her laughter, her love—clinging to me like a memory I couldn't outrun. Even as she left, I realized she wasn't truly gone. She had always been a part of me, woven into the fabric of my soul, a thread I couldn't unravel no matter how hard I tried.

The wind picked up, the cold air biting at my skin, but I didn't move. I stood there, alone now, the ocean stretching endlessly before me, the horizon a blur in the distance. I closed my eyes, letting the tears I had been holding back fall freely. They weren't just for her. They were for me, for the parts of myself I had lost in the wake of her absence.

And slowly, painfully, I began to understand. I had to let go.

DOWN AND OUT IN BYRON BAY

THE SUN SANK LOW, CASTING the world in a soft glow of orange and pink, and with it, something inside me shifted. The weight I had carried for so long—of grief, of longing, of unspoken goodbyes—began to lift, like a tide pulling away from the shore. Ella was gone, and for the first time, I allowed myself to accept it.

I stood still, breathing in the salty air, and smiled at the horizon. It wasn't the smile of someone who had lost, but of someone who was finally free. Free from the ghosts that had haunted me, free from the fear that had shackled me to a past I couldn't change. It felt like a release, a deep, guttural letting go, as though my soul had been holding its breath for far too long.

I looked out at the waves, crashing against the rocks in their eternal rhythm. Each wave, each swell, was a reminder—life keeps moving, keeps changing. I could no longer pretend I could control it. I had to surrender to it. To the ebb and flow of time, of existence, of who I was becoming.

For the first time in years, I felt like I could breathe again. I was no longer tethered to the past, no longer defined by what I had lost. I was free. And in that freedom, there was peace.

An Inheritance of Silence

I leaned against the weathered railing of my old porch, staring out at the undulating waves of Byron Bay. The ocean was a churning blue, glinting with shards of sunlight that pierced through the morning haze. I took a deep breath, letting the salt air fill my lungs, but today it felt heavier—charged with something unnameable, a whisper of inevitability.

Just moments before, I had received a phone call that shattered the fragile calm of my morning. My grandmother, a silent sentinel in my life, had passed away. The news came wrapped in a thin layer of formality, delivered by a distant relative whose voice trembled like a falling leaf. "She left you something," they had said, their words stumbling into silence, leaving an echo that reverberated in the pit of my stomach. "I left the box on your front lawn." She hung up.

The sun had already begun its descent, casting long shadows across the yard, when I noticed the box. It was old—faded brown cardboard, the edges curling as though it had been through more than one storm. I hadn't heard anyone drop it off, but there it was, waiting for me like some forgotten relic of a past I was struggling to leave behind.

I hesitated, standing in the doorway for a long moment, before I finally crossed the threshold. My heart felt heavy in my chest as I knelt to pick it up. The box smelled faintly of dust and old wood, a smell that took me back to my grandmother's house. The moment I set it down on my coffee table, the lid popped open, revealing a jumble of photos, trinkets, and knick-knacks that looked like they had been packed away decades ago. My hands trembled slightly as I pulled out the first photo—a black-and-white image of my grandmother, young and radiant, standing beside a man I didn't recognize. She was smiling, her eyes full of a hope that seemed foreign to me now. I wondered who he was—was he a lover, a friend, or someone from a time before I could remember?

I sifted through the pictures, one by one. Some were of my parents, before they had me, their faces caught in moments of laughter, a time when they were still strangers to the weight of responsibility. Other pictures were of family gatherings, birthdays and holidays—faces I barely recognized, their names a blur of distant relatives who had come and gone, their lives briefly intersecting with mine before fading into the past.

There was a trinket next—a small porcelain bird, cracked along one wing. I had seen it on my grandmother's mantelpiece, always positioned so carefully, as if it were a symbol of something. Maybe the fragility of life, or the way she had held on to every moment, every memory, even when the world around her seemed to slip away.

I reached for something else, a delicate locket. It was tarnished now, but I could still make out the engraving on the front: For the one I love. I opened it cautiously, half-expecting to see a picture of my grandfather, the man I'd only heard about in stories. Instead, there was a faded photo of a woman I didn't recognize. She was young, standing in front of a house I couldn't place, a bouquet of flowers clutched in her hands. I stared at it for a long while, feeling the tug of some unknown connection. Who was she? My grandmother's sister? A lost friend?

I let the locket fall back into the box and closed my eyes for a moment, trying to summon the memories that had always felt just out of reach. I remembered my grandmother's hands—wrinkled and worn from years of work—but always gentle, always steady. How she used to hum as she moved through the house, a soft, comforting sound that made everything feel safe. I could still hear her voice sometimes, a whisper in the back of my mind, urging me to keep going, even when it felt like everything was falling apart.

The box felt like a time capsule, holding pieces of a life I had only touched on the surface of. But now, in the quiet of my living room, I was surrounded by fragments of her world—memories I had never known, stories I had never asked about, lives that were part of the fabric of her existence but were completely foreign to mine. I felt like an intruder, sorting through the remnants of something I hadn't fully understood.

ALEX TELMAN

The clutter of the box seemed to overwhelm me, the weight of it pressing down. It wasn't just the things inside it, but the unspoken questions they raised. Why hadn't I asked more about my grandmother's past? Why had I assumed that the woman who raised me had no story beyond the one she'd shared with me? Why had I let her stories fade into the background of my life until it was too late to learn them?

I could feel the ache of regret deep in my chest, a pull that seemed to stretch between the past and the present. The memories that were now scattered across the floor felt like a silent reproach—a reminder of everything I had missed by not paying attention, by not asking the right questions when I had the chance. I wanted to know who my grandmother was outside of the role she played in my life, to understand the woman she had been before she became the version of herself I had known.

The box was a testament to the fragility of time, and the way we only see the full picture when it's too late to piece it together. It was filled with things that meant something once—things that had been held close, kept safe, waiting for a time when they would matter again. But I had no idea what to do with them now, no idea how to make sense of the scattered pieces of her life in front of me.

I stared at the box, lost in thought, as if waiting for some kind of sign. A realization slowly crept over me, one I had been avoiding for too long: the only way to understand her was to let go of the distance I had kept between us. I couldn't keep carrying the weight of my assumptions and regrets. I needed to piece together her story, not just for myself, but for the sake of the legacy she had left behind.

I closed the box, quietly, as if sealing something precious inside. For now, it would stay there, a reminder that the past is never truly gone—it lives on in the objects we hold, the stories we share, and the questions we choose to ask.

My grandmother's home had been a sanctuary, filled with the scent of chamomile tea and the creaking of old floorboards that whispered secrets of generations past. She had been the keeper of stories, each one a thread in the tapestry of my family's history, yet her life had been marked by a series of silences—secrets buried deep like roots in the soil.

"Why didn't you tell me?" I whispered to cardboard box, the question hanging in the air like a ghost. "Why did you choose silence?"

My mind raced as I contemplated the implications of her legacy. Silence was both a refuge and a prison. It was the space where pain could fester, unaddressed and ignored, yet it was also a shield—protecting us from the raw edges of truth. I could feel the weight of unspoken words pressing down on me, as if the very walls of my grandmother's home were soaked in the essence of everything left unsaid.

The phone rang, a sharp intrusion that pulled me from my reverie. The phone's sudden ring jolted me, its shrill tone cutting through the quiet air like an unwanted visitor. I stared at the screen for a moment before my gaze flicked to the caller ID. The words Caller Unknown blinked back at me, stirring an immediate sense of unease. Hesitating, I lifted the receiver, a strange knot tightening in my stomach.

"Hello?" My voice came out quieter than I intended, the weight of the moment pressing down on me.

"Good afternoon, is this Finn Sullivan?" a deep voice asked, slightly muffled as though coming from behind a desk.

"Yeah, this is Finn." My thumb hovered over the button to hang up, but something told me I needed to hear this out.

"This is Peter Hawthorne, a lawyer with Hawthorne & Bellamy. I'm calling regarding an inheritance from your grandmother, Annabelle Carter." His words hung in the air, and the sudden mention of her name hit me harder than I expected.

I stood still, my mind a blur, trying to connect the dots. Inheritance? My grandmother? It was so out of left field. What else could she possibly have left for me?

"Sorry, an inheritance?" I repeated, needing to hear the words again.

"Yes, that's correct. Your grandmother has left you something in her will. Your mother instructed us to reach out and ensure you were made aware of the matter. If it's convenient, could you come down to my office this afternoon? I have the documents ready, and I'd like to go over them with you in person."

I took a shaky breath, trying to piece together what I was hearing. My mother. The mention of her stirred up its own swirl of emotions. There was always tension there—complicated, never quite settled—and now she was involved in something I didn't even understand.

"I... I wasn't expecting this. What exactly is it about?" My voice cracked despite my attempt to keep it steady.

"I'm afraid I can't go into specifics over the phone, Mr. Sullivan. I'd really prefer to explain it all in person. If you're free, I can see you this afternoon—say, in the next hour or so?"

His polite tone felt almost too impersonal, like the kind of voice you use when you know you're about to say something that might change someone's life. And maybe that's exactly what was happening now.

"I... I'll be there," I managed to say, my throat dry. "I'll head to your office now."

"Good," Peter replied. "I'll be expecting you. The office is at 27 Bayview Street, just past the café on the corner. Take your time. We'll be here."

The line went dead, and I stood frozen, the phone still pressed to my ear. What had just happened? Inheritance? My grandmother had left me something, something of significance, enough for her lawyer to be involved.

I walked to the window, looking out at the streets of Byron Bay, still bathed in that lazy afternoon light. The air felt thick all of a sudden—full of unspoken things. My grandmother's ghost had been all afternoon, in the trinkets she'd left behind, in the faded photographs I had just uncovered, but now... now there was something more. Some part of her had been waiting for me to find this. Waiting for this moment.

I shook my head, trying to shake off the flood of uncertainty rising in me. Was this some kind of mistake? A mix-up? And what did my mother have to do with it?

I grabbed my jacket and pulled the door open, stepping out into the warm air. As I walked towards town, a heavy unease settled in my chest. I didn't know what to expect from this meeting, but the knot in my stomach only tightened with every step I took.

The walk to the lawyer's office felt like it took forever, the shops blurring past me as my mind raced through a thousand scenarios. I had always thought my grandmother's life—and her death—had been relatively simple, straightforward. A woman who lived in Sydney, who purchased the small plot of land I lived on 60 years ago, who put up a cottage I call home, who never came to visit, who passed away quietly after a long life. But now, with the mention of an inheritance, a part of me wondered how much of her I had really known. How much had she kept hidden? Why was she leaving me something, and why had my mother been involved?

The lawyer's office was located in an older building just off the main street. The kind of place where the windows had yellowed with age, but the sign outside still gleamed in the afternoon sun. My breath was shallow, my pulse quickening.

Inside, the office smelled faintly of leather-bound books and old paper, the air thick with the scent of history. Peter Hawthorne was waiting behind a desk, his face polite but unreadable.

"Mr. Sullivan," he said, standing up as I entered. "Please, take a seat."

I sat down slowly, my hands resting in my lap as the lawyer set a thick envelope in front of me. The seal on it was old, worn—definitely my grandmother's handwriting.

"This is the will," he explained, pushing it toward me. "As I mentioned, there are things in here you'll need to understand. Your grandmother's wishes were quite clear."

I took the envelope in my hands, but my fingers shook slightly as I turned it over. Whatever was inside—whatever this was—it was about to change everything.

I felt the weight of my grandmother's silence, but now it felt different. It was not just an absence; it was a call to action. The stories that remained untold were now mine to uncover. The inheritance was not merely a collection of photographs or artifacts; it was an invitation to confront the silence, to share the burden of memory, and to reclaim the legacy of our family.

I closed my eyes, inhaling deeply. A storm loomed not merely on the horizon, but within me, a flicker of hope ignited—a hope that perhaps the silence would finally be broken, that the stories would be told, and that the legacy we inherited would not be one of absence, but of connection and understanding.

I sat there for a moment, my fingers gripping the envelope tightly, its rough paper texture grounding me to the present. The air in the office was stale, and the quiet seemed to amplify the pounding of my own heart. A million thoughts swirled in my mind, but none of them seemed to make sense. What had my grandmother left for me, and why now? Why had she waited until after her death to reveal this part of our story? It was as if, through some unspoken agreement, she had been waiting for me to become ready.

For the longest time, I had lived under the shadow of her memory—her absence, her quiet wisdom. But now, sitting across from this lawyer, it felt like she was standing right beside me. This wasn't just about money or possessions. This was about legacy. This was about unlocking the door she had kept closed for so long, behind which lay truths that I'd never had the courage to seek.

The silence in the room grew heavier as I stared at the envelope, my thumb tracing the edges of the seal. It wasn't just a legal document; it felt like a puzzle, a map, a key to something I couldn't yet comprehend. Was this the moment where everything shifted? Where I stopped being the boy who drifted through life, haunted by regrets, and started becoming the man who could truly understand his roots? The man who could finally give voice to the questions that had plagued me for so long?

I looked up at the lawyer, who was watching me closely but gave nothing away. His face was calm, professional—too professional. I wanted to shout at him, demand answers, but I knew this wasn't his story to tell. It was mine. Whatever my grandmother had left for me, whatever she had been trying to say, it was now my responsibility to understand it, to give it meaning.

The thought terrified me. I wasn't ready. How could I be ready? What if I opened the envelope and found only more questions? What if it was too much for me to carry?

I could hear the faint sound of traffic outside, the world still moving on, oblivious to the moment unfolding in this small office. But the world felt different now, and I wasn't sure whether I could still play the part I had been cast in. Was I meant to continue the path my grandmother had set for me? Or was this inheritance some kind of rebirth, a chance to begin again, but on my own terms?

I couldn't stay here forever, frozen in indecision. I needed to make a choice.

I slid my finger under the seal, breaking it gently. The crackling of the paper felt louder than it should have. The envelope opened with a soft sigh, revealing a stack of papers, neatly folded and tied with a ribbon that looked like it had once been red but had faded with time. I hesitated, my breath catching in my throat. I didn't know what I was looking for. I didn't know what to expect. But I knew it was something that would change me—something that would change the course of my life.

Slowly, almost reverently, I unfolded the top page. The writing was elegant, the ink slightly faded, but the words were unmistakable:

"To my beloved grandson, Finn..."

I paused, reading the words again, letting them settle in. My grandmother's handwriting, her familiar loops and flourishes. She had written this for me. Her voice was here, within these pages, calling me forward into a future I hadn't anticipated but was now undeniably a part of.

I felt a tremor run through me, not from fear but from a deep, resonant sense of... recognition. This wasn't a gift. It wasn't just something left behind. It was a responsibility. A legacy. One I had to honor.

I glanced up at the lawyer, who was still waiting, still silent. His eyes were kind, but I could see a flicker of something there, something that suggested he, too, had seen this before. He knew what it meant to find a part of yourself that had been hidden, buried beneath years of waiting, of hesitation.

"You said there were things I'd need to understand," I finally spoke, my voice more steady than I felt. "What does this mean? What is this—really?"

His expression softened, but he said nothing. It was clear now: the answers lay not in him, but in me. The inheritance wasn't just something material—it was a shift, a call to dig deeper into the past, to bring the hidden things to light. And I had to be the one to decide what to do with it.

I set the papers down gently, the weight of them heavy in my hands. This was it. The beginning of something new, something terrifying and beautiful. I had no idea where it would lead, but I knew I was done running. Done pretending that I could stay on the surface forever, afraid to dive in.

My grandmother had given me the keys to unlock the door. It was up to me now to open it.

But what was on the other side?

ALEX TELMAN

I stared at the pile of papers, my grandmother's delicate handwriting, the words scrawled in ink that seemed to tremble with their own truth. These were the stories she never told me aloud, the truths hidden beneath years of silence. Her silence. My silence.

I felt the weight of the inheritance she'd left me. It wasn't the land, the cottage, or the small fortune she'd tucked away over the years. It was something heavier, something intangible: silence. The silence she'd lived with, the silence that had been passed down, unspoken but understood. The silence that suffocated everything real, everything raw.

It had always been there, a presence in the room, a presence I hadn't wanted to face. The way she never talked about my father, the way she never spoke of her own past, her own griefs. She had taught me to survive in it. To keep things inside. To keep quiet. To look straight ahead and pretend that everything was fine, even when it wasn't.

And now, here I was, standing at the precipice, holding the key to unlock all the things we had never said. The questions I'd buried for years—about my father, about my family, about myself—swirled in my head like ghosts. The silence had been a shield, yes, but it was also a prison.

I knew the moment I opened this door, I couldn't go back. There would be no more pretending. No more safe distance between me and the truth. Whatever was hidden in these papers, whatever had been left unsaid, was going to shatter the carefully constructed version of myself I had held together for so long.

But I also knew it was the only way forward. I couldn't live in the silence anymore.

Was I ready for what I might find?

I looked at that first sheet of paper again, my fingers trembling slightly. The words on the page seemed to pulse with a life of their own as if they were waiting for me to read them, waiting for me to finally listen to what had been buried beneath the surface for so long.

I had been holding my breath for years. But now, I had to exhale. Now, I had to face what had been waiting in the silence.

I took a deep breath and began.

Homecoming

The sun dipped low over Byron Bay, casting a golden haze across the familiar landscape. I stood at the edge of the sand, the grains warm beneath my feet—a sensation I'd taken for granted in my youth. The waves rolled in, rhythmically kissing the shore, their whispers reminding me of a simpler time—before adulthood muddied the clarity of my heart. I was back, yet the town felt both achingly familiar and painfully distant, like an old friend whose face I had forgotten.

I took a deep breath, the salty air filling my lungs, mingling with the scent of jasmine wafting from nearby gardens. It was an intoxicating blend that evoked memories of long-lost summers—a time when laughter echoed through the streets and I felt invincible, chasing sunsets with a surfboard under my arm, dreams vast as the ocean itself. But now, those echoes had faded, replaced by a lingering ache—a regret I couldn't shake, a shadow of choices made.

Looking out at the horizon where the sky met the sea, I saw a vast expanse that seemed to swallow everything whole. This place, once a sanctuary, now felt like a cage. I had spent years trying to escape the weight of expectations, the suffocating embrace of conformity. But here I was, facing the ghosts of my past, each wave crashing against the shore a reminder of the life I had walked away from.

The laughter of children broke my reverie, a haunting melody mingling with the calls of seagulls overhead. They played near the water's edge, splashing joyfully, oblivious to the complexities of life. Their innocence was a balm for my fraying spirit, but it also stung. I longed for that simplicity, yet I knew too well the cost of such freedom. The tides of life had pulled me far from the shores of youth, leaving me stranded in a world of my own making, filled with questions that echoed louder than any child's laughter.

I turned away from the sea, drawn to the small café that had once been a favorite haunt. The walls were painted a cheerful blue, but the paint was peeling now, revealing the weathered wood beneath. I pushed open the door, the bell above chiming softly—a sound that felt like a welcome and a warning all at once.

Inside, the aroma of strong coffee mixed with the sweetness of pastries. The barista, a young woman with inked arms and a warm smile, recognized me immediately. "Finn! Haven't seen you in ages!" Her voice was bright, cutting through my haze of nostalgia.

"Yeah, it's been a while," I replied, forcing a smile that didn't quite reach my eyes. "Just... came back to see how things were."

She nodded, understanding unspoken between us. "You know how it is. The town keeps changing, but some things stay the same. It's good to have you back."

I nodded, the words hanging heavy between us. I ordered a coffee, the taste bitter on my tongue, mirroring the bitterness of my unresolved feelings. As I sat down at a small table by the window, I watched the world outside. Couples strolled hand in hand, their laughter intertwining with the wind, while a group of surfers debated the best breaks for the day. I felt like a ghost in my own life, trapped in a moment of stillness while everything else flowed seamlessly around me.

In the café's quiet corners, I found remnants of my past—old photographs hanging crookedly on the walls, moments captured in time. I traced the lines of a black-and-white image depicting a group of friends, their faces lit with unrestrained joy. I barely recognized the carefree boy in the picture, the one who believed the world was full of possibilities. That boy had vanished, swallowed by the tides of time.

As I sipped my coffee, my mind wandered to the decisions that had led me here—the love I had lost, the friendships that had faded, the paths not taken. Each recollection was a thread woven into the fabric of my life, yet I felt the fray—an unraveling that left me exposed.

I recalled a conversation with my mother, her voice trembling with concern. "Finn, home isn't just a place. It's a feeling. You need to find it within yourself." At the time, I dismissed her words as sentimental nonsense.

But standing here now, with the weight of the past pressing down on me, I wondered if she had been right all along.

The rain began to fall, pattering softly against the window. I watched the droplets race each other, each one a small journey of its own, merging and splitting in a delicate dance. Life was much the same—a series of choices, some leading to joy, others to regret. Yet in each drop, I saw a glimmer of beauty, a reminder that even the storm could be transformative.

"Hey, everything okay?" The barista's voice pulled me from my thoughts, her brow furrowed with concern.

"Just... thinking," I replied, my voice barely above a whisper.

"Yeah, it's a lot to process," she said, setting down a fresh pastry in front of me. "But don't forget, sometimes it's okay to just be. To feel the weight of it all."

I smiled, grateful for her understanding. "Thanks. I guess I've just been trying to figure things out."

"Life's a mess, isn't it? But that's where the beauty lies," she said, her eyes sparkling with a wisdom beyond her years. "You'll find your way, Finn. Just give yourself time."

I watched her walk away, her words echoing in my mind. There was a freedom in acknowledging the mess, in accepting that home wasn't a physical location but a state of being. It was the warmth of connection, the comfort of familiarity, and the acceptance of imperfection.

With renewed resolve, I took a deep breath, the air thick with the scent of coffee and rain. I could feel the storm within me settling, the tumult giving way to clarity. Home was here, in the laughter of children, in the embrace of old friends, in the quiet moments of reflection. It was the acceptance of my past, a recognition of the beauty in my scars.

As the rain fell heavier outside, I stepped back into the world, ready to face the future. I would paint again, write again, live again—embracing the uncertainty, navigating the chaos, and discovering the beauty that lay within the heart of it all.

Byron Bay remained the same yet changed, and I understood now that I, too, was both a part of it and separate from it—a mosaic of moments stitched together by memories, regrets, and dreams. Homecoming was not a destination but a journey, and as I walked toward the surf, the ocean whispering my name, I felt a sense of belonging rising within me like the tide.

I now owned a home.

Roots and Wings

I sat on the weathered wooden steps of my small cottage in Byron Bay, the salty air wrapping around me like an old friend. The cottage, with its faded blue paint and peeling shutters, felt like a relic of simpler times—a monument to dreams once bright, now softened by the relentless sun. I could hear the distant crash of waves, their rhythm echoing the turmoil inside me. This place, with its sandy streets and bohemian charm, was both a sanctuary and a cage—a spot where my roots intertwined with the desire to spread my wings.

It was late afternoon, the sun dipping low, spilling golden light that danced on the surface of the ocean. The sky became a canvas of oranges and purples, a promise of twilight. I traced my fingers along the rough wood of the steps, lost in thought. I had lived in Byron for years, yet I often felt like an outsider, adrift between the life I had built and the aspirations that pulled at me like the tides.

Flickers of childhood memories danced in my mind—my father's rough hands, calloused from labor, and my mother's laughter, a balm that soothed the stings of a hard life. They had instilled in me a sense of responsibility, a grounding that tied me to this earth. Yet, as I grew older, the weight of their expectations began to feel suffocating, anchoring me in a world I no longer wanted to inhabit.

"Finn!" A voice broke through my reverie. It was Jess, her tone a blend of warmth and sorrow, pulling me from the depths of my thoughts. I looked up to see her and Ricky walking toward me, the sun catching in her dark hair, casting a golden halo around her. Ricky trailed behind, hands shoved in his pockets, his expression unreadable. The sight of them together made my chest tighten.

Jess smiled, but there was an edge to it, a kind of finality that had been building between us over the past few days. They had told me this moment was coming. It was inevitable. They were leaving Byron Bay. After all the years of living here, it felt like the end of an era, not just for them, but for me, too. Jess had always been the free spirit, the one who was quick to pick up and leave when the world called her name. Ricky, on the other hand, was more grounded, always hanging on to the past a little longer than he should.

"I thought you might be out here," Jess said, her voice gentle, almost apologetic. "Can we talk?"

I nodded, though my throat felt tight, a lump forming at the back of my mouth. I gestured for them to sit, my gaze flicking to Ricky, who lowered himself onto the step beside me, his body language tense, as if he was bracing for something.

"I can't believe you guys are really leaving," I said, the words feeling strange in my mouth. They seemed so final, so irreversible. I had known this moment was coming, but hearing it aloud felt like the wind had been knocked out of me.

Jess sat down next to me, a little too close, as if trying to bridge some gap that had formed between us over the past few weeks. Ricky remained silent, his eyes focused on the horizon, his jaw tight.

"It wasn't an easy decision," Jess said, her eyes glistening in the dying sunlight. "But it's time for us to move on, Finn. We're not like you—we can't just stay here forever, tied to the same place, the same routines."

Her words struck me harder than I had anticipated. They were right. They couldn't stay. Jess and Ricky had never been the type to settle, to put down roots in one place for too long. They were the dreamers, the adventurers, always seeking the next horizon. Meanwhile, I had been standing still, frozen in place by my own indecision, watching as they slipped through the cracks of the world. And now they were leaving.

"Are you sure about this?" I asked, my voice quieter than I intended. "Byron's been home for both of you for so long. Why now? Why leave it all behind?"

Ricky shifted uncomfortably, finally speaking up. "It's not about leaving, Finn. It's about finding something new. We've been here for years, man.

Byron's got its charm, but it's not enough anymore. It's like... we've outgrown it."

The weight of his words hung heavy between us. Outgrown it. It hit me like a punch to the gut. Maybe that's what I had done too—outgrown it. But I was still here, still holding on to something that didn't fit anymore. I had made my peace with Byron once, but the longer I stayed, the more I realized it wasn't the place that had changed. It was me. I was the one who had grown restless, unable to move forward, and now, like Jess and Ricky, I was just waiting for the tide to pull me in a new direction.

I turned to Jess, trying to swallow the lump in my throat. "So, what's next? Brisbane?"

She smiled faintly. "Yeah. We're heading there. We've got some friends, a place to stay. It's a new start. A chance to see what else is out there."

I could feel the sadness in her voice, but there was also a sense of excitement, of possibility. It was the same look she had had when we were kids, standing on the edge of the beach, looking out over the endless ocean, imagining the adventures we would have. Back then, she had always been the one to push me to take the leap, to stop holding back, to follow my heart. Now, it was her turn to go, and I couldn't help but feel abandoned.

"Are you guys really just... leaving?" I asked, the words tasting bitter in my mouth. "Without even saying goodbye properly?"

Jess reached over, putting a hand on mine, her touch gentle but firm. "Finn," she said, her voice soft, "we've been saying goodbye for a while now. Every day we've stayed here, it's been harder to ignore what we're both becoming. This town... it's been great to us, but it's time to move on. We can't keep holding on to something that's slipping away. You know that."

Her words cut through me like a knife, leaving a jagged wound that I wasn't sure how to heal. They were right. The world was changing, and I was stuck, unwilling or unable to let go.

I stood up abruptly, running a hand through my hair, feeling the heat of the day settling into my bones. "I don't know what to say, Jess. I don't know what to do anymore."

Ricky stood up beside me, his hand on my shoulder, a rare gesture of camaraderie. "It's not about knowing what to do, man. It's about doing it.

You've got to stop waiting for something to change and start making the change yourself. You can't keep living like this."

The words felt like a punch to the gut, but they were true. It wasn't about waiting for things to get better. It was about taking responsibility for my own life, about choosing to move forward.

"I get it," I said finally, my voice rough. "I'll figure it out. You're right."

Jess smiled, squeezing my hand before letting go. "I know you will. You always have a way of figuring things out, Finn. Just don't wait too long this time. Life's too short."

With that, she and Ricky turned toward the road, their figures slowly fading into the dusk. I stood there for a long moment, watching them go, feeling a strange mixture of grief and hope.

I now owned a home.

I was now financially independent.

Byron Bay had always been my home, but I could feel its grip on me loosening, like a tide that was pulling away. Maybe it was time for me to leave too.

The Final Wave

I stood on the edge of the world, the sea at my feet, a canvas painted with undulating blues and frothy whites. The sun was rising in the sky, a molten orb prodding the horizon, gently kissing the familiar stretch of sand. Byron Bay was a place that had changed, morphed like the tides that ebbed and flowed against its shores. The bustling cafés, the thrumming music scene, and the kaleidoscope of bodies that once gave life to the beach now felt like echoes of a past I could barely grasp.

I had awoken in the first light of morning when the sky still inky, with only the faintest touch of gold creeping over the horizon. The sun hadn't fully risen yet, but the promise of a new day was already stretching across the sky like a slow exhale, warming the air in its own quiet way. I could hear the soft rush of waves in the distance, a constant, rhythmic reminder of the world outside the small, cocooned space I had spent so much time in.

I rolled over and glanced at the window, the soft glow of the early light spilling through the slats of the blinds, casting thin shadows across the room. The world outside felt untouched, serene, as if it had been waiting for me to wake up and face it.

It was a new day. I could feel it in the air, in the way the room felt just a little brighter, a little clearer. There was something about the early morning—before the world had fully come alive—that seemed to hold all the potential of what could be. The stillness, the quiet, almost sacred time before the demands of the world crept in, offering a moment of peace before the chaos.

I sat up, the cool wooden floor beneath my feet grounding me. My thoughts from yesterday—Jess and Ricky leaving, the weight of their goodbye still heavy on my chest—seemed distant now. The world had shifted overnight, without warning or invitation. I knew I couldn't keep clinging to what was slipping away. The edges of my own reality were blurring, and it was time to face that.

I got up slowly, pushing myself off the bed and walking toward the window. The colors of the sunrise began to deepen, streaking across the sky in shades of pink and orange. It was a moment of fleeting beauty, and for the first time in a while, I let myself absorb it without overthinking.

My bags were packed.

It was time to stop waiting for something to change and start making the change myself. I wasn't sure where that would take me, but in the soft glow of the morning light, I felt a glimmer of possibility.

Byron had been my anchor for so long. But now, as I stood there, watching the world wake up, I realized something: perhaps I had outgrown it, too.

The salty breeze tugged at my unkempt hair, the familiar scent of the ocean mixing with the bittersweet aroma of impending twilight. I closed my eyes, letting the roar of the waves wash over me. Each crash against the shore felt like a whisper, a reminder of the life I had lived. The laughter of friends, the late nights spent sharing stories over cheap beer, the heartbreaks that carved deep lines into my soul—all of it churned within me like the restless ocean.

"Hey, Finn! You coming?" Lila's voice broke through my reverie, pulling me back to the present. She was a vibrant flicker in the fading light, her presence grounding amidst the swirl of my thoughts.

"Yeah, I'm just... thinking," I replied, forcing a smile. The truth was that I had been grappling with memories that felt like anchors, dragging me down into depths I wasn't sure I wanted to explore.

"Thinking about what?" she pressed, her eyes sparkling with curiosity.

"Everything," I said, the weight of the word lingering between us. "Byron has changed so much. It feels different. I feel different."

Lila shrugged, a nonchalant movement that suggested she understood all too well. "Change is the only constant, right? Besides, it's just the surface. You're still you underneath."

"Am I?" My voice cracked like dry earth. I had spent years shaping myself to fit the world around me, bending like a palm tree in a storm. But beneath that facade lay a core of uncertainty, an aching desire to belong while feeling perpetually adrift.

The sky deepened to a bruised purple as the sun finally kissed the horizon. "Look at that," Lila said, pointing to the vibrant colors bleeding into one another. "It's beautiful. Just like you can be. You've got to find a way to let that out."

Her words hung in the air, heavy yet delicate. I felt the stirrings of a connection, the weight of shared experiences pulsing between us. It reminded me of the laughter, the mistakes, the way life felt in vivid technicolor before the shadows crept in.

"I don't know if I have the strength to start again," I confessed, my voice barely a whisper. "It's exhausting, fighting against the tide."

"You've already fought so hard," Lila had said earlier, her voice full of conviction. "You've got scars that tell stories. But that doesn't mean you can't reshape your narrative."

Her words echoed in me, like a mantra I had been needing but had never allowed myself to hear. For the first time in what felt like forever, I didn't feel anchored to the past. I could feel my heart moving forward, pulling me along, like the pull of the ocean that had kept me here for so long.

We walked in silence for a while, the sound of the waves crashing against the shore in the distance. It was a peaceful kind of silence, the kind that comes when two people are so deeply connected that words feel unnecessary. We were heading toward the minibus that would take us north, to places unknown, to a journey that neither of us could fully predict. But the weight that had been pressing on me for so long—like a fog that blurred everything around me—was beginning to lift. With every step, the fog thinned, and the path ahead became a little clearer, brighter.

I felt Lila's eyes on me, a quiet encouragement in her gaze, urging me to keep walking, to keep moving forward.

"Let's do this," I shouted, a fire igniting in my chest. "Let's GO!."

Lila grinned, her eyes lighting up. "Now that's the Finn I know!"

Her voice cracked through the thick air, and for a moment, I felt a surge of energy that radiated from my core out to every corner of my being. The Finn who was too afraid to leave, too afraid to change, was fading, retreating like a bad memory. And in his place stood the Finn who was finally ready to step into the unknown, to face the future head-on.

With that, we continued our walk toward the bus, the road now feeling more like an invitation than a burden. I glanced back over my shoulder, taking in the view. Byron Bay—this place that had been home for so long—was slowly fading behind me. The ocean stretched out in front of me, the waves relentless and powerful, yet strangely soothing. The sound of the surf was always the same, constant and eternal, a reminder that life, like the tides, was always in motion.

I took a deep breath, feeling the salty air fill my lungs. "Here's to new beginnings," I whispered to the sun, which was now just breaking the edge of the earth, casting golden light across the sand.

I wasn't just leaving Byron; I was leaving behind a version of myself I had long outgrown. I was stepping into a new chapter, and I had no idea what it would hold, but I knew that I was ready. For the first time in ages, I was free. Free from the weight of expectations, free from the chains of regret, free from the shadow of fear.

Lila and I reached the minibus, and I stopped for a moment, running my fingers over the weathered exterior of the bus. This would be my home for the next chapter, my sanctuary from everything I thought I knew.

"Are you ready?" Lila asked, her voice gentle but firm, as though she could see right through me, to the parts that still hesitated.

I nodded, my heart pounding in my chest. "Yeah," I said, more sure than I had been in a long time. "I'm ready."

As I climbed into the minibus, I took another look at the shoreline, the waves forever crashing and retreating. In a way, it felt like Byron Bay had been the starting point for my journey—not the end. The ocean would always be there, a reminder of where I'd come from, but it was time to see where the road would take me. Time to embrace the uncertainty, the chaos, and the beauty of it all.

I could feel the heat of the early morning sun on my back as Lila closed the door behind us, sealing in the warmth of a new beginning. The engine hummed to life, and the bus slowly rolled away, carrying me forward toward whatever came next.

DOWN AND OUT IN BYRON BAY

As we veered left onto Jonson Street, my heart sank. It was the wrong way, a quiet rebellion against the order of things, but in that moment, it felt right—an act of defiance against the path I had always followed. The one-way street, the rules I had spent my life abiding by, all seemed irrelevant now. I glanced back one last time at the ocean, the waves shimmering under the sunlight. The water crashed and retreated, relentless in its cycles. Maybe, like the sea, I too had to go against the current to truly find my way.

In that moment, I realized I was not defined by the changes in Byron Bay, but by my ability to adapt and grow. I would carry my roots with me, but I would also reach for the sky, crafting a narrative that was uniquely my own.

"Here's to new beginnings," I whispered to the sun, feeling the strength of the ocean echoing within me. I was ready to ride the waves of my own journey, no longer afraid of the final wave, but eager to greet it with open arms.

Don't miss out!

Visit the website below and you can sign up to receive emails whenever Alex Telman publishes a new book. There's no charge and no obligation.

https://books2read.com/r/B-A-YBSCC-HIUHF

BOOKS 2 READ

Connecting independent readers to independent writers.

About the Author

Alex Telman, a Brisbane-based healer with over 45 years of experience, is celebrated for his profound impact on both the mind and spirit. From the age of three, Alex's fascination with Spirit set him on a path of healing and insight, blending traditional spiritual practices with modern therapeutic techniques. With degrees in Law, Arts, Hypnotherapy, and Education, Alex's expertise extends to psychic phenomena, past life knowledge, and entity impact and removal.

Parallel to his healing practice, Alex is a prolific poet specializing in sonnets, sestinas, and modern poetic forms. His poetry vividly captures the essence of city and country life, exploring the psychological and philosophical depths of the human condition. His notable work have been widely recognized for their profound insight and resonance. Alex's poetry often serves as a therapeutic tool, blending realism with deep emotional understanding.

An esteemed author and public speaker, Alex's dual mastery of healing and poetry not only inspires but also guides individuals toward greater clarity and self-awareness. His unique approach and community engagement further underscore his commitment to both personal and collective transformation.